LORD OF THE WYRDE WOODS

BOOK ONE

ESCAPE FROM NEVERLAND

NILS VISSER

Lord of the Wyrde Woods Book One
ESCAPE FROM NEVERLAND
1st Ingram Edition.
December 2014 Amsterdam

ISBN/EAN 978-90-823229-7-2
Netherlands NUR-CODE 336

INGRAM #9014557

A C.B.S. Green Man Publication
Cider Brandy Scribblers
Burnham-on-Sea, Somerset, England

Text copyright © 2014 Nils Visser
The Wyrde Woods Chronicles TM

Registered at the *Depot van Nederlandse Publicaties*
Koninklijke Bibliotheek, Den Haag, The Netherlands

First published in print in Amsterdam in 2014 as:
(Lord of the Wyrde Woods Book One) ESCAPE FROM NEVERLAND
ISBN: 978-90-823229-4-1

First published digitally on Amazon Kindle in 2014 as:
Lord of the Wyrde Woods Book One: ESCAPE FROM NEVERLAND
ISBN 978-90-823229-2-7

Instructions for use: Start at the beginning and read all the words one after the other until you come to the very end and then stop. Holding the book the right way up will enhance the quality of reading. Not suitable for microwave, washing machine, dishwasher or toaster. Do not read and cross the road at the same time.

This book is dedicated to

Zoë Heukels-Morffew

In gratitude for many years of sharing,

loving, laughter and fun.

Table of Contents

One for Sorrow

Two for Joy

Three for a Girl

Four for a Boy

Five for Silver

Six for Gold

Seven for a Secret

Never to be Told

Prologue

"So what did you do to end up here? Murder someone?"

Michael looked puzzled. Quite endearing really, what with his half-long dark curls and boyish glasses completing the quizzical look. He looked a bit like a grown up Harry Potter.

"Nothing I think," he replied. "I volunteered for this position."

I stared at him in flabbergastation.

All of fourteen years old I had already been at Nowhere Place for about six months and considered myself a veteran. Michael was a new therapist, this was our first session. I had seen them come and go - or stay for that matter. The old tired ones shunted to yet another position in a place which was known to be a dead-end. Then the young ones who came in with boundless optimism. You know the type maybe, it's like you can almost see the neon angel's halo which their own mind projects on their self-image. Michael had that optimism, but without the self-saintly smugness. He also wasn't that young, over thirty so pretty ancient in fact. I was becoming curious; he didn't fit in my staff categorisation.

"You volunteered?" I asked, raising my eyebrows in disbelief.

Michael nodded amiably. "How about you Wendy? What did you do to end up here? *Quid pro quo.*"

"Quid what?"

"Give and take. Tit for tat."

Gotcha! I recognised an opportunity when offered one and provocatively stuck out my chest, making my small boobs appear as big as possible.

"So you're offering me a quid to see my tits?" I enquired sweetly.

To his credit Michael continued to look in my eyes. Nor did he become uncomfortable like most male newcomers did when the females of the Forlorn Hope tested them with a bit of lewdness. Always good for a story to regale in the common room amidst peals of laughter afterwards. Perhaps more importantly it allowed us to identify the pervs, those who thought it was okay to look at us like we were candy.

"I think you know very well what I mean Wendy."

He continued smiling in a manner which could be nothing but sincere. I was taken aback and finally sat down in the seat he had offered me when I had walked in and started being insolent.

"You aren't supposed to tell me anything about yourself you know," I told him. "This *quid pro quo* business of yours suggests we exchange information. That's against regulations. You should maintain a professional distance and all."

"I know." That smile again. He closed my open file which lay in front of him. "But I sort of tend to do things my own way. This means I talk to you just as if you were a regular human being, not a lab rat."

I was still sceptical. This was Nowhere Place in Neverland after all. There was no escape. If you talked about escaping from Neverland the folk around here would tell you to quit daydreaming and accept reality for what it was. Then they'd get back to guzzling cheap lager by the gallon, stoning themselves into oblivion or losing themselves in the mindlessness of the bloody junk that is shown on telly night after night.

In my case I lost myself in books, I read a lot, which was my escape. It allowed me to forget about Neverland for a while which is why others drank, took drugs or allowed themselves to be brainwashed by the telly. Around here we all want to forget about Neverland, in one way or another.

The Council Estate where we serve these life sentences has an official name, but I'd be buggered if I know it. Google would have an answer I suppose, the right tag words to use would be: Crime statistics, unemployment, domestic violence, teenage pregnancies, child abuse, alcoholism, drug abuse, rape statistics and suicide. It's a concrete pen for the poor in the county town of Odesby.

Somewhere in the early Seventies over half the brick shacks of the working class slums had been torn down to make room for concrete tower blocks. These threw their shadows over the old pub called the Neverland Arms which had given the estate the name everybody used. It was an apt name really; the kind of place in which you would never achieve much and where you really didn't want to be found dead in the first place.

I always appreciated the association with Peter Pan's Neverland. There was a cynical irony to it. In my Neverland Tinker Bell would be found strangled in the old Gas Works, wings ripped off her back and knickers around her ankles. Peter would be in hospital, battered and bruised, because the menfolk around here wouldn't stand for a lad wearing green tights. As for the Lost Boys? Why, they'd be in the professional hands of Youth Care, and that would be enough to mess up their minds forever and ever.

I know this because that was what Nowhere Place was. Its official name was the Odesby Juvenile Care Home but we had renamed it since it was on the end of the road to nowhere. A last resort for kids who had run the entire Youth Care gauntlet; been through all the other regional homes, hospitals, juvenile detention centres and clinics, you name it. We were incurable, irredeemable and past reformative recall. One of the history teachers at school called us lot the `Forlorn Hope'. I liked the sound of it. I looked up the meaning once, it had something to do with being the first to charge onto a breach in a fortress wall. It could have meant anything; from being insanely courageous to being the daft buggers sent in as a sacrifice in one of those bizarre and lethal testosteronic rituals men are fascinated with.

Michael was of a different mind. He sincerely believed there was a future for me which did not necessarily involve Neverland, prison, a hospital or an early grave. Over the next two years I started to believe him; it was a combination of being talked to like a human instead of a lab-rat and his contagious indefatigable optimism which slowly eroded my cynicism. However, when I did make my escape from Neverland it wasn't in a way which either Michael or I had envisaged.

Part Eena: One for Sorrow

1. One for Sorrow

The common room of Nowhere Place was packed for it was half-term which meant a lot of lounging about in apathy. Nowhere Place was a ramshackle old building of some previous importance, situated right next to the Neverland Arms. Tall ceilings and windows reminded us of the building's former dignity, dating way back to the early part of the last century - just as the plumbing did. Now it was shabby, bordering on derelict and beyond repair like its inhabitants.

Hanging about Nowhere Place instead of having to attend school was no punishment. There was a sense of community amongst the Forlorn Hope. We were the Untouchables of Neverland. Not in the sense of that movie about those coppers taking on the Mafia in Chicago mind you. This is more like the Untouchables from India, at the very bottom of the food chain, like we were subhuman.

The tenements that surrounded Nowhere Place on three sides were hostile territory and for physical safety we banded together against the rats in the flats. In the same manner we formed an alliance against the pedantic rats in the staffroom at school, the security rats at the local supermarket and the rats who ran our so-called care home.

I was leafing through some glossy magazine my best mate Sharon insisted I have a look at, though I couldn't fathom why; more than half of it seemed to consist of ads for make-up and fashion and the other half of photo-shopped super girls who couldn't possibly be real.

Michael poked his head around the corner of the common room and asked if he could speak to me. I was kind of surprised; our scheduled talk was always on Wednesdays. I raised my eyebrows to the Forlorn Hopers who were faffing about and I sighed to indicate my general weariness with the unfair demands of the staff. Just keeping up appearances; pretty daft of me as he was reasonably popular with most Forlorn Hopers but there you go. Welcome to my world.

I dropped the act as soon as we entered the hallway. I liked talking to Michael so an extra session wasn't a hardship. He never asked stupid questions. He would answer questions I asked but he didn't probe my mind, he just waited patiently till I chose to tell him things. Better than that even, he let me supply my own interpretations too, rather than assuming he knew better as to what a mess my head was in. He acknowledged that I was an expert on this matter.

Moreover, he had a pendant for honesty but only smiled vaguely if I tried to throw verbal shit at his colleagues, even the ones whom I sensed he disdained a bit. That I liked, I could depend on his honesty or else his graceful silence if he felt unable to tell me something. Honesty like that was a rare jewel in the midst of all the dishonesty that pervaded my life on all levels. Michael did just as he promised; he never spoke to me like I was a lab rat. Until this particular Friday morning at the beginning of April that is, when he turned my life in Nowhere Place upside down and inside out.

§ § § § § §

We went into our regular consulting room. I was relaxed until I sensed a distance in him and I became wary. Then he dropped his bombshell.

"You're leaving?" I stammered.

"I am afraid so Wenn, I've been reassigned to Stancaster."

My eyes grew wide and I felt a constriction on my chest, found it harder to breathe.

"Well tell them you don't want to go!" I shook my head. "Tell them you want to stay here."

Michael remained silent, eyes down. At first I was surprised, he had never come across as a coward and surely he could tackle his superiors. They were just paper pushers after all.

Then the meaning of the silence dawned on me.

"You want to go?"

I was incredulous. I began to swallow convulsively, felt my feet turn to lead. The beginning of a panic attack. I didn't want Michael to leave, I needed him. Surely he understood that?

Then, for the first time, he became snooty. His tone was reasonable as he started explaining away about career growth and opportunities like it was the most plausible and rational thing to do but in doing so he became condescending, as if he had to explain some basic concept to a small child. Or a lab-rat.

"You Twack!" I became furious.

"Wenn." He protested, raising his hands.

"You are a BLOODY RAVTILE! How dare you come in here and make me faxing trust you and then just announce you're bloody well walking out on me? That's just faxing douchebaggery you BLOODY FAXING SPAKE!"

I was so angry that raving at him was all I could manage to do. Had I been more articulate I might have avoided the F-word and tried to explain to him that he should have considered the implications of lightly throwing away the trust he had worked so hard to gain. To a kid like me that spells rejection. Kids like me have overdosed on rejection so often that we avoid it by letting nobody come close. Because if you do, as Michael had just proved, you would just have your guts ripped out again. And if they shied just short of doing that themselves, it could be a death warrant anyway, an encouragement to walk into Neverland at pub closing time wearing a t-shirt that read: *Kiss me, I'm drunk.*

"Wendy, when all is said and done, I'm just a therapist and you are one of my clients. There is no guaranteed duration…"

"You should've faxing said that to me before!" I was on my feet, my face was glowing and I was squeezing back tears. "YOU KNOW IT WAS MORE THAN THAT YOU FAXING GOBSHITE!"

I stormed for the door in an attempt to escape before I started blubbing. Too late. By the door I stopped and turned, a few tears already rolling down my cheek.

"YOU," I suddenly lost the will to shout and hoarsely whispered the rest. "You made me care. Don't you understand? You made me faxing care."

I looked at him pleadingly. He was about to say something, then shut his mouth again and shrugged helplessly, desperately unhappy with the situation but seemingly of no intent to change his plans.

I fled into the hallway, pushing aside a staff member who had come to inspect the source of the screaming. It was Miss Watson.

"Now just a minute young lady," she said sharply. "Come back here."

There would be no end to it now, no safe haven in my room upstairs and I couldn't stand to be harassed by staff involvement right now: A circle talk so everybody could discuss my faxing feelings or some such crap like that. I made a beeline for the front door instead. Another staff member emerged from the little office in the front hallway but I was much faster, out of the front gate before they even made it to the door.

I began to run blindly, barely able to see through a haze of tears, barely able to think through the red fury in my head and barely able to breathe as panic continued to grasp me in its claws.

§ § § § § §

Finally I slowed down. By now I was out of the range of staff pursuit. The protocol was to assume that a storm-out would return in twenty-four hours, after that they notified the police and waited to see what would happen.

It wasn't a great day for a stroll really. The sky was leaden, filled with the promise of drizzle or rain and I hadn't had the time to grab my coat. I was just wearing a blue summer dress which looked sweet till you came close enough to discern that the seemingly innocuous white patterns were swirling human skulls large and small. Black stockings and combat boots completed my attire. I reached for my mobile, thinking I could call my mate

Sharon and ask her to bring me my coat. I grimaced when I realised that I had left my mobile in the common room, and then grimaced some more when I realised I was well into tenement territory.

I sputtered to a halt on a courtyard between the concrete monstrosities. Normally I would have scoped out any such place rather than rushing in blindly like a complete idiot and I was immediately reminded why. There was a small playground in one corner of the courtyard, with broken swings and a battered metal slide. A bunch of chavs had gathered around a bench overlooking the playground and were swigging from a bottle of vodka. I forced myself to walk on. Usually the Forlorn Hope didn't venture into the tenements by themselves; I had come to a potentially dangerous place. This awareness temporarily banished my feeling of wholescale desolation. Michael's face across the table in the consulting room was already a thing of the past; the here and now demanded my full attention.

The chavs had seen me and two of them started walking, casually following a course parallel to me in the way young blokes walk, broadening their shoulders and swaggering as if they were packing 20 inches in their jeans. They blocked my exit. I resisted looking around me, knowing I shouldn't show fear and having already noted the only escape route from this concrete courtyard was the way I had come, which was now blocked by some of the other yobs. The hundreds of tenement windows overlooking the courtyard were no reassurance. In the Neverland tenements no one ever saw anything. At all. Ever.

"Look here, a treat," one of the chavs in front of me said. He was pretty tall, his hair closely cropped and his face disfigured by a broken nose. His hands were in the pockets of his bomber jacket, offering no immediate threat.

"OTF," the other shorter boy grinned. I saw that he was missing a front tooth. He waved his hands in an outward curve over his chest. "Tits out for the lads?"

"We's gonna smash your panties," Broken Nose said with a leer.

"Juice you up good," No-Tooth said; clutching his crotch while thrusting his hips forward.

I hesitated. I didn't know this lot and was trying to ascertain their degree of threat. They were about my age and might still have been too young to be doing much more than impressing themselves and their mates. On the other hand, they might have already crossed the border to a much more dangerous category of tenement rats: The young men for who might was right. Those yobs weren't afraid of anything, did as they pleased and took what they wanted. Either way, I decided, there really only was one sensible course of action.

"You're both too small in the game for me," I said calmly. "So piss off."

"Don't fade us you slunt," No-Tooth curled up his nose in anger, his eyes flashed.

"You bet," I answered, then drew back my right arm and delivered the hardest punch I could, which was pretty bloody hefty as I was seething with unreleased anger. My fist landed squarely on his nose and he crumpled, blood welling up from his nostrils. Broken Nose's mouth fell open and before he could do much more than that I spurted past him.

"GERONIMOOO!" I hollered defiantly as my feet pounded the pavement. The pervasive grey concrete passed by in a blur, faint shouts of anger reached my ears and my lungs gasped for fresh air, each breath an intake of foul odours from the rent open rubbish bags piled up against the tenement walls.

I suddenly felt liberated, flying like a piratical sea gull in total freedom. I knew I'd probably go to hell for feeling satisfied about punching that boy but I couldn't help the satisfaction. I grinned and then I ran and ran; my mind a mad whirlwind blowing my body in a random direction, which happened to be straight out of Neverland.

2. Willick

I slowed down my speed till I was just jogging, adrenaline still in a tidal surge which made it hard to slow down more than that. My mind did start to reassemble, gradually descending from the whirl it had been in. I started to note my surroundings again. I had just passed the Old Gasworks (not a good place) and jogged into the industrial estate that was located conveniently close to the working class estates of Odesby. This area contained many old brick buildings, all deserted with glassless windows and surrounded by tall weeds and rusty chain linked fences. Some fences were still shiny and bright; they shielded modern buildings, lots of corrugated iron, lorries on the lots and occasional visible human activity. More than half of the buildings were empty though, unemployment was rife in Odesby.

I made my way down to the North Canal and jogged right up to the sudden drop down to the water. I came to a halt and decided I had to continue by balancing on the very edge with two inches of solidity to work with, the rest just thin air.

If I lost my balance I'd either become well acquainted with the asphalt or else I'd plunge five feet down into the canal. I am a good swimmer but the sluggishly flowing murky water did not look appetising. I'd probably die of instant toxic poisoning. Or I might survive, and be found downriver towards the sea by some kids who would take me to their Tudor manor farm. I'd be nursed back to health and, impressing the whole family somehow, be adopted and live happily ever and after.

I gave falling in some consideration but an opportunity to experience family life was ruined by my good balancing skills. When I reached the large bridge which carried the northbound traffic out of town onto the A267 I lost interest in the game and walked on normally. I had to make a sharp 90 degree turn to follow the canal northwards, passing underneath the dual railway bridges and the road bridge of the westbound Nickleby

Road. The shadows underneath the bridges concealed piles of empty beer tins, shards of broken bottles and casually discarded used condoms. This was Make-out Corner, a romantic destination of peace and tranquillity if you lived in the Neverland tenements.

After passing underneath the bridges the chain fences guarding Odesby Chemicals Ltd. were to my right, guarding a complex assortment of industrial structures, including ducts which spit out flames and smoke like a dragon's nostrils. This was the largest employer in town and suspected of illegally dumping their waste products in the canal which I well believed after seeing it up close. To my left though, across the canal, I could see the sumptuous green fringe of a forest which I knew was called the Wyrde Woods and I started walking faster, brightened somewhat by the prospect of escaping Odesby altogether. I had never been this far, negotiating the tenements and the industrial estate was too much of a hassle on any given regular day.

There was a forest on the north-east corner of Neverland which earned the name forest only because there were trees there. I had visited a couple of times but had been put off by the fact that half the estate used it as an illegal rubbish dump and it was also a place where a handful of hard core crack-heads congregated. So usually walks consisted of a stroll up and down the High Street to visit shops where it was easy to nick things. The woods here were surely far away enough from Neverland to have escaped that fate. It was one thing taking your date to the bridges, another to lug an old fridge all that way and then even further.

The industrial estate ended abruptly and suddenly I found myself on a path leading into the Wyrde Woods. Within twenty paces I was swallowed up by fresh lush spring green and Odesby ceased to exist altogether, except for the noise of the traffic but that had competition in the form of chirpy birdsong. I felt like I had passed through some weird Sci-Fi portal into another world altogether and began to breathe easier. Why had I never come here before?

The path ambled deeper into the forest over reasonably flat terrain. The woods were airy and bright, the young leaves sprouting from trees yet to form dense foliage. As the path meandered back towards the canal I turned a corner and gasped. The trees were further apart from each other here and the ground was carpeted by blue bells, forming a purple haze everywhere I looked. The path narrowed and I felt the flowers lightly brush my black stockings as if in a fond greeting. Just then the clouds overhead split and the sun burst through, lighting up the bluebell sea around me to reveal their perfect glory. The beauty of the purple-blue carpet was stunning and to top it off the noise of the traffic had faded too. For a moment I felt simply happy. Something good had come out of this day after all.

§ § § § § § §

I decided to stop for a while and perched myself on a fallen tree trunk by the side of the path. I fished a half-empty pack of rolling baccy from the small right pocket of my dress, just about all which would fit in there, and then retrieved a pack of rolling paper from the other pocket. As I made my roll-up I grinned at the foolishness of celebrating nature's fresh air by having a smoke.

"It's like I can't handle too much oxygen at once," I told the tree trunk. "Not used to it see. This is vital breathing apparatus for me."

I fished out a lighter from my bra and lit the gret, then sat happily on my tree, smoking and surveying my new empire; drinking in its purple splendour and fully understanding why all those wee birds sounded so damn cheerful. Maybe I would just stay here, build an outlaw camp and flip the world my middle finger. I didn't need them anyway and they certainly didn't need me. I grinned as I observed the antics of two squirrels that were playing hide and seek; circling a broad tree trunk again and again, ever in astonished surprise when they spotted the other.

After a while I continued on my way and soon had to bid a regretful goodbye to the bluebells as the trees thinned out and grassy patches first indented the flower carpet and then replaced it altogether until I was walking through a meadow. The grass was tall and dotted with white and yellow wildflowers resplendent in the sun which was now gaining enough strength to stroke my bare arms and shoulders with pleasant warmth. A few rabbits dashed away when they became aware of me. Another surprise awaited me as the path turned to run parallel to a river; its slow water was so clear I could see it tugging the water plants on the river bed. Logic dictated that this river was the same body of water as the canal which I had walked past earlier, but the contrast between the two couldn't have been greater so it was hard to believe. I happily made mental notes to tell Michael about my passing from one world into others today. He liked that sort of...

Michael.

I became solemn again as I recalled the morning's eventful start. The sadness was calmer now. Michael was a wise lesson, I decided. Not to trust anybody or depend on anybody. Ever again.

I had slowly opened up to Michael since our first session two years before. I had begun to trust him more and more and with his help began to envisage an actual future for myself, one that looked further than just the end of the day. Also one that didn't involve getting pregnant so I could get a council flat and some state income; the usual level of social enhancement for girls in Neverland. He helped me find things I was good at and after our sessions I even tried my hand at school for a day or two, usually repressed by one of the Neanderthal teachers who would remind me that my lot in life was to remain ignorant and stupid. They would literally say: "I don't know why you bother girl, you're too thick to ever amount to much in life."

It saved them extra correction work I suppose, though Michael would endeavour to instil new motivation in me, waxing on about my qualities. I sometimes doubted him, I mean; he was the only one who had ever noted qualities in me. I didn't even know I had qualities, up to then all I knew about qualities was that most of the lads reckoned girls had two qualities and mine weren't big enough for their taste.

None-the-less, I liked it when Michael praised me, it made me feel better about myself. Now and then I even stopped looking at myself like a worthless piece of shite. Not by much, but that little bit made a huge difference.

All gone now. Back to square one.

The meadows on both sides of the river became broader and seemed to have other waterways because I could see stretches of water here and there, as well as a great many ducks, geese, swans and herons.

"I am on my own," I told a passing butterfly which was entirely disinterested, lured instead by some bright flowers. I eyed its passage with a sad smile; such a beautiful creature had no business hearing ugly thoughts.

Best to be alone. It was a lesson I had first learned when I was around six. I had adhered to it on a structural basis until Michael had come along and convinced me that humanity's disregard of me might not be universal. So much for that then. Maybe he had even done me a favour by reminding me of reality. I tried to toughen up but couldn't entirely get rid of a wistful layer of grief that settled on my heart. More emotional scars, why the fax not? I was practically made of faxing scar tissue.

The cloud cover had broken up fast, the sky was now a steady blue dotted with a few drifting clouds and I relished the sunshine.

My attention was drawn to strange shapes that loomed up ahead. Small blobs of grey at first to which I paid little attention but as I got closer and they grew larger their contrastive oddity started puzzling me. The grey colour formed the biggest contrast at first because the forms seemed organic, curling and folding in a natural manner. As I got closer however it became clear that they didn't grow out of the earth but were manmade like some sort of abstract sculpture. It wasn't till I was only separated from the forms by an old moat that I recognised the remnants of buildings.

I had always thought ruins were far more angular, the rubble pillars and walls here were rounded by exposure to weather and time. The irregular sandstone rocks they were built with had weathered into grey, though various hues of ochre still showed here and there. The broken arches of former windows and doorways reached outwards like limbs, forming outstretched fingers and pointy beaks.

I was intrigued and I followed the path along the moat until I came to a small wooden bridge that led across. There was no signpost giving further information about the place -or forbidding access- so I walked across the bridge and some way into the complexity of the ruins till I had reached what seemed like the middle. I was surrounded on all sides by weird curvaceous serpentines of sandstone, some rising as much as twenty feet into the air. Definitely a rollie-mo and I started hunting for the necessary materials.

"We doant get much in the way o' visitors here," a man's voice startled me. "So what does ye reckon? Worth the trek from town, surelye?"

I spun round, almost dropping my baccy and papers. The man was old, in his sixties I guessed, an amiable face creased by laugh wrinkles with the most remarkably clear and bright blue eyes. They seemed to speak volumes. Intelligence for one, but also omniscient knowledge, like he already knew all about me. His hair was grey with remnants of blond and reasonably short; I could only see some of it as the rest was covered by one of those old fashioned working man's caps. He wore a green wax coat and brown corduroy trousers which were tucked into leather boots that looked ancient and worn. A brown linen bag hung from his shoulder.

"How do you know I am from town?" I asked guardedly.

His eyes twinkled and he looked me up and down in an exaggerated fashion, as if that was enough to answer my question.

"Anyhow, what business is it of yours?" I added, peeved by his manner.

"By Geemeny! We've ournself a tough nut here, surelye. Streetwise alikes a middling alley cat from Brighton," the man beamed. "Should I be afeard o' ye?"

He talked funny, using weird words in a sing song intonation, stressing his 'r's and switching some his 'i's and 'e's. But smiles are my weakness. If they appear genuine I am rapidly disarmed. The man seemed harmless enough though his speech was odd and I relaxed somewhat.

"Outyer tis considered good manners to greet a passer-by and scorse pleasantries," he added but not in a manner which was reproving, just a matter of fact statement.

"I am from town," I agreed.

"And a quick learner I does reckon," he smiled approvingly. "Runaway are ye?"

"Yes. No!"

He raised a quizzical eyebrow and I almost had to laugh. I put some baccy in a rolling paper and rolled it up, just to avoid that all-knowing look for a few seconds.

"I just needed to get away for a bit," I explained. "Place is like a rat cage you know?"

He looked serious for a moment, then nodded.

"Aye, that I does. There is everything o' something and something o' everything there I reckon. But a fair shatter o' smeech, surelye."

I didn't get any of that but somehow it sounded like an accurate description so I nodded.

"Folk call me Willick, Willick be mine forename, and Maskall be mine aftername." He looked at me expectantly.

"Wendy," I mumbled.

He frowned.

"Is that a problem?" Irritation crept into my voice.

"Aye, tis," he said. "I doant mean yern problem Wendy. Tis an unnacountable curiosity o' mine."

He pronounced his 'y' like 'eye'.

"How's that then?"

"I've a difficulty with folk's names that end in 'eye'," Willick explained.

" 'ie', not 'eye'."

"Quiddy?"

"Wend'ie'. Not Wend'eye'."

"Aye, that were what I said," Willick smiled. "Tis a problem for me all-along-o' that it seems a slight beliddling. As if there's naun need to take them serious. Ye reckon I ought to take ye serious Wendy?"

I stared at him, half-a-sneer ready to form on my face if it turned out he was dissing me. Willick just looked back brightly, he appeared entirely sincere.

"Does ye mind if I names ye Wenn?"

I considered this. It had been Michael's name for me. Our own special thing as it were. Then again, Michael had pretty much squandered his rights hadn't he?

"Sure," I conceded. At the same time I was considering a problem. My lighter was back where I usually kept it, in my bra. Bloody useful things to carry small items in. I really wanted to light up the gret, but it seemed kind of improper in front of a stranger. Bugger it, I decided and fumbled around for a second until I retrieved it. Willick didn't bat an eyelid.

"Well, I be pleased to meet ye Wenn," he said as if he meant it. "Ye've an aftername?"

I frowned.

"Yes, it's the only thing my parents gave me," I explained. "I don't use it."

He nodded in understanding. Somehow I perceived that he wouldn't mention it again. I was beginning to warm to him at a speed which surprised me.

"And what brings you here? To the woods I mean?" I asked.

"Oh, I live thereaways," he waved vaguely in the direction of the woods looming over the northern side of the ruins where the meadows reached an end. "I be hoping to meet Puck down disyer way today, howsumdever, I reckon that young mawkin have loped off again."

"Puck?"

"Aye, he looks alikes a wodewose. Seen him have ye? "

I shook my head. The last people I had seen up close were the tenement rats in that sad excuse for a playground and I doubted that Willick meant either one of those two scumbags when he said *wodewose*. The word reminded me of the Woses who helped the Rohirrim through the forest of Drúadan in *Lord of the Rings* and I pictured a smallish man covered in mossy green grinning over his freshly poisoned arrow tips.

Willick looked around at the ruins.

"Nice enow place on a sunny day disyer St. Lewinna's Priory," he remarked. "Howsumdever, naun a place to visit after the sun sets."

"How did it get these shapes? Who is St. Lewinna? Why isn't it nice? Is it a ghost story?" I demanded.

Willick laughed and his eyes laughed with him.

"Tis an old place, gwoan all the way back to the Dark Ages, long ago," he explained. "I doant hold much with shims, surelye. Howsumdever, disyer woods have all manner o' places that…well, they be energised as 'twere. They hold unaccountable energies."

I remembered the feeling I had when I passed the Old Gasworks earlier that day and nodded.

"And this isn't a positive place then?" I asked. "There are good places too? Where?"

Willick examined me inquisitively, like he was seeing me for the first time again. Then he came to a decision and nodded.

"Best ye come along then I reckon, tis anigh." he said and then strode off towards the bridge across the moat without looking back to see if I was following. I didn't hesitate. Somewhere even I had been conditioned to be wary of following strange men to unknown destinations but I felt comfortable with this bloke, the rarity of which was somehow doubly reassuring. Moreover, I had a natural appreciation of danger. I mean, I was scraping the very bottom of the barrel of life as it was. There wasn't much further to plunge. If he turned out to be an axe murderer then that would just be another interesting life experience.

Willick had a healthy stride for an old man and I had to rush to keep up with him as he took a left and led us onto a path that wandered into the woods. Once again I was struck by the beauty of the bluebells which grew in abundance here as well but now offered a visual spectacle of extra dimension because the ground began to rise and fall and then became hilly altogether.

"How come those ruins don't have info signs or anything?" I wanted to know.

"Ye be axing why English Heritage doant build a parking lot, a ticket booth and a souvenir shop there?"

"Exactly." I recalled some school field trips to just such destinations where some poor enthusiastic teacher would be rewarded for efforts to get us out of classes for the day by collective disinterest and acts of vandalism.

"Tis private property," Willick explained. "Ye were trespassing to be sure. Howsumdever, the owner, she doant bother to have it fenced off all-along-o' so few folk visit the priory. Also, I doant think there's no-ways she've ever been out in the woods hernself since hern were a liddle chavee."

"Who's the owner?" I felt a sudden pang of jealousy. Just imagine owning a place like the priory.

"Lady Malheur," Willick said in a neutral tone.

The name rang a bell.

"From the castle?" I asked. There was a great big fancy moated castle north of Odesby called Malheur Hall. I'd never been there myself but had seen a few pictures of it on postcards on display in the High Street.

"Jes so. Malheur owns most o' the Wyrde Woods. They've never encouraged visitors. Except those what pay to visit the castle grounds." Willick sounded guarded, like he felt uncomfortable talking about the Malheurs.

"Are we trespassing now?" I felt a secret thrill.

"Naun, woods and hills be privately owned, but even Lady Malheur is to respect the right o' public way. Puck now, he be trespassing all-along-o' that him opted to live on hern land without axing. The young scaddle is to be evicted."

I didn't understand much of the latter part of his explanation and decided to ignore it.

"Good. Where are we going now?"

"To the Giant's Grove."

"What's that?"

"Ye'll see soon enow," Willick looked sideways at me. His face was still friendly enough but there was sternness in it now. "Ye be realising we've already passed three deer?"

"Really? Where?" I looked behind me.

"Aye, anigh disyer path. Fallow deer. Howsumdever, they'll freeze, ye see, all-along-o' that they hear us coming."

"You think I talk too much?" The implicit criticism felt like a blow. I wanted him to like me and as usual was ruining everything already. For a brief moment a familiar anger flared up. Anger at Willick, at myself, at the world in general.

"I reckon," Willick regarded me thoughtfully. "That ye'd be benefitting from yern escape from the rat cage more if ye doant jes walk through the woods, but tries to experience it. Ye does seem to jump from one thing to another…" He waited till I reluctantly nodded affirmation, and then continued, "Try to focus on the woods, soak them up as 'twere."

"'Kay," I agreed as demurely as I could manage. I wanted to see what that Giant's Grove was about so I kept quiet and tried to focus on the woods around us as we continued on our way, into a world far away from Neverland.

3. Here be Giants

The path climbed steeply to the top of a low ridge where a grassy clearing offered a wide view. I stopped and looked around in wonder. We had climbed higher than I had realised and behind me I could see St. Lewinna's Priory at the edge of the broad meadows through which meandered a multitude of waterways. These joined into a single river that flowed to Odesby, which seemed almost quaintly picturesque on the horizon. To my left I saw the edge of the woods bordered by a patchwork of farmland and to my right the woods seemed to roll on forever, lapping like a green sea against the shores of islands formed by prominent grassy rounded hills, one closer by and two further away.

I determined that I would climb those hills as soon as possible. I turned around, the path led steeply downwards again and Willick was waiting patiently by a gaping cave-like entrance in the tree line. The tree tops descended into a narrow valley and then rose again to a hill that was somewhat higher than the one I was on. The top of the hill was crowned by a clump of trees which were spectacularly tall, rising twice over the surrounding forest. That had to be this Giant's Grove where Willick was taking me.

Driven by anticipation, I skipped down the path toward Willick.

"It's beautiful here!" I exclaimed.

"Aye, tis lamentable purty," he sounded pleased.

I was full of questions of course, but remembered what Willick had said about experiencing the woods so I kept my mouth shut again, though the bluebells failed to captivate me for the first time that day and the other trees seemed dull and boring now. I couldn't wait to get a closer look at the Giant's Grove and soon enough we were climbing once again. The forest thinned out somewhat and suddenly the giant trees came into view, much closer now and all the more impressive. The trunks were unbelievably wide and rose up in vertical perfection, forming two score or so of red columns that supported large green cones so high up I couldn't even identify individual branches or leaves when I stood a mere ten feet from the nearest giant.

I felt humbled and awed by the trees, they must have been ancient. I threw an inquiring glance at Willick. He nodded.

"Tis alright for ye to bid them a good day."

I resisted a What-The-Fax moment; there was no way I was going to hug a tree. But I was kind of curious to see the tree closer up so I walked to the nearest one. As I got to it I looked upwards and my head started spinning. The trunk seemed to rise upwards forever. The upper branches and conical crowns seemingly just as distant from me now as when I had first spotted them. I swayed on my feet as I tried to comprehend the height of the trees which left me in vertigo. I lowered my head to face the tree normally, shaking my head briefly as if that would readjust my giddy brain. I stretched out my arm to let my hand rest on the bark for support. I was expecting steel solidity but to my surprise the bark was so soft it felt like a sponge, gently absorbing the pressure of my hand.

"It's like it's a living being," I exclaimed, immediately realising the stupidity of it. Trees are living beings. DUH.

"Tis generally-always so," Willick nodded but he didn't laugh at me.

I smiled foolishly.

"I meant…trees generally just stand there all day. Sure, they do important stuff with oxygen but they are not fun like cats or dogs. These trees seem like fun though."

I looked up again. These would be a challenge to climb.

"Most-in-general trees be fun when ye stop for a proper gander," Willick's eyes sparkled. "Howsumdever, ye're right about the Giant's Grove, they be bettermost trees."

Willick squatted and took two wrapped packages and a bottle of water from his linen bag. He unwrapped the packages to reveal a loaf of bread and a chunk of hard yellow cheese. My mouth watered, I hadn't eaten since breakfast and that had only consisted of half a slice of toast with some marmite. Willick produced a pocket knife and he began to cut the bread into slices.

"Would ye be hungry lass?"

"Yes," I affirmed heartily and walked over, squatting too. Willick gave me a thick slice of bread with a generous amount of cheese on it and I bit into it eagerly. It tasted good; today's long walk had given me an appetite. I was thirsty too and the water was refreshing. For a while we sat on our haunches chewing while we looked at the trees.

"These be *sequoia sempervirens*," Willick pronounced the name carefully. "Californian redwoods."

"In England?" I asked incredulously, mouth still half full, my eyes resting on the evidence right in front of me.

"Aye," Willick positively beamed. "A hundred and fifty years old these be, surelye. Long ago, in Victorian days some unaccountable folk, rich eccentric ones, collected trees, so they does. They'd saplings or seeds brought in from all over the wurreld: Asia, the Americas, Australia and thereabouts, a middling stride from Sussex, surelye."

"One of the Malheurs?" I guessed and stood up to walk a bit closer to the trees.

Willick nodded, "There be a dozzle more odd bits and pieces in the woods, howsumdever, disyer trees crown the collection."

"The Giant's Grove," I looked back at him.

"Aye, most local folk think they've been round longer than that, they associate these giants with them giants on the twin hills. Howsumdever, twere Oscar Malheur what planted them here, naun those two giants on the hills."

"You mean to say there are giants here?" I snorted. "Pull the other one."

"Oh all sorts here in the Wyrde Woods Wenn. Witches, forest sprites, giants, wodewoses, dragons and a Faere Fey with seven Farisee maidens."

"I thought you didn't believe in ghosts, are you parring me?" I felt a wave of irritation rise; did he think I was a fool? Damn, the guy had a good poker face; he just kept on beaming sincerity and speaking in a tone that was utterly serious. But I felt like he was treating me like a small girl now, telling me fairy tales, dissing me. I was a Neverlander, we knew better than that.

"Shims, naun. Them others, they've been here for dunnamy years."

"Yeah right, and they all lived happily ever after."

Willick's face briefly contorted into an expression of grief and pain that unsettled me.

"Naun all o' them," he spoke softly, casting a glance at the redwoods. Then he cast an inquisitive look at the sun and resumed his normal tone, "If ye be wanting to make it back to Odesby afore dark, ye'd best be thinking o' making a start dappens the sun sets."

It was no more than a friendly suggestion, not a command. But being treated like a small kid had made me become unreasonable. I did that a lot. It was frustrating, because I was fully aware of overreacting at those moments, but it was like my common sense could only look on in dismay as it was overridden by something else inside of me. Something that spoke of disappointment, of never being good enough. That something now convinced me that his suggestion was typical adult behaviour, telling me what to do, sending me off and dismissing me. Like everyone else he'd had enough of Wendy already. I wanted to snarl at him that I was already sixteen, a pretty big milestone as far as I was concerned. Moreover, whereas those sixteen years may not have amounted to much next to the Californian redwoods' age, I sure as hell felt like I was every bit as old as their 150 years in my mental age. I'd been through a lot more than most folk. That made me about three times Willick's age and he was treating me like a small kid.

"I am not afraid of walking through town after dark," I curled my lip, irritation surging through me now like an unstoppable tide.

"Ah doant think ye be afeared o' that Wenn," Willick spoke calmly. "But have ye considered the Wyrde Woods? How well does ye know yern way around?"

I had walked pretty much north from the railway bridges, returning was a matter of going south. It didn't seem to be too complex to me.

"I can manage just fine," I straightened my back, making myself as tall as possible, which, to my everlasting frustration, wasn't very tall at all.

"Ye be certain now?" His eyes seemed to know better. "The Wyrde Woods can be a strange place at night time."

"Full of dragons and wodewoses who will hunt me down for a snack?" I asked, forming an amused little smile on my lips.

"Ye never know what ye'll meet in the Wyrde Woods Wenn," he did not respond to my tone other than sound bemused.

But his words struck me. Was he threatening me? With what? Puff the Magic Dragon? The Big Bad Wolf? I suddenly felt uncomfortable.

"I'll tell ye what," he smiled. "I'll walk ye back to St. Lewinna's, the way to Odesby be middling easy from there."

"I'd prefer it if you didn't," I said bluntly. "I don't feel that comfortable around you."

He was taken aback for a moment.

"We dursn't have that, though ye're misagift about me," he said thoughtfully. "Letbehow'twill. I'll be gwaon then and ye can cut yern stick. Good day to ye Wenn."

With that he gathered the remnants of the meal and strode off northwards. I watched him go with a sinking heart as my anger subsided and I realised that I had been pretty rude. This guy hadn't been some sicko from the tenements like the ones that followed me and Sharon around when we had to pass through the rat-blocks to get to the supermarket. My first instinct had been a strong feeling I could trust him, he had been kind, generous with his time and he had broken bread with me like I was his guest. For a moment I was tempted to run after him, to thank him for the meal and the giants. But that would look so foolish now, make me look cray. Better to be alone, I decided, always better to be alone. I turned away from the soft-skinned redwoods to start my long journey back to Neverland.

4. Hindesideafore

I took a wrong turn soon after leaving the Giant's Grove, or rather, kept on going straight when I failed to spot the left turn I should have taken. One of my points of reference was a small footbridge across a stream and as my new path also featured one of these I didn't even realise I was heading westwards, rather than southwards. Had I been more focused I would have realised the water was flowing in the same direction it was when I had first crossed the bridge, as if the small river had decided it was time for a change and reversed its course.

There might have been time for me to realise my mistake and backtrack to the Giant's Grove to start anew if it hadn't been for a small clearing around a large chestnut tree on the other side of that bridge. I could not resist the invitation of its stairway of thick chunky boughs and limbs. I have an aptitude for climbing trees. Got that when I was around nine and was stuck in a clinic in Stancaster which had ample grounds around it, including trees with branches overhanging the fencing that surrounded the complex. I came and went as I pleased there and that feeling of freedom was invoked again as I began to climb the chestnut. It was easy at first but as I climbed higher the branches became thinner and negotiating my way to the top became a matter of careful calculation. I was charged with full focus, all a tingle. A brill sensation to begin with, but for me it also had the added bonus that for a blessed moment it shut out the whirlpool of all the cray thoughts and random weirdness that permanently pestered my mind.

By the time I got down again I was satisfied but exhausted. I rested with my back against the tree as I enjoyed the sun's warm caresses while I could before it was going to be cut off by the band of clouds slowly drifting in from the horizon. I had a rollie after which I promptly dozed off in that last sunshine.

§ § § § § §

I must have slept for some time because when I woke everything was not only unaccountably cold but also unexpectedly pitch black and I panicked instantly. I wasn't used to this degree of darkness, in towns there was always some light, dim maybe, but enough to see by. I don't like darkness, have an irrational childish fear of it. All my life I had been chided for leaving the lights on wherever I went. Unnecessary costs, a waste of energy. Yeah right, was my standard mental response. Let there be light baby. As soon as possible I would drift through hallways and rooms turning on as many lights as I could.

Night in the Wyrde Woods was one of total darkness, for a moment I even felt like I had gone blind. I lifted a hand in front of my face but couldn't even see that. I fumbled in my bra for my lighter, but couldn't find it. I cursed at myself for wasting time by fumbling my own boob as clumsily as an unexperienced lad when I should have remembered that last gret I smoked. I began patting the ground around me till I finally located my smoking gear. The relief I felt when I flicked on the lighter was only brief, for all I succeeded in doing was create a minute globe of light which allowed me to see my hand but seemed to increase the intensity of the surrounding darkness. Cursing again, I killed the flame and tried to distract myself by making a roll-up. My hands were shaking badly and all I managed to do was spill precious baccy on the ground. Giving up, I pressed my back against the chestnut and sat there; shivering and peering into the darkness.

I was not sure if the shivering was because of the rising panic or the night's chill. Probably both as the cold was fierce. My bare arms felt blue and my stockinged legs weren't in a much better state. I pulled my knees up and folded my arms around them, pressing myself against my upper legs.

I became aware of sounds all around me: Rustling in the bushes, a strange high-pitched series of grunts off to my left, and the hoots of owls competing with the screeches of other birds in the black sky. The woods seemed to be teeming with life; hunting or being hunted, a gruesome game of life and death. I tried to reassure myself that England's main predators walked on two feet, like tenement rats and douchebags with lecherous hands. Unlikely to be in the woods tonight. Out here there'd be what? Foxes and as far as I knew those wily creatures didn't hunt and eat humans. So nothing was going to pounce on me out of the eerie total eclipse of light.

I decided that I found the pressure of the chestnut against my lower back comforting. We knew each other now, this tree and I. I had unlocked one of its secrets after all and if that many teethed monstrosity -which usually lurked beneath my bed at night- came whiffling out of the murk I could shimmy up the tree in no time. The tree would protect me, I felt absolutely sure of that.

Reasoning with myself thus I calmed my breathing somewhat, the initial fear subsided and the cold become the predominant problem. I didn't have a clue as to how long I'd slept and what time it was now. If it was still early in the night then that night would last an eternity. Much as I drew comfort from the chestnut I realised that I would have to leave it. Without warm clothing it would be madness to remain stationary. Better to move, maybe even get back to Odesby. Suddenly I missed my room, my duvet and the extra blankets on my bed as well as the awareness of the Forlorn Hopers all around me. It was the first time ever that I actually thought of Nowhere Place as a safe place of some sorts.

I made up my mind when I realised that the total obscurity of the night was becoming less relentless for I began to discern different degrees of darkness around me. I stood up, gave the chestnut a pat, and then marched bravely down the path. The shapes I perceived were partially visual but also a sense of another sort, just a feeling they were there. That feeling increased manifold when I left the clearing and the forest swallowed me up. It became darker again and the trees and foliage seemed to crowd up on me. The temptation to rush back to the chestnut and climb into the embrace of its branches was great and I overcame it only by thinking of that duvet and those blankets on my bed.

Slowly things improved. Though I was still shivering a little I felt a bit warmer now that I was on the move and I got used to the sensation of the trees pressing in on me from all sides. My eyes had also adjusted to this new shade of night and I somehow managed to make out where the path was, even there where it twisted and turned. I felt renewed confidence, I was going to simply own this return journey. Willick had made a fuss over the woods at night, but I was coping wasn't I? If only I had a coat it would have been a piece of piss. As it was the absence of one offered plentiful motivation to keep on moving.

I'd walked for about 20 minutes or so when my mind started gnawing, eroding my resolution. By now, I figured, I should have reached the open water meadows, sensing open space that would widen even further once I was past the priory. Once across those meadows Odesby would be tantalizingly close.

Maybe I had misjudged the distance I decided and walked on, though my steps began to falter in their determination somewhat. The view I had seen earlier from atop that ridge drifted in my mind's eye. The Wyrde Woods had seemed to stretch forever in three directions from there. If I had taken a wrong turn somewhere this walkabout might yet become something of an ordeal.

The temperature dropped with a startling suddenness and I halted. I took two step backwards and immediately felt warmer. For a moment I hesitated, the word thermal air layer popped into my head but I thought those were horizontal layers, this was a vertical wall. I decided it might have to do with the type of trees that grew here -even though I couldn't actually see much of them- and continued, albeit more cautiously. In no time goose bumps covered my entire arms and I was shivering badly again.

The clouds above broke and a perfectly rounded moon slowly drifted in sight, casting a remarkable amount of illumination. Suddenly I had regained a great deal of my sight. Then I spotted the pale grey of a monastic looking tower and sighed a breath of relief.

It lasted less than a second at most. I froze in my tracks.

Something was wrong. The ruin should have been further away from the trees. On the other side of the path. Rounded, not rectangular like this one.

Maybe I had missed an outbuilding on the way to the Giant's Grove? Maybe not. With trepidation I walked on and soon registered that I had definitely not seen this place before. There was no clearing as such, ghostly pale birch trees thinned out irregularly, with clumps that stretched out like forest fringe fingers right up to the walls of a small roofless church with a seemingly intact squat tower. There were no other buildings nearby, just a low irregular wall which ran adjacent to the path on either side of the church.

An icy fear gripped my heart, could it be…?

Of course, it was. Even though I kept to the far side of the path the wall was low enough for me to spot old mossed gravestones in the moonlight. Some standing upright, some flat on the ground, others tilted at cray angles. I jumped when an owl suddenly hooted right overhead, bringing into sudden focus how all the other sounds of the night had ceased. I heard the owl's wings as it flew onwards and hurried my stride. This place was dead scary and I was pranging out big time. I broke into a jog, eager to leave it behind. I remembered how Willick had spoken of focal points of energy in the woods and realised I must have stumbled upon one of these. Not a good one.

A sense of dread and foreboding slowed me down again, I wondered if it was my imagination instructing my intuition to sense the menace which now seemed to ooze out of every stone of the ruined church and every phantom like birch. I resisted the urge to curl up in a ball on the ground and cry and then almost screamed as an owl whooshed over me at low altitude emitting an angry screech.

"Fax shite arse fax FAXEDY FAX FAX!" I cursed the owl and started running, fear urging my legs to pump up and down faster, irrationality bidding me turn my head to check if that shapeless dour malovence which preyed upon this place had taken form and was in pursuit. There was nothing behind me that hadn't been there before except for an overriding hostile emphasis that I was not welcome. The shape that began to slowly take form was not one I could see with my eyes, it was a pervading presence in my mind's eye: Dark and hunched up, full of heinous spite. It began to stretch out. Growing wide upper limbs. Raising a rounded head. Opening its eyes. Blood red eyes which shone with ancient malice.

Another owl hooted and its nefarious call was the signal for an ominous cacophony of high pitched screeches as if the air had filled with owls. I gave a yelp of fright and sobbed. The sound stopped again and then I heard the wings. Like before, swooping down, but now much louder. The sound grew louder yet; I looked behind me, then to my sides and back to the front in desperate agitation. There, on the ground, I could see my moon-shadow. And a larger shadow with outstretched wings behind me, closing up fast.

I jerked my head sideways to look over my shoulder.

The thing that flew towards me resembled an owl of sorts but it was far too large, with an incredible wingspan and a body that was out of proportion to those massive wings, much too long and trailing long legs with claws attached. Predatory red eyes focused on mine, locking me in its gaze. Its long sharp claws stretched forwards, reaching for me. I shrieked and pissed myself at the same time and then ducked, hugging the ground in frenzied desperation. I felt the airflow of the creature as it hurled itself through the space which I had just occupied. It rose again emitting loud angry screeches.

I scrambled up and ran, ran as fast as I could, screaming all the while. Either I had gone fully delusional or else something intended to casually shred my life. It didn't matter, both possibilities were terrifying to the extreme and I stampeded hysterically down the path.

The owl-thing's wings sounded closer again; evidently it had turned and was coming in for another run. It sounded and smelt real; surely this could not be a by-product of my poor mind.

"No, no, no." I whimpered, my face running with tears and snot and my knickers soaked by warm piss as I put every ounce of energy I had left in my headlong flight. The wings beat louder, the owl-thing was closing in.

"FAX YOU TWAT!" I shrilled defiantly. The creature screeched back at me menacingly and flew on unperturbed but then suddenly halted its pursuit and rose upwards again.

I ran on. Though there was no longer a physical detection of pursuit, those red eyes had burned themselves into my awareness, a recollection that was just as terrifying and seemed impossible to outrun.

I came to a river and dashed straight in. For the first six yards or so it was only knee deep but then the riverbed dipped steeply and I stumbled headlong into the water. For a moment I was completely submerged, stunned by the cold and thrashing wildly, not sure where the surface was. When my head popped up the current had already carried me downstream somewhat but it wasn't overly strong and with powerful strokes I reached the other side. I scrambled up the riverbank and wanted to take a deep breath when an owl's screech ruptured the sky. I gave a garbled choke and started sprinting away from the noise, almost tripped by tree roots and repeatedly whipped by mean thin branches. I didn't care; all that mattered was to get away from those red eyes boring into my brain. I slowed down a few times, entangled in brambles which would not easily yield passage and the thorns ripped into my flesh, tearing considerable gashes though I could barely feel the sting of the cuts and was only vaguely aware of the blood that flowed from them.

I don't know how long I ran, or in which direction. At some point I was utterly exhausted and sank against the trunk of a broad tree, curled up and then passed out. That is how Puck found me the next morning: Rolled up like a hedgehog, shivering violently with cold, dried blood concealing scores of small cuts and when he took hold of me and tried to shake me awake my eyes opened and rolled around in a frightened frenzy.

Part Deenah: Two for Joy

5. Two for Joy

"Kleak-kleak."

I opened my eyes and looked straight into the ink black eyes of an owl.

"Kleak-kleak," the bird repeated.

"MwhuaAA no No NO!" I trashed about trying to draw away from the creature but my movements were impeded by a smothering layer of blankets. The owl –it was only a small one- had been perched on my chest and seemed greatly offended by my sudden animation, it hissed a protest, spread its wings and hopped up, hovering over me for a few seconds before flying away. I managed to sit up against the backboard of a bed and registered two things at once; one that sitting up caused my head to spin and two that I was naked. I clutched one of the blankets over my breasts and then sank slowly back into the bed.

"What the…" I mumbled. I tried to take in my surroundings but it was all a blur.

I closed my eyes, trying to remember…at which point two fiery red eyes materialised, fury personified. I whimpered as I recalled my experience by the ruined church and cemetery, vaguely remembering a panicked scramble through the undergrowth, going arse over tit in a river and then a wild flight into exhausted unconsciousness. The red eyes glowed and I whimpered again, raising an arm as if to shield myself.

"There, there lass," a woman's voice said kindly. "Ye be safe now."

A hand stroked my clammy forehead. The voice and hand were reassuring and I opened my eyes. The woman sitting on the side of the bed was about Willick's age, her face was lined with wrinkles which failed to disguise that she must have been a real eye catcher once. Her hair was grey with remnants of auburn in it and her eyes were ruby green; sparkling with life and lending her a strangely youthful ambience. What was most noticeable though was that her face was covered in tattoos, some faded, and others intense with colours yet. Strange symbols, runes, small depictions of animals. It was like an artwork.

"Where am I?" I felt totally disorientated and shook my head trying to clear it. "Who are you?"

"Folk calls me Joy, and ye be in The Owlery in the Wyrde Woods," the woman answered.

"OWLS." I struggled upright again. "There were owls..."

She looked at me thoughtfully.

"Aye, I've been thinking ye've probably been at Tuckersham Church. All-along-o' the state ye be in."

I stayed silent. Apparently there was something about this Tuckersham Church which this woman called Joy knew of. So maybe I had not lost my mind completely. But how could I possibly speak of what I had seen? Any sane person would have me sedated and locked up.

"And ye dursn't talk about it," Joy gave me an encouraging smile.

"It's...there was..."

"Ye met him doant ye? Ufmanna. The owl man," she said quietly, holding my eyes with hers.

My mouth nearly fell open. Now I was sure that I hadn't passed through that flimsy barrier between sanity and howling madness, though the alternative that this Ufmanna actually existed was just as chilling.

"You know about the owl man?" I asked in a small voice.

"Aye," Joy nodded. "Ufmanna've been there forever and longer than that. I have seen him with mine own eyes, I have."

"Were you scared too?"

"Naun liddle one," Joy gave me a look of sympathy. "I were prepared. More than that I have an understanding with owls. Yernself now, he would have seen as an intruder, trespassing and all, surelye."

"It tried to kill me!" I shivered when I recalled the attack.

"In mine recollects Ufmanna aint never killed naun, he were jes chasing ye off." Joy stood up and smoothed the faded apron she wore over an old fashioned black dress. "Now I am gwaon to fetch some charm-stuff for ye. Can ye does me a favour lass?"

I nodded absentmindedly, still chewing over the information about the owl creature while I was also surprised to register I liked the 'lass' and 'little one' Joy was using. I guessed that she just had that gift or else I felt so vulnerable that it was comforting to be spoken to as a child.

"Cover yern teats lass, or I'll gwoan green with envy," Joy chuckled. "All purty and perky whilst mine sag, tis unaccountable."

I realised the blanket had fallen down and pulled them up again, a blush spreading on my face along with an awkward grin. Joy laughed at the expression on my face.

"Tis naun to be ashamed o' lass, ye'll drive the lads all mucked up with those, surelye."

Joy walked away and disappeared around a corner. I looked around me. The bed was tucked away in an alcove of sorts, from which I could see a large room with a low beamed ceiling. A huge stone arched fireplace took up most of one wall, barely leaving space for the doorway Joy had disappeared through. A little fire burned merrily in the fireplace, casting a warm glow on the low cluttered table, rocking chair and sagging couch arranged around the fireplace. I saw my dress and other stuff hanging over a small drying rack on the far side of the fireplace. Other items of ancient looking furniture were scattered haphazardly around the room; threadbare armchairs and battered cupboards piled with books and magazines. Bunches of dried herbs hung along the walls as well as a few faded paintings. Two small windows in the wall opposite me -on either side of what looked like the front door- let in daylight. Most noticeable were four wooden boxes attached high up on the walls, placed away from each other. They were open and three held owls, the fourth was empty and I presumed it belonged to the bird which had me all shook up when I came to.

None of the owls were very big. One of them had various hues of brown in its coat, orange around its eyes and white stripes on its forehead and around its beak. Its ear tufts stood straight up giving it a surprised expression. The second was smaller, with a white belly and white and grey markings on its wings. It had a funny little face, with a dark grey Zorro-like mask around its eyes which lent it a perpetual frown. The third had a white heart shaped face and a beige belly and a yellowish brown and grey coat, just like the one which I had found peering into my face when I had come to.

That last one sat perched on a large wardrobe opposite the fireplace, its head turning here and there as it examined the room with an inscrutable look. It did not deign to look at me. I started making clucking noises, trying to get its attention, having decided that the owls here were of a different temperament than the lot I had encountered in the woods. The owl on the wardrobe continued to ignore me, but the others now all looked my way and became restless.

"It'd be bettermost if ye doant make that sound sweetie," Joy returned with a steaming mug. "That'd be the type o' sound they associates with theirn prey."

 I stopped immediately; I had my fill of being owl prey.

"What does folk call ye?" Joy asked.

"Wenn," I said without hesitation, deciding that Willick's name for me would be my Wyrde Woods name. I liked playing around with names.

Joy held the mug in front of me and I tucked the ends of the blanket behind my back so I could take it with both hands and keep my boobs covered. The mug was scorching hot. I gave Joy a questioning look.

"Charm-stuff?"

"Jes a tea sweetie," Joy smiled. "With meadow sweet for pain relief, Corsican borage for fever and cold, doant want ye catching hot now, and French tarrogen to calm ye. There be honey and mint as well, all-along-o' the taste."

"Wow," I exclaimed and took a sip. It tasted odd beneath the dominant honey and mint but it wasn't bad. "Are you like a witch?"

Fortunately Joy didn't take offense at the question, she just chuckled again.

"Tis naun magic lass, jes medication o' natural sorts."

"Pain relief, fever, cold…" I mumbled.

"Quite a state ye were in, aye. All dishabill." Joy confirmed. "Soaking wet, shivering and shaking, babbling oakum and scrazed badly, ye'd been bleeding."

"Bleeding?" Of course, the brambles. I examined my arms; these were lacerated with cuts which looked surprisingly deep.

"Be time for another poultice dappen ye finishes yern charm-stuff."

"More herbs?" I asked, starting to sip from the mug.

"Yarbs, aye. Purple loosestrife, sweet woodruff and yarrow," Joy nodded. "Ta treat it, keep it clean, dull pain and prevent infection."

"How do you know all this stuff?" I asked, fascinated.

"Born and bred in the Wyrde Woods, in disyer Owlery, surelye. Mine Mam learned me."

"How did I get here? I don't remember a house."

"Oh naun, ye fainted a whiles away." Joy shook her head. "Puck found ye and brought ye here. Carried ye all the way so he does. Puck be a bettermost sort o' lad."

I was beginning to get intrigued by this Puck bloke. So he had met me and I couldn't recall a single instance of it. Carried me? My mind's eye formed a strong young man who had scooped me up in his muscular arms as my head rested on his broad chest…

"Tossed ye over hisn shoulder," Joy grinned like she had read my mind. "Like a bag o' taters."

I smiled sheepishly.

"When did this happen?" I asked.

"Somewhen t'other-day," she answered, leaving me none-the-wiser. I must have looked puzzled for she added, "Ye were out for a good day-an-half."

I nodded, if I had been brought here yesterday morning I had been gone from Nowhere Place for more than 48 hours already. There'd be hell to pay I realised. I would have to think of a tall tale to justify my absence. I smiled to myself. If I told them the truth they'd accuse me of lying. Or else beef up my meds to zombie level. Probably both.

My meds! Shit-fax-bother. I had been missing those too. It wasn't that I'd turn into a homicidal maniac if I missed them for a few days. Sometimes I even sold them to Biggs, a lad on my corridor, when I was in dire need for cash. But I might subside into gloom and doom a bit deeper than I liked. I yawned, suddenly feeling too tired to fuss.

"Tis disyer drink," Joy nodded. "I'll treat yern arms and legs and then ye'd best rest some more, ye still be beazled lass."

I nodded, drowsy already and I barely registered the calm soothing effect of the poultices when Joy applied them to my arms, after which she lifted the blankets to treat my legs which were also crisscrossed with scratches and cuts.

"As lean as a rake ye're. And all callow below, is that the fashion?" She tutted.

I mumbled incoherently.

"Never mind sweetie." When she was done she tucked me in and I remember thinking that nobody had ever done that before. It was comforting and safe.

I was safe here, I realised with a numb smile before I fell into a deep sleep.

§ § § § § §

My dreams were vivid: A landscape of foliage guarded over by giant trees and other entities which remained vague in shape. Ruined serpentine walls of age-old stone which started flowing like liquid, curving into shapes that separated themselves and floated upwards. People from another time who spoke a tongue familiar yet strange. A purple carpet spread out beneath the trees through which strode a handsome boy, broad shouldered with slim flanks and dressed like a farmer of yore. Green woods filled with watchful eyes, some of wary animals, others almost human but filled with swirling colours. A full moon revealed by parting clouds shining silver upon a hilltop where large fires formed golden beacons. These were surrounded by animalistic wild dancers driven into frenzies by incessant loud drums. Then a suffocating tidal wave of grey wet concrete which carried me away. When I went down, still clawing at the smothering surface, I was suddenly surrounded by tower blocks and looking into the angry faces of No-Tooth and Broken Nose. Their mouths moved with rapid anger but I couldn't hear them at all. Neither was there noise when I screamed for help; Michael shrugging helplessly in response. No-Tooth and Broken Nose grew wings and rose into the air and then just hovered, staring at me with fierce piercing red eyes. I felt as vulnerable as a mouse waiting to be pounced upon but could not move, transfixed by those glowing red eyes.

I woke with a start and shot upright in the bed, gasping for breath. Looking at the windows I could see that it was dark outside. The fire had been stoked higher and a bunch of lit candles provided a surprising amount of illumination. The fourth owl was now in its box. I heard somebody rummaging about through the open doorway in what I assumed was the kitchen. The blankets had fallen away from my upper body again and I decided it was time to get properly dressed. I swung my legs over the side of the bed, stood up and then walked to the drying rack next to the fireplace, where I put on my knickers and bra and then pulled the dress over my head. I examined the stockings for a moment but they seemed a total loss, the brambles had torn them pretty badly.

I saw my boots but decided to leave them be. I wasn't going anywhere just yet as I felt somewhat shaky merely from the exertion of getting out of bed.

I sank onto the couch close to the fire, and appreciated the warm glow. I wanted a smoke badly, but my baccy had become a ball of goo and the papers were ruined. Joy came in with a bowl of thick and creamy soup and a chunk of bread and my belly started rumbling. I realised I was famished and accepted the meal gratefully. Joy sat on the rocking chair and beamed as she watched me wolf down the food.

"Thank you," I said when I finished the last of it. "Thank you so much."

"That be fine sweetie, will ye be wanting more?"

I shook my head, content with my full belly and the warmth of the fire, though the food seemed to have energised my thoughts.

"Joy?"

"Aye lass?"

"I met someone in the woods; he spoke of places which were like sources of energy..."

"...and filled with shims."

I recognised the word; Willick had used it a few times.

"No, he didn't believe in ghosts." I said.

Joy started laughing heartily.

"Mus've been Will Maskall ye met then. He be the only one round here what doant hold with shims."

"Yes, him I think, he said his name was Willick Maskall. But those places, like St. Lewinna's and that cemetery are there more places like that, bad ones?"

Joy regarded me thoughtfully for a while. "Does ye know the Wyrde Woods well?"

"Not really, I walked to St. Lewinna's from Odesby and then Willick took me to see the Giant's Grove. That's about all."

"Does he now?" Joy seemed surprised.

"He was kind," I bowed my head, feeling shame when I recalled our parting.

"Then he mus've liked ye. Will doant take to Sheere-folk much, howsumdever, some-one-time he makes exceptions."

"Sheere-folk?"

"Them that doant come from disyer parts," Joy frowned. "There be a snoule o' places like ye said. The Blood Stone and Devil's Tarn best be seen in light o' day. The old Westwood Manor House and Devil's Bottom. The Raven's Roost in Wolfden and the mill at Roreford. Then there's Malheur Hall o' course and most o' Odesby as far as I be concerned."

I burst into laughter. Joy looked quizzical.

"Oh, I totally agree about Odesby. I live there." I kept grinning. "Malheur Hall is bad?"

"Crawling with shims, which be the reason Willick doant admit to them o' course, middling old fool that he be."

She lost me there, I couldn't understand what Willick's refusal of ghosts had to do with Malheur Hall but I let it go.

"And Lady Malheur?"

"Unaccountable brabagious draggle-tail," Joy snorted, her face momentarily disfigured by an intense dislike.

"Right," I nodded though I hadn't understood a word of that either. The context was clear though. There was something neat about the way Joy and Willick spoke, but it required some effort to understand them. Sometimes it was like I understood them without understanding them. Was it the same for them when I spoke? How much contact did these people actually have with the outside world? With the *Sheere-folk*?

"And these ghost stories? The shims?" I loved ghost stories. "Can you tell me a few?"

Joy looked at me in an odd way.

"I would no-ways tell them this deep in the night Wenn," she said softly. "Alltsinit that I think they best be left in peace, naun reason to call their attention to us I reckon. Tis different at daytime."

It cost me some effort not to raise a sceptical eyebrow. Joy had been kind and generous and had won my devotion the moment she tucked me into bed, something I had never experienced before. I wanted to avoid the mistake I had made with Willick at all cost. If that meant obliging her in her wish not to tell ghost stories late at night it was a price I was happy to pay. Besides, there might well be something to it, I realised with a shiver, recalling a dark red eyed shape swooping out of the dark sky.

"Joy," I asked shyly.

"Aye lass?"

"Can you...would you tuck me in again tonight? When I go to sleep?" I felt like a right idiot asking it, it wasn't as if I was six years old anymore. But I really wanted her to.

"O' course I'll tuck ye in sweetie," Joy nodded. "I'd be happy to does so."

§ § § § § §

I felt my old self again the next morning. Not much to write a non-existent home about to be sure, but I could walk steadily and needed to get back to Nowhere Place before I got into so much trouble that I'd put my placement there at risk. I gave Joy a brief explanation of my background and was relieved that she attached no judgment in her responses. To her I was just Wenn, regardless of where I lived. She walked me northwards on a dirt road that led to a tarmac road and a bus stop. She paid for the bus ticket when the double-decker showed up and then it was time to say our goodbyes.

"Can I come back?" I was suddenly reluctant to leave.

"I'd be middling disappointed if ye doant child, I mean that." Joy took my hand in hers and gave it a squeeze. "Ye're always welcome, surelye. Always."

"Hurry up girl," the driver called impatiently and I got on the bus which drove through the woods to the village of Nickleby and then on to Odesby.

I got off on the High Street across from the ruined keep of Odesby Castle. Standing in the middle of a busy street was weird, it all seemed loud and fast and oddly wrong. I felt very much out of place. I looked at the sandstone walls of the keep and saw the castle to which I had never paid much attention before in a different light. There was something familiar about it, its age and history seemed like a connection to the Wyrde Woods.

"Then I dursn't deny it, surelye," I said aloud with a grin, then grimaced. It was time to start the walk back to Neverland.

6. Nowhere Place

By the time I reached Neverland it was almost as if I had never been away. I could have walked the concrete jungle blindfolded. I might have made a few bob organizing wild life safaris there. As expert resident zoologist I could have told tourists a thing or two about the complex social structures which most Odesby residents had no clue about. They looked down on all Neverlanders without recognising the all-important distinctions that influenced the estate's hierarchy. The landlord of the Neverland Arms was king of the heap, and then came those who lived in the old part of the estate, in the old working man's cottages. Though their houses were as dishevelled as Nowhere Place and the garden plots the size of postage stamps they didn't live in the tenements and that made all the difference. Next were the handful of Indian shopkeepers who ran a few corner shops and off-licenses. Then came the tenement rats. The tenements were warrens of stairways and corridors where the lights were permanently busted and everything smelled of stale urine. Separated by flimsy walls were minute boxy apartments where every possible human tragedy was played out 24-7. I suppose everybody has to feel superior to someone and the tenement rats looked down on us. They lived in something resembling family units, no matter how insanely dysfunctional they were. We didn't.

The Forlorn Hopers were wanted by no one and everybody knew it and that made us the least-of-the least in Neverland. Which was pretty much how we thought of ourselves anyways, so there was little dispute about it. That said, the majority of the people who lived in the tenements were decent people in difficult circumstances, it was a dominant minority which loudly brayed their existence and gave the estate its reputation.

"Well look what the cat's dragged in," Miss Watson said when she intercepted me after I had walked through the front door of Nowhere Place, half hoping to sneak unseen to my room for a shower, change of clothes and a chance to bum a smoke off somebody before facing the music.

Watson placed her hands on her wide hips and examined my bedraggled appearance.

"And where have you been young lady? We have been worried sick about you."

Yeah right.

"Out and about," I answered. "I am back now."

"I can see that," Watson snapped.

"I'd like to have a shower," I said hopefully. I really did, I smelled pretty foul.

"You can bloody well wait until we have sorted out the mess you caused," Watson said tersely. "I'd like you to go to the consultancy room now and we'll be by for a chat."

"WENDY!" Sharon shouted happily from the top of the stairs. I gave her a friendly wave. She was about to storm down the stairs when Watson turned and gave her a stare that caused her to freeze in her tracks.

"I think I will have that shower first," I said resolutely and took a step towards the stairs.

Watson grabbed my arm, she was surprisingly strong and her grip hurt me.

"HEY!" I protested angrily. She responded by steering me down the hallway to the consultancy room. When I struggled she tightened her grip so much it hurt. I bit my lip, not wanting to give her the satisfaction of hearing me whimper. I couldn't place this. I had never been manhandled by the staff of Nowhere Place before, only at previous institutions when I'd sometimes been so insanely wild I had to be restrained, sedated and placed in the isolation cell.

Watson opened the door of the consultancy room with one hand and shoved me into the room. I nearly stumbled, regained my feet and then turned to look at her angrily.

"You..." Watson said.

"What the FAX do you think you are doing?" I shouted. Now that I was released from her grip I felt anger welling up inside of me.

"YOU MIND YOUR TONGUE!" Watson bellowed, and then added "Because of you poor Michael Hassock left the OJCH in tears. After all he had done for you. He deserved a little better don't you think?"

I saw her eyes moisten. Bloody hell, had she fancied Michael then? I was about to ask when she slammed the door shut and locked it. I ran to the door and shook the door handle, and then beat on the door with my fists.

"LET ME OUT!" I screamed, I hated being locked up. It was to no avail of course and for once common sense took charge and led me to the table. I sat down, gripping the table edge in clenched hands and started to take deep breaths. If I lost control I'd only make matters a lot worse. Right now, I told myself, most of that had been Watson's personal feelings surfacing.

Watson was what we called a 'Lifer'. These were veterans just like we were and in a funny way we were in the same leaky boat. Just like we couldn't sink much lower in the system, they ended up at Nowhere Place because they couldn't possibly sink lower in their careers. Their motivation for their work was usually sub-zero, they knew that the Forlorn Hope were beyond saving just like their careers. Their main focus was on keeping up the appearance of rehabilitation by demanding that we attended group talks, counselling and therapy as well as try to stay out of hospital or prison. We submitted to this without much resistance, knowing that the next stop was likely a young offender institution, the kind of place that made a juvenile detention centre a piece of cake. Besides, nobody took the therapeutic sessions seriously, both staff and Forlorn Hopers just went through the motions and as a reward we received the meds which was all that stood between us and total mental oblivion.

Lifers were mostly caretakers, with a few therapists thrown in. We had shrinks too, but the Freud Squad were different, they were detached to Nowhere Place for a day or two every week and mostly just rubber-stamped whatever the Lifers asked them to, not having a great deal of interest in us at all.

There were also Snooties on the staff, students or first-job optimists whom we generally despised. They made sincere attempts to make contact with us sure enough, much more so than the Lifers. This seems friendly enough perhaps but would inevitably be followed by attempts to burrow around in our psyche in a none too subtle manner. Snooties always thought they were being clever but tended to forget that most of us grew up with continual psychological probing. We knew the script inside out and we had developed the skills to run circles around expensively trained and well-paid counsellors, therapists and psychologists if we chose to do so. Which was all the time. Some well-meaning but stuck-up first-timer who just got his or her nose out of the books was no match for our cunning. Biggs, called that because he was enormously fat, was a bookie on the side and we would all place bets with him when a fresh Snooty arrived. The safest bet was that it would take us less than two weeks to break a Snooty in and cause him or her to assume a permanent look of despair.

Anyhow, Watson was just a caretaker, not a therapist or shrink who had far more to say. So her anger wasn't necessarily indicative for the measure of trouble I was in. Going AWOL simply wasn't the kind of thing that bought you a ticket to a young offender's institution, unless you did it on a structural basis. There'd be lots of blahblahblah and if I just acted contrite I'd get away with it. If I started fighting then they'd fight back and the system always won. It was that simple.

They made me practice that patience for more than an hour, I am pretty sure they let me wait intentionally and I tried to stay calm by singing the lyrics of songs, tapping on the table with my fingers for the beat.

At last Watson returned, with one of the Freud Squad in tow as well as a man I didn't know. The shrink was a weasel faced pedantic bitch called Mary Hare. The Forlorn Hopers hated her collectively and called her Hairy Mare on account of her thin moustache. The new guy was a heavy set man in his thirties with dark brown hair; his cheeks, upper lip and chin were dark with the shadow of a beard. His mouth was set in an amiable smile but I immediately distrusted him because of his jet-black eyes, which conveyed no friendliness, just cool calculation, predatory almost. I dubbed him Stubbles as he and Hairy Mare sat down on the other side of the table. Watson remained standing by the door, her arms folded in front of her and a grim look on her face.

Stubbles and Hairy Mare took their time, laying files on the table, opening them, rereading bits of them and consulting in whispers once or twice whilst pointing out items of interest. I leaned back in my chair; arms folded, and regarded them stoically.

"Well then," Stubbles said at last, folding his hairy hands in front of him on the table and beaming a fake smile at me whilst his eyes scrutinised my face.

"Well then." I repeated.

"We haven't met yet Wendy, my name is George Dagle and I am Michael Hassock's replacement. I understand you were particularly attached to Mr. Hassock, but I am sure you and I are going to get along just fine once we get to know each other."

He spoke in a deep voice that was somehow reassuring but didn't lessen my distrust of him. I didn't respond, just stared at him. He stared right back at me without blinking even as he continued speaking in that fake jovial tone.

"Before we can do that though, we need to establish just what happened with regard to your unauthorised absence. Let's see, you left these premises..."

"The day before yesterday," I filled in. It sounded like a short time ago, had I really only been in the Wyrde Woods that briefly? It felt much longer. "Isn't Mrs. Hare superior to the therapist? Shouldn't she be leading this talk?"

Stubbles and Hairy Mare exchanged glances, Hairy Mare giving him a prissy 'I told you so' look. Watson snorted by the door.

"I don't really think you need to be concerned with professional procedures Wendy," Stubbles said with a condescending smile, though his eyes conveyed irritation. "Now let us turn to your whereabouts, shall we?"

"We would like you to tell us where you have been these past three days," Hairy Mare added in her shrill nasal voice. It was one of her professional assets. I knew Forlorn Hopers who would just talk and talk in sessions with Hairy Mare, telling her whatever she wanted to hear in order to spend as little time as possible listening to that voice. I threw her a poisonous look. I realised my intention to cooperate was fading fast, their attitudes steering me to the edge.

"I would like to register a complaint," I said.

"All in good time Wendy," Stubbles said. "Right now we have other business to discuss."

"I was physically abused by a member of staff just now when I got back," I stared pointedly at Watson who just snorted again.

"That is a serious allegation Wendy," Stubbles said. "Do you have witnesses?"

"Sharon was watching," I said.

Stubbles looked at Watson.

"I have had a talk with Sharon already," Watson said. "She has nothing to report."

"It appears that your witness will speak against the accusation," Hairy Mare shrilled, and then shook her head and tutted. She opened her notebook to a blank page and made some notes.

"It is my contention that you are trying to change the subject Wendy," Stubbles said. "I would like to know if you are going to co-operate in this de-briefing or not?"

He managed to say this in a manner that was simultaneously pleasant and threatening.

I glared at him, tensing my arms as I tried to contain the rising bile.

"If you would rather not be here, I would understand," Stubbles gave an emphatic smile. "You can have as much time as you need to mull things over in the Reflection Room."

The 'Reflection' Room. I felt a cold chill. It was a politically correct name for isolation cell. I had never been in the one in Nowhere Place, but previous encounters in other institutions have provided me with a lifetime's worth of nightmares. I closed my eyes and took a deep breath, trying to recall my resolution to co-operate.

"We are waiting," Hairy Mare chirped. I opened my eyes. The shrink had a triumphant smile on her narrow face, sensing victory no doubt. Stubbles just sat there, giving encouraging smiles, but his eyes told me that he knew he had won.

"I was with a friend," I mumbled, casting my eyes down again.

"Where?" Stubbles inquired.

"Tenements," I lied.

"Who is the friend?" Stubbles asked.

"I am not going to tell you, I don't want trouble for them," I looked up again defiantly.

"Probably Katy Marston," Watson said. "They used to be inseparable before Katy left."

"It wasn't Katy," I shook my head.

"Was it a boy then? Or a man?" Stubbles asked.

"I am not telling."

There was a pause as both Stubbles and Hairy Mare started scribbling in their notebooks.

"I will presume you were in male company then," Stubbles said. "And take your silence as an affirmation."

Even Watson raised an eyebrow at this. I shrugged and stayed silent.

"Has somebody hurt you?" Stubbles asked, pointing at the scratches on my arms.

"She has them on her legs too," Watson supplied helpfully.

"Nobody hurt me," I said.

Though a monstrous owl man tried to disembowel me by a graveyard in the light of the full moon.

I giggled.

"Have you been hurting yourself again Wendy?" Hairy Mare asked pointedly.

I shook my head.

"Miss Twyner is noncommittal as to whether her wounds are self-inflicted or not," Hairy Mare intoned as she wrote in her notebook.

I shrugged.

"Now Wendy," Stubbles said. "I think we know why you departed in an emotional state. Perhaps you were too attached to Mr. Hassock. In such situations, it is not uncommon to find solace with…company elsewhere."

I just stared at him. Did they think I fancied Michael? The guy was ancient.

"If so, we need to know if said man, or men, is a minor or an adult. There are legal implications." Stubbles continued. Hairy Mare scribbled in her notebook like a madwoman.

"You seriously think I was boning somebody?" I asked in disbelief. Even if I had been it was none of their bloody business.

"Then will you tell us with who you were, how you were hurt and what you *did* do during the past days?" Stubbles said sharply.

"I already told you."

Damn, this was totally out of order.

"I was upset and stayed with a friend, that's all," I added.

"We'd like a few more details than that," he insisted.

"Well you're not getting them," I shook my head.

"Then you leave us no choice but to fill in our own interpretation of what happened," Stubbles shrugged as it were of no importance to him.

I took a deep breath. Co-operate, I told myself. They'll decide what happened and what goes on in my head regardless of what I say.

"I think further consequences are best discussed in a group session," Stubbles said, nodding slowly. "But as a matter of precaution we need to make an appointment with the G.P. to examine Wendy as quickly as possible. Possible bruising around the thighs. Traces of semen. Venereal disease. Pregnancy."

"That is a good suggestion," Hairy Mare's tongue flicked out and she ran it along her moustache, "I will arrange an emergency appointment today."

"No shower for you then Wendy, not until you have been examined," Stubbles said. "Miss Watson would you lock the upstairs shower rooms for the duration?"

I was used to a great deal of unprofessionalism at Nowhere Place, but this really beat it all. Three professional caretakers and two of them were just concurring as the third was projecting some sort of pervy fantasy. I considered my thoughtless accusation of Willick.

Instant karma is gonna get you.

"How do you feel about this Wendy?" Stubbles asked, his eyes probing me. I closed my eyes and saw Willick's face, those honest sharp blue eyes, and his willingness to share his woods with me. My bitchiness at the end.

"Ashamed," I spoke truthfully and opened my eyes just in time to see Stubbles and Hairy Mare exchange a meaningful look before they both started scribbling in their notebooks again.

§ § § § § § §

The group session followed straight away, the rest of the Forlorn Hopers whom I shared a corridor with were already gathered in the common room. Stubbles and Hairy Mare marched me there and we all took a seat in the circle. Most of the kids hung over their chairs listlessly, looking bored. Some nodded a non-committal greeting at me, others ignored me. A few of the lads just stared at Sharon who was considered hot spice and well-stacked, far more interesting than anything to do with me. That particular disinterest would stay; the rest of the boycott wouldn't last long. Right now they were pissed because this was costing them free time on account of me. I'd feel the same.

Biggs was bobbing up and down as he tried to catch my eye, he adored the ground I walked on, a situation which I sometimes took shameless advantage of. I ignored him, locking eyes with Sharon instead. She gave me a pleading look, wanting to know if I was pissed off by her submission to Watson. I smiled at her and nodded an okay and she looked relieved.

"We all know why we are here," Stubbles started the meeting, proceeding to explain how my abrupt unauthorised departure from the OJCH had meant that I had placed myself in a vulnerable position, possible prey to all sorts of depravity. He actually used that word: Depravity. Sharon looked shocked and threw me a concerned look. I subtly shook my head and rolled my eyes and she smiled. Hairy Mare, in the meantime, tutted and nodded wisely.

"Just as grave perhaps," Stubbles preached, "Wendy's absence has meant that a lot of you were quite upset as well, there has been an unusual amount of agitation in the group. People have been very concerned Wendy."

He looked pointedly at me.

I looked around the group; half were still comatose. Biggs smirked guiltily and some of the other lads grinned. I understood they had milked the situation to the max; being upset was a great reason to break the rules of course. I could hardly blame them as I would have done the same.

"I am so very sorry guys," I opened my eyes as wide as possible and spoke in a high falsetto tone. "I made a terrible mistake, I certainly didn't mean for you all to be worried and upset. Please accept my apologies and give me another chance. I want to better myself."

Hairy Mare started nodding her appreciation of my confession, Stubbles shot me a dirty look and some of the Forlorn Hopers burst out into loud laughter.

"We forgive you Wendy," Thomas, one of the swag lads, sniggered and winked at me.

"I forgive you too," Biggs said eagerly. I flashed him a smile, I would need to borrow some money off him for baccy later.

Sharon looked less happy, I realised she might well have been genuinely concerned for me, but I knew that once I had been examined by the G.P. and had my shower I'd spend most of the evening in her room smoking crow and getting blunted and I would tell her of my adventures, barring Ufmanna that was. I'd just say I got lost in the woods like the utter fool I was.

Stubbles wasn't satisfied yet and persisted in continuing to list in detail the various consequences of my anti-social behaviour towards the group. In vain though, cohesion had been re-established and it was business as usual: Us against the rats. I just kept on apologising and being forgiven. Hairy Mare, in her obtuseness, positively beamed, in her book this was remarkable group progression. In the end Stubbles gave up and announced that there would have to be some sort of consequence to help me reflect my behaviour and suggested that the group would vote on a two-week house arrest. I frowned; it was a faxing cloober as I'd be stuck here during next week's second half of the midterm. Then again, it could have been much worse. When the voting started I was the first to raise my hand and the rest duly followed suit.

"Very well," Stubbles said. "I hope you all appreciate how the consequence is a collective decision and not something decided by the staff alone."

He looked around expectantly. We all nodded our great faxing appreciation and then the meeting was over.

§ § § § § §

Sharon told me later that nothing out of the ordinary had happened during my absence, barring that Michael had been led from the consultancy room looking pale -supported by an over-concerned Watson- and George Dagle had arrived. He had immediately started to stamp his own view of things on Nowhere Place in an energetic fashion that had impressed most of the Lifers, including the Head Supervisor. He'd had his first sessions with a few of the Forlorn Hopers and these had been filled with sexual insinuations, earning him the nickname 'The Perv'. As for the rest, it had been the usual general mayhem of sex, drugs and rock-n-roll -minor infractions mostly- with the main difference being that I had been blamed for all of them.

The two weeks of house arrest passed by slowly. Both Stubbles and Watson worked on Mondays, Wednesdays and Thursdays, meaning I made sure I spent those days in my room assuming an angelic look whenever they came to check on me, and those two did so often. I didn't mind, it gave me time to read which meant I escaped the intention of their punishment. Hairy Mare considered herself too well qualified to demean herself with such visits, that's what the rest of the staff was for. On the other days I went downstairs and slipped out of the back window of the laundry room for short expeditions to the High Street, coming and going as I pleased.

I had my first session with Stubbles. I spent the hour in sullen silence, staring at the curtain rails where they had come loose from their attachment to the wall. This had been the case for two years, nobody bothered to fix such small dilapidations in Nowhere Place so it wasn't like I hadn't noted it before, but I find that a stare can be maintained better if there is a clear fixed point to focus on. I shut Stubbles out entirely; his voice had become a distant and indistinct drone as I tried to recall the exact route up and down a favoured chestnut tree.

"Having a bad spell," I mumbled when the time was up. He nodded understanding but his smile was thin and his eyes angry and that gave me satisfaction.

In the first post-punishment weekend Sharon and I persuaded Biggs to finance a train trip to Stancaster for a Shop-Saturday. He was delighted and stood beaming in several camping and outdoor stores as we stuffed various items in the pockets of the parka coat which he always insisted on wearing, or down his jumper and trousers. None of the security guards noticed that he had got considerably fatter when we left the stores, even when we stuffed a sleeping bag halfway down his trousers. The alarms went off, of course, but we solved this by having Sharon walk out simultaneously with Biggs. The alarm would beep and Sharon would make an immediate loud admission of guilt, fussing over a new purse which had not had its magnetic tag removed properly. Being blue-eyed, blond, pretty and having a scrumptious cleavage helps a great deal in these situations, the security guards transformed into helpful gentlemen who came to her aid as Biggs and I made a quick getaway.

We had acquired the purses from a big department store where I had thrown them out of the ladies' bathroom window into an alley where Biggs and Sharon had been waiting to collect them. When we left Stancaster Sharon had four new purses, I had a new sturdy backpack containing a Wyrde Woods survival kit and Biggs' self-image was much improved as we praised his sirageous bravery and invaluable help all the way back to Odesby.

On Sunday Sharon and I went to visit our friend Katy in the tenements. Katy had been my best friend in Nowhere Place during my first year there, even though she was a good two years older than I was. Last year she had got herself preggers and after the baby had been born she was allocated a flat and an allowance. She was pleased to see us and delighted in showing off her new possessions, some cheap furniture but mostly of course, the baby. She talked of little else and Sharon listened attentively and cooed over the brat at appropriate times. I just sat there noting the smell of dirty nappies which pervaded the whole flat and listening to the couple next door having a huge row, the couple overhead having some sort of kinky sex whilst the floor shook because the downstairs neighbour was making the most awful racket on an electric guitar.

"Don't you think little Markie is adorable?" Katy asked me for the sixth time.

"Oh yes! OH YES! OH MY GOD YES!" A woman's voice shouted from the ceiling.

"USELESS PIECE OF SHIT!" A woman's voice contributed next door, followed by the sound of something thudding into the wall and shattering into pieces.

"SMOOOKE ON THE WAAAAAAAATER!" The downstairs guitar player bellowed.

"He's so cute!" Sharon gushed for the sixth time.

I looked at the brat, who squirmed around in a play box, its prune like face had turned red and it was gathering breath for another round of incessant wailing.

"Very nice," I said to please Katy.

"WHO'S YO DADDY?" A man's voice roared above.

"YOU ARE! YOU ARE! YOU ARE!"

"STOP NAGGING ME STUPID BITCH"

"FIRE IN THE SKYE-HIIIIIGH!"

§ § § § § §

My head was fair ringing when we escaped at last and made our way back to Nowhere Place warily, continually looking around us like soldiers on a patrol. This was habit rather than immediate necessity, it had been raining for days on end and still was, leaving the streets inhabited only by unmanned cars, mostly old ones with visible rust stains, one of them nothing more than a burned out wreck.

"I want what Katy has too," Sharon said happily.

This wasn't shocking to me; we'd had this conversation before.

"You shagged Thomas already then?" I asked.

"Almost," she beamed. "He's sooo bear sic. Totally piff."

"You know what boys are like; they'll run a hundred miles if you get preggers."

"Have you seen his six-pack?"

"Darling, everybody in Odesby has seen Thomas' six-pack. He takes his bloody t-shirt off on the High Street in the middle of the winter if he can think of a bloody excuse for it. He's not going to settle down till he's ancient and has a faxing beer gut you know."

"Thomas is different Wendy," Sharon looked at me with conviction in her blue eyes. "He's ever so bostin. He'll stick round."

"They're sweet when they want to get in your panties Sharon," I sighed.

I had applied all the arguments before, but I knew it wouldn't be long before I lost Sharon just like I had lost Katy.

I didn't like change much. Every time I was shunted to a new location I had to struggle to find some sort of comfort zone and every time I accomplished that I would have to cope with changes imposed by things beyond my control. Like losing Katy or possibly Sharon. I felt like an autumn leaf, blown willy-nilly by a cruel cold wind, ever further from the branch to which I had been attached and which I missed terribly, even though I wouldn't be able to recognise it if someone beat me over the head with it. Things weren't helped by my impulsive rash actions of course. In the end I was usually the one that set off the spark which would blow the remnants of my hard-fought comfort zone to Kingdom Come.

I sensed that change had already been set in motion though this was a different kind of change; I wanted it. Sure, I was busy living my Nowhere Place life, getting stoned with Sharon, shoplifting, finding new ways to fool the Lifers, flirting money out of Biggs, trying to prevent myself from going ballistic…but things had been different since I had got back from the Wyrde Woods. My dreams were full of trees and green things. Freedom. I had tried to talk to Sharon about these things but her eyes had just glazed over, this was a million miles from her world, she couldn't understand that I was finding life in Neverland ever phonier, in her mind there was no other life.

I was the biggest phony of all of course. Being Wendy meant being a bitch. I had never minded this much; it was the way I kept my head above the flood waters. It was also an integral part of me just like every other girl I knew, no matter how much they tried to sugar-coat it with being sweet and peachy. But now I had met Wenn. I had liked being Wenn, especially at the Owlery. There were plenty of flaws still, but I simply knew that Wenn was capable of improving herself, making changes Wendy could never make.

In other words, I was just biding my time till I could return to the Wyrde Woods.

7. The Green Man

One problem was that I hadn't figured out when to explore the woods again. Till now I had never really wanted to leave Nowhere Place for a longer period of time. Weekend day passes and the occasional stolen hour to wander about the High Street or the supermarket had sufficed. There was also the fact that the staff considered me to be on an informal probation period of sorts. I couldn't really go AWOL again which only left the day pass. That didn't leave me a whole lot of time as I would have to hike to the woods and back in that time.

I pondered for a week, studying local maps on the internet. The maps only showed the major landmarks. There was no reference to the Giant's Grove let alone Joy's cottage. Malheur Hall was marked as were the courses of the two main rivers, the Rore and its principle tributary called the Taunflow as well as the three hills I had seen. It was the Taunflow I had crossed when I had failed to take the left turn back to St. Lewinna's and I figured it was probably the Rore I had plunged into during my flight from Ufmanna. I didn't want to go stumbling around blindly again. Joy had mentioned a fair number of places best avoided. At night-time, sure, but those red eyes still haunted my sleep so I reckoned it would be best to avoid them in daylight too by avoiding the unknown.

I decided that catching the bus that would bring me to the bus stop near the Owlery was one option and I opted to do that the next weekend, which was a home leave weekend, when Nowhere Place emptied because most Forlorn Hopers went on family visits. This Saturday I'd use my weekly day pass and catch the bus to Nickleby. There was a marked walking path to the solitary hill which was called Arthur's Fort and it wasn't too far to walk. It would be a good opportunity to try out my new gear as well.

I laid it all out on my bed on Friday evening. Apart from the backpack and sleeping bag I had two pairs of green army trousers, a wool jumper, a fleecy vest, a pocket knife, a canteen, a mess kit, a small torch, spare batteries, matches, a compass, a poncho, and a small towel. There were also a few survival gear gadgets for which I couldn't even begin to fathom the purpose but they looked neat and professional. Besides that I had liberated tampons, tissue paper, two bottles of spring water and a pack of muesli bars from the supermarket.

I felt incredibly chuffed as I saw all the gear laid out neatly. It was in total contrast to the rest of my room which looked like a tornado had swept through it, sucking up everything and then scattering it in a random debris pattern. I decided to pack everything on my bed into the backpack –barring the clothes I'd wear-, even though most of contents of the backpack were superfluous for a short outing. It would be good to see how I coped with the weight on my back.

I managed to wake up early on Saturday and walked to the High Street in good spirits. The sun was up already for it had finally stopped raining and the streets were still relatively quiet. The bus was nearly empty and before I knew it I was in Nickleby. The footpath began behind a pub called the Earl's Barrel which was an old timbered building which looked like it had been teleported in from a fairy tale. The path started at the far end of the pub car park. As I walked on to it I felt sheer exhilaration to be back in the woods again, it was as if my mind was set free of at least some of the shackles which so often dragged it down.

The woods here had a much denser appearance because the leaves had filled out a lot during the past three weeks though there was sparse undergrowth, barring colonies of ferns which grew here in large numbers, swaying serenely in a soft breeze I could barely register.

I was well aware of the weight of the backpack on my back but after a few adjustments I had got the straps just right. I'd have a proper breakfast once I got up the hill, I decided; water and a muesli bar would do just fine but I made a mental note to acquire a thermos so I could bring coffee next time. I kept up a good pace while the path ran east, level with the Nickleby road on which I could hear occasional cars rush by. At some point though the path turned north and changed radically in its nature, rising and falling steeply along with the strange folds of the land which formed low ridges interlaced with four to six-foot deep gullies. These ran down to deep holes, craters almost, often containing a pool of stagnant water.

The trees were crowded together here but their smooth grey trunks had few lower branches and high canopies which shaded the lower levels of the forest meaning there was little undergrowth apart from small clusters of young trees so that there was a sense of space.

There where the path ran on horizontally for a dozen yards or so at a time puddles had gathered. These weren't like the puddles we had on the uneven dilapidated streets of Neverland. Here in the Wyrde Woods the puddles had dug themselves into a lair of mud and were deceptive. Some looked harmlessly shallow but concealed surprising depths. Others seemed to be surrounded by solid earth but this gave way on first contact with my boots to turn into sludge before my eyes and I had to make sudden sideways scrambles to firmer ground as the sludge slid into the puddle. The gradient of the slopes increased and as it did so the mud got worse, covering the ground in a continuous thin but treacherous sheet. This meant I now had to also contend with the stuff on the steep paths which zigzagged down the even steeper slopes. Some of these I could manage only by using my hands to clutch on to the young trees which were clustered by the sides of the path and saved me from falling more than once as my feet started slipping.

I came to the largest hollow I had yet seen, easily thirty feet deep with a large dark pool at the bottom and halted for a moment. Despite all my enthusiasm for the woods I had not forgotten Ufmanna and this place had an eerie feel to it. I looked around, there seemed to be no easier path around the hollow as the undergrowth had become denser and more restrictive. The path I was on led steeply downwards to the sullen pool where it took a sudden 90 degree turn and departed through a gulley. The rest of the slopes around the pool were by far too steep to climb. I started down carefully but within a few feet my boots slipped and this time there was no vegetation to hang on to.

My subsequent descent was a rapid series of events. I slid down using my boots as skis while my torso swayed from side to side and my arms flailed in the air to keep balance. I swayed so far to the left that for a few seconds I was supporting myself on just my left leg, the right joined the instinctive movements of my arms. I thought that heralded the inevitable fall but somehow I managed to get back on two feet. Albeit, only for a few seconds because now I swayed so far right that my left foot lost all contact with the ground. This time I fell hard but I managed to land on my bum and immediately started sliding downwards at increasing speed.

I registered that my course was taking me straight to that pool and I could now see through enough of the water to note that it was deep. I started digging my heels into the ground, at first producing nothing but a spray of mud which hit me full frontal, but then I found grip and my boots started burrowing themselves into the mud. Deeper and deeper they went and I started to slow down. Not fast enough, I thought in alarm, but then my left boot was snagged on a root and I swung sideways, sliding to a halt just by the water's edge.

I turned and scrambled up, away from the pool and into the gully. There I found a fallen tree which offered some solid surface and I sat down, panting and temporarily blown.

I looked down at myself. My army trousers were caked in mud. My bottom felt distinctly wet from the slide and my duffel coat had received a splattering. There was even a fair bit of mud on my face and in my hair. I felt behind me, the backpack appeared to be dry. Then I laughed.

This was FUN! I was really enjoying myself. I was glad Sharon had refused point-blank to come when I had suggested she accompany me. I had been a bit disappointed at the time, wanting to share my new world with her, but I now realised she would have hollered blue murder if she'd been down a mud slide and got this filthy. We would have had to go back to Neverland; she would have given up by about now. I smoked a gret before continuing on my way, slip-sliding away and sometimes walking with my hands, swinging from branch to branch like Tarzan when the ground offered little solid support.

At some point I realised that I wasn't descending anymore and had climbed relatively high already, which must mean that I was now on the slopes of Arthur's Fort. Before long I emerged from the tree line and found myself on a grassy slope which led up to the summit. I had almost forgotten that it was a sunny day, so preoccupied had I been with water and mud. The ground was much drier here and I made fast progress. I'd bask in the sun for a bit once I reached the top, I decided, it was warm enough. Dry out a bit and just relish the freedom. There wouldn't be time for much further exploration today; the walk had lasted much longer than I had anticipated.

The path led through two sets of embankments which circled the summit. I got to the top and saw that the treeline on the other side began much closer by. The view was stupendous. I could see faraway farmlands which were interrupted briefly by the grey smudge that was Odesby and turning to my left I overlooked the vast expanse of the Wyrde Woods, which occasionally revealed stretches of the rivers that conjoined at the water meadows. Behind the meadows I could make out the distinctive crowns of the Giant's Grove. Turning further left the sea of green became choppy as the terrain grew increasingly hilly, culminating in the twin summits which rose high above the woods.

I gasped, and covered a delighted grin with my hand. Willick's voice echoed in my head.

Oh all sorts here in the Wyrde Woods Wenn. Witches, forest sprites, giants…

So far so true.

I had never seen the hills from this angle before, the road taken by the bus from the Owlery had offered no views except for the trees which edged the road closely along its entire length to Nickleby. Like parts of Arthur's Fort, there was a low tree line, leaving the greater part of the hills covered only with grass. However, the turf had been removed here and there, right down to bare rock thus creating patterns on the hillside. Patterns which formed two huge figures, one on each hill. The hill on the left depicted a standing man, arms upraised to either side of him, the face profiled so that he appeared to be looking at the other hill and his penis upright in full erection. The man must have been well over a hundred feet long and his member seemed to me well out of proportion, easily covering a quarter of that. The other hill depicted a woman; her face was profiled so that she looked back at the man. This figure was much shorter for it was seated, with huge bulbous boobs and her legs spread widely to reveal enormous half-opened labia.

As drawings the images looked like they had been drawn by a primary school kid, crudely etched lines at most without perspective or much regard to correct anatomy. The size of the giants however, was impressive; it must have been quite a feat to achieve a recognisable resemblance on such a large scale. I knew that hill figures were old, from a culture that was long gone. What I hadn't realised was how extremely explicit our distant ancestors had been. The woman seemed to be welcoming the man walking towards her, both displaying their enlarged genitalia in unmistakable purpose. On the one hand it was extremely crude, on the other there was an erotic suggestion there which didn't miss its mark.

"Stone age porn!" I exclaimed. I was far from a prude nor a virgin but still couldn't observe the figures without a half-embarrassed grin. I took off my backpack and rummaged about for my water and snack. I didn't bother to use any of the water to wash the mud on my face. I could feel it drying on my skin and felt like a warrior with face paint on to intimidate the foe. It felt like it was some sort of recognition of my persistence, so I was happy to leave it be. I gazed over the entire woods as I drank and ate and felt pretty much like a successful conqueror. I grabbed a second muesli bar as I was famished and would be burning calories all day anyway. When I had finished I put the empty wrappers in one of my side pockets and started making a rollie.

I heard an out of place noise and looked puzzled until I realised it was singing. Somebody else was climbing Arthur's Fort today, approaching from the nearby northern tree line. I realised this rambler would encounter me covered in mud but shrugged. There was not much I could do about it now; I opted to wait patiently to see who would emerge from the woods.

The singing became louder, definitely a man but one with a surprisingly good singing voice. Someone who could sing so well must be harmless I decided, but checked the pocket in which I had deposited my pocket knife for reassurance.

Armed and dangerous.

"That's me," I grinned evilly.

The singing stopped and for a moment only the birdsong reigned in the trees. Then the voice launched into a new song, a cheerful upbeat ditty. I could make out the words now and smiled.

Now, this is number one
And the fun has just begun.
Roll me over, lay me down,
and do it again.

Suddenly a dog erupted from the tree line, a border collie which streaked across the grass barking joyfully and proceeding to run a figure eight on the slope below the summit.

Roll me over, in the clover,
Roll me over, lay me down,
and do it again.

The collie spotted me and dashed towards me. About ten feet away it came to an abrupt halt and crouched on the ground, looking at me expectantly, panting with its tongue hanging lopsidedly from its mouth and wagging its tail. I smiled.

"Come here then." I patted the ground next to me in invitation and the collie rushed to me, a quick bundle of energy that twisted and turned around me in a joyful greeting. I petted it with both hands and the dog sat down next to me with a contented sigh, leaning its lithe body against my side as I stroked its back.

Someone emerged from the trees. It was a boy, I estimated 17 or 18. He was dressed entirely in green, from his wool knitted green cap to a green army jumper to army trousers like mine and then green Doc Martins with green laces. He was tall but skinny, his chest was puny and he hardly had shoulders to speak of. A goatee and moustache decorated his face, isolated tufts of reddish brown hair which ridiculed the notion of a beard. He wore a pair of dooby green rimmed glasses with round lenses. He hadn't spotted me yet and continued to sing as he climbed towards the summit. The collie thumped its tail on the ground.

He spotted me and stopped singing immediately.

"Lady!" He shouted.

I frowned; I was anything but a lady.

"Here girl, come on Lady."

The collie thumped its tail some more but looked up at me in complicity and stayed where it was. I grinned.

The boy shrugged and walked on a few yards till he was about 10 feet away.

"Well met!" He raised his hands in greeting, spreading his open palms towards me.

"Watcha," I responded, giving a lacklustre wave.

"A fine day for a walk," he said cheerfully, peering through his glasses to examine my state thoughtfully for a moment. "Mind if I join you?"

He didn't wait for an answer, came closer and sat on the other side of my backpack.

"Did you know the locals have more words for mud than Eskimos for snow?" He asked happily. His green eyes reminded me of Joy's, they were bright and lively. He had a posh accent somewhat eroded by common Kentish with the incongruous addition of the occasional word pronounced in a northern accent.

"Really?"

"Well, I am not really sure how many words Eskimos have for snow to be honest. I know it's a lot. But round here in Sussex they have a bunch of words for mud and all sorts of mud-related activities. They say they have the best mud in the whole nation, no other county can compete."

"The best mud huh?" I was amused.

"Yup, categorised according to texture mostly: from the light stuff that just gets you dirty all the way to the downright vicious stuff that grabs you right by the legs and tries to drag you under, cursing at you all the while. I am pretty sure tales of folk abducted by the Faere Folk are actually a way to explain the disappearance of people swallowed up whole by Sussex mud."

I laughed, he was funny.

"Mud from a horror flick," I said happily. "That's sirageous innit."

"I am surprised the movie hasn't been made yet," He drew a square in the air in front of him with his hands. "ATTACK OF THE MUD FIENDS."

"REVENGE OF THE MUD!" I exclaimed.

"RETURN OF THE MUD PART SEVEN!" He responded. Lady gave a happy bark.

"Do you know any of the mud words?"

"Some, there's garm which is real sticky and smells foul, though gubber aint too fresh neither. There's ike which is a whole bunch of mud together. Then there is pug, slab, sleech, slob, slurry, smeery, stodge and stug, to name a few."

I laughed again. He smiled at my trousers.

"And the reason you are so grabby and gormed up, is probably because it was slobby and you slubbered."

"Oh yes," I nodded seriously, "I slubbered a lot."

"Thought so. Fun isn't it? Slubbering?"

I nodded enthusiastically.

"You come walking over from Nickleby?" He asked.

"Yes."

"I think I'll go back the way I came then. Much as I like slubbering you look like you had an overdose and Lady will look like a mud creature from one of our movies, she loves rolling around in it. Thanks for the advance warning Wenn."

"You're wel…wait a minute, how do you know my name?" I was suddenly alert.

"Joy told me."

"There could be any number of girls going for a walk in the woods today." I was suspicious as hell and on my guard.

"Oh yes, the Wyrde Woods are currently filled with hundreds of city girls slubbering about," he laughed and I couldn't help joining him. Lady thumped her tail in approval.

He stopped and looked at me.

"We met before Wenn, though you probably don't remember me."

"PUCK?"

"One and the same," the boy called Puck beamed and I stared at him.

I could have guessed it I suppose, but my mental image of him was so different that I had not connected the dots. This skinny bespectacled runt had carried me halfway through the Wyrde Woods to Joy's house? He must have been stronger than he looked.

"Well, thanks for taking me to Joy's," I said. "Dunno what would have happened otherwise."

"Oh you had mild hypothermia which would have turned into moderate hypothermia. Movements become slow and coordination becomes hard, then you turn pale though your fingers and ears and such could turn blue. Your mind goes all sluggish first and then becomes active with very mad shit."

I stared at him for a moment. He was a bit of a wazzock, I mean, who walks around with information like that in their head? It was interesting though.

"Very mad shit?"

"There's a fair few people who get so confused that they start what they call paradoxical undressing, they think they'll get warm if they take their clothes off," Puck grinned. "The next step is terminal burrowing; they try to get into a small enclosed space, start digging into the ground if necessary."

"So you could have found me stark naked, blue and trying to enlarge a rabbit hole?" I asked, partially disbelieving. Then again I was capable of doing such a thing without having hypothermia, cheap vodka can be funny stuff.

"Righto," Puck rubbed his absurd beard with his hand pensively, "Maybe I should have waited another hour."

"Oi, spaz!"

Puck laughed, and then turned serious.

"You could have died. It happens more often than people think, and not just in wintertime. I see that you came more prepared this time?"

He threw a look at my backpack.

"Yes," For a brief moment I was pissed off by his implicit admonishment. It wasn't as if I had chosen to freak out after being attacked, who the fax did he think he was? Then I remember Willick's offer to walk me to the priory. Maybe I had, in a weird way, chosen for what happened. Regardless of that I owned Puck one, getting angry at him was a poor repayment.

"So you know Joy?" I asked, changing the subject.

"Yes," he smiled warmly. "She's hoping you'll come back you know?"

"Really? I can get away for a day next weekend, on a day pass from Nowhe…The Home. Everybody else goes home to their families all weekend so the day passes are easy to come by for those who stay, to sorta compensate like."

He nodded, though I wasn't sure he could make head or tail of my confused description. I tried again.

"I was hoping to catch the bus there next Saturday."

"She'll be pleased to see you; she took a liking to you." Puck nodded and smiled again, he had an endearing smile really, shame about those odd tufts of goat hairs on his chin. And that gangly body. He smelled kind of funny, there was no chemical deo that I could detect and there was a strong musky odour which I couldn't quite place. It wasn't bad, just different.

"I kind of have to think about heading back," I said reluctantly. "There'll be hell to pay if I don't get back in time."

"There is an easier way to Nickleby," Puck said. "A bit longer in distance perhaps, but it'll be quicker if the path yonder is anywhere near as muddy as you are. You'll end up on the Lusty Giant's Hills car park, but from there it's tarmac and the bus stops close by."

"Lusty Giant's Hills?" So that was what it was called.

"You might have kind of noticed?" He chuckled and pointed westwards. I glanced there only briefly and then looked back at him.

"I am much too young and modest to be looking at that."

"Yeah right," he gave me an amused smile. "So no thoughts on the Wyrde Woods peep show?"

I grinned and looked to my left, taking in the giant chalk figures once again.

"It's kind of unsettling," I answered. "Fascinating on the one hand, but cloobering sleazy too."

"They weren't into the taboo of it much in those days; it was just a natural part of the cycle of life. Just like death."

"So they were liberal lefties?" I tried to joke.

"Definitely. I think it fascinates because it triggers our subconscious; prime motivational drive and all that."

"I thought that was food, water, shelter and internet."

"I reckon this," he pointed at the Lusty Giants, "came before shelter and internet, but you're right about the other two. Shall we say all three are equally important?"

I nodded, it seemed a reasonable compromise.

"Come on then, we have to get you to that bus stop."

I was about to protest and say that I could find my own way, but I remembered those two red eyes in the depths of the woods and I decided green eyes were preferable and a guide wasn't a bad idea. Besides, I didn't mind spending some more time with Puck, he was funny. He had jumped up already but waited patiently till I had gathered my things and packed them in my backpack while Lady frolicked around us in boundless enthusiasm.

§ § § § § §

The northern slopes of Arthur's Fort were far gentler and the state of the path, though still muddy, required less effort. The woods were different here, the trees much older, wide in their circumference and impressively tall, their crowns cutting off all sunlight except in the occasional spot where one had fallen and there was a sudden intrusion of bright gold light with young saplings competing for space. The older trees were mossy and some of the moss and lichen was so old and expansive that it seemed to cascade from the dark branches and trunks like motionless green waterfalls. It was spooky but also serene. I began to realise the Wyrde Woods was far from a single entity, every time I turned a corner it seemed to take on a different aspect.

I threw a sideways glance at Puck who had a faraway dreamy stare. We hadn't spoken since we left the summit, normally something I interpreted as awkward in company. To find silence in Nowhere Place I would have to withdraw into my room, and even then plug in my ears for music, as most kids in the corridor simply left their bedroom doors open and held conversations by hollering at each other as loudly as they could to be heard over the beats of at least five stereo systems going full blast. With Puck it seemed okay, I could sense that he was enjoying the woods and this appreciation was something we could share in silence. Lady was all over the place, rushing forwards to scout the terrain, and then dashing back to some interesting scent before joining us for a minute afore she rushed off again.

We move through an area abundant with lightfalls of gold sunshine and I could see numerous well decayed large trunks scattered around like some giant had plucked them up from the ground and then casually tossed them aside.

"1987," Puck said.

"Quiddy?"

"There was a big storm, huge."

Now that we were talking I decided to grill him. I wanted to know why he had chosen to live in the woods, he wasn't all that much older than I was, did he go to school? Did he have parents?

"Someone told me you lived in the woods?"

"Yes, I do. Almost two years now."

"He said you have to be evicted."

"Ha, so you met old Fluttergrub?"

I was puzzled. "Erm, no, that wasn't his name."

"Fluttergrub is the one who is supposed to evict me, but he hasn't got a clue where I live and the Wyrde Woods are large."

"So where do you live?" I asked curiously.

"Ah," he chuckled, "One of the reasons nobody knows that is because…"

"Yeah okay Puck. I get it." I was sullen for a moment, even considered telling him he could trust me. But he hardly knew me and I sometimes forget I am cray, hardly the most trustworthy person you could encounter.

"But where are you from?"

"The Boulevard of Broken Promises in Busted Dreamville," he answered.

I must have looked annoyed for he added: "Sorry Wenn, I don't like to talk about it much."

"'Kay," I nodded, if anybody should understand that it was me, I was just dreadfully curious.

"Curiosity killed the cat," Puck said, trying to lighten the situation. He had Joy's knack of reading my thoughts it seemed. Must be all that clean air or something.

"Yeah, but satisfaction brought her back Puck," I responded in kind.

We came to a crossing of sorts. A narrow path turned left to head westwards. Puck pointed at the path and I hesitated for a moment when I saw the murky darkness that surrounded the path.

"You don't have too," Puck's face dropped for an instant. "But if had I intended to…" His voice trailed off and he looked embarrassed.

"No, show me," I said quickly to ease his mind. He was right of course. As I walked behind him on the narrow path I wondered what was different between him and Willick, whom I had happily followed further into the woods. Probably that Willick was ancient, I decided, as I watched Puck's buttocks move underneath his trousers. Meaning that, once trusted, Willick fell into a different category than the boy. Harmless rather than one that held faint possibilities I decided and then came to the conclusion that Puck had a cute ass.

After about 20 minutes we came to a dirt road which we followed until we came to the base of the Lusty Giants' Hills. They were far less spectacular here as it was difficult to make out the forms of the white lines so close up. The visitor centre was already shut and the car park was empty. Puck pointed at the tarmac road leading southwards from the car park.

"Follow that and you'll get to the road going to Nickleby. There's a bus stop at the junction, there's one every half hour still, so you shouldn't have to wait too long,"

"You're going?" I pulled a face.

"Gotta get back, there's things that need doing," he shrugged. "I'll let Joy know you plan to come when I see her."

"Thanks, I'll definitely come. I really liked her a great deal. I have even been missing her." I felt awkward for a moment. "Well, see ya Puck."

"See ya Wenn," he said cheerfully and then went back up the path. Lady gave me a quizzical look, and then followed him.

I stood there watching them till they disappeared from view.

§ § § § § § §

I walked through the front door of Nowhere Place and was about to knock on the office door to report my return when I heard Stubbles' voice. He wasn't supposed to be here on Saturdays and I frowned.

"Ah, there it is, I knew I left my phone here somewhere. Good thing I dropped by." He came walking out the door and halted when he saw me. He was about to speak but then he registered the layers of caked mud that covered me from head to toe and his mouth fell open.

"Hiya," I said, and then shouted into the office, "TERRY I'M BACK."

"Okay Wendy," a muffled voice replied.

"And what, pray, have you been up to?" Stubbles recovered his insincere smile, his eyes suspicious.

"Oh, it was slobby and I slubbered," I answered lightly.

"Excuse me?"

"That's why I am all grabby and gormed you see," I continued cheerily. "But slubbering is fun; you ought to try it some time. Bye now."

I started walking, he looked at his watch. When I reached the stairs I heard him speak to Terry.

"Please make a note that Wendy was two minutes late in returning."

I rolled my eyes, my gut started to churn in anger and I took a deep breath. Stay calm, stay ca…oh bugger it. Half way up the stairs I put up my right hand and raised my middle finger at Stubbles.

8. Tales of the Unexpected

The second session with Stubbles was no improvement on the first. He harangued me at length for my insolence upon returning from my day out and produced a list of other misdemeanours he had issue with. I made a sincere effort to explain to him that I sometimes acted impulsively without knowing why. He cut me short and told me that was not something I could use as an excuse to explain away deviant behaviour and then started reading aloud a number of my crimes. All the while he insisted that I 'understood' why he was hounding me.

I was genuinely puzzled. On the whole I had been on my best behaviour, I knew that crossing the line would probably mean that my right to a day pass would be revoked, or worse, and the prospect of returning to the Wyrde Woods again had given me the motivation to behave. I really did miss Joy. No one had ever been kind to me in the way she had been and I was hoping to enjoy that a bit more.

Stubbles' list consisted of minute infractions, like being back two minutes late. *Two bloody minutes.*

"Yesterday you gave half your dinner to Jeffrey Clarkson," Stubbles said accusingly.

Clarkson? "Oh you mean Biggs, yeah well he was hungry and I wasn't."

"I would prefer it if you didn't call Jeffrey that name."

"But," I shook my head, "that's what he calls himself."

"It isn't good for his self-image and we all need to help each other."

"Okay," I said, not meaning a word of it.

"As for the meal…"

"I told you, I wasn't…"

"Hungry, yes. However, I must insist you finish your own meals, every last bite."

He chuckled like he had just told a joke but I was getting really browned off with this clinker. He must have been digging around in my files. I'd had these spells before, where I ate little or nothing at all, even making myself gag to chuck up whatever I had managed to work into my mouth. But I never possessed the determination to carry on as such for long. Usually it was a collective effort, a passing vogue between the girls which turned into a bit of a competition for a few weeks but then gradually passed only to return again a month or three later. I wasn't like the girl in one of the other corridors who looked like a broomstick but only saw a blob of cellulite when she looked in the mirror. She subsisted on less than a few hundred calories a day whereas I just didn't have a big appetite, though I had actually been eating better since my visits to the Wyrde Woods had begun, wanting to be strong enough for the long walks.

"Also," Stubbles peered at his list, "School called, there was…"

"How long is that list?" I was getting fed up.

Stubbles put down the list and gave me the stare. I stared back defiantly.

"We haven't got off to a very good start, have we Wendy?" Stubbles folded his hands in front of him. The pedantic tone was gone, it was all friendliness now. You had to give Stubbles that, I supposed, he was a true voice artist who could manage to sound sincere, concerned and reassuring when he wanted to.

"No we haven't." I was pleased that there was something we could agree on.

"I understand it must be hard for you," He nodded sympathetically but as usual his eyes remained unreadable, what was going on in that mind of his?

"What is hard?"

"To accept somebody who has come to replace a therapist you had such a deep connection with."

He made it sound almost perverse.

"Oh yeah, Michael." I said as nonchalantly as I could, though I still missed him sorely. I would have loved to tell him all about my adventures in the Wyrde Woods and he would have been happy to sit there and listen to me chatter for an hour, instead of listing my flaws.

"Indeed, Michael." Stubbles was oozing understanding now. "It's a jolly good thing you know, when a therapist and patient can build up such a degree of mutual trust."

I shrugged and impatiently tapped the table top with my fingers.

"I just want you to know, Wendy," Stubbles went into reassurance mode, "That just because Michael is gone now doesn't mean that you can't have such a connection again."

I nodded, thinking of Joy. I wondered what she was doing right now. It had definitely felt like there was a connection there.

"I mean it Wendy," Stubbles suddenly reached out his furry hand and laid it over mine. I got instant goose bumps and shivers and froze. He leaned forward a bit and suddenly those inscrutable eyes were much closer. "I want to be there for you just like Michael was."

I snatched my hand away underneath his. Sirens were causing a cacophony of alarms in my head.

"OI! Hands off!!" I snarled.

Stubbles leant back in his chair.

"Now, now, Wendy," he said in a tone of reasonableness. "I just wanted you to stop tapping your fingers. It was very distracting you know."

I just looked at him. He looked back and gave a twisted little smirk. They would believe him, I knew. If it were my word against his, I'd have bugger all chance. Everybody knew cray girls made things up to get attention.

"We will address your anger management issues another time. I think this is enough for today," Stubbles said. "A productive session, even if I say so myself."

I took this as a dismissal and rushed out of the room and up the stairs to get as far away as possible from that twisted deceitful excuse of a human being.

"Heya!" Sharon was in the corridor, bright with excitement. "Guess what?"

I ignored her and ran into my room. There I locked the door and leaned against it for a moment. Nowhere Place was changing fast and I felt increasingly trapped. I gathered my blankets from the bed, curled up underneath my desk and stared at the wall for hours.

§ § § § § § §

It was Friday afternoon and Nowhere Place was abuzz, Forlorn Hopers talking excitedly as they packed their things for the home leave weekend. This lasted from Friday afternoon till Sunday night, provided you were collected and deposited by a family member. I hated these weekends because I was left mostly to my own devices as Sharon, Biggs and just about everybody else on my corridor was gone, barring John and Jasmin. I didn't even know if my parents were alive, let alone if I had brothers, sisters, aunts, uncles or cousins and the like. All I had was my father's surname and the knowledge that Youth Care had seen it fit to remove me from my parents' care aged three due to their complete inability to cope with me and life in general. That was it. No pictures and blurry memories that were so vague they gave me nothing to hold on to.

The usual departure related fuss on these Fridays reminded me that in this I was different from most other Forlorn Hopers. Even the other kids on my corridor who stayed behind had family. John, who never spoke a word but just wandered aimlessly through the house practicing kick-boxing movements with an invisible friend, was simply never collected by his father except at Christmas.

Jasmin's parents did show up faithfully on these Fridays, but as usual she had been dragged kicking and screaming to the Reflection Room after trying to assault them. Her father had led her sobbing mother away again and Jasmin would be drugged to the eyeballs for the duration of the weekend. I was pretty sure that these drugs didn't help her mental state a great deal; she was absentminded most of the time to begin with. The only time she was focused was during some of the Hindu holidays. She could have got leave to visit her family on those occasions but refused to do so with the same fury she displayed when her parents tried to pick her up at home leave weekends. But she'd be in the communal kitchen for hours preparing all the foods which she associated with the holidays. Every now and then we'd be offered the most delicious dinners for a few nights. Jasmin served these in her Sari, the only time she wore one, and although I wasn't really into girly stuff I loved the materials. But this weekend she would be totally spaced out, her mind far beyond reach.

John and Jasmin would be poor company; I didn't like the kids from the other corridors who stayed behind so I lay on my bed, envied the others and sulked.

My phone beeped and there was a cryptic message from a number I didn't recognise.

J.W. will play Nyle's mum. Play along.

It made no sense to me whatsoever, I didn't know anybody called Nyle so I figured it was a wrong number and put my phone away again. The battery was running low but I couldn't be buggered to recharge it now, I'd do that later.

Thomas made an appearance in my doorway, wearing a sleeveless t-shirt so that everybody could appreciate his biceps. He was incredibly fit, I had to admit, but he was a real swag and considered himself buff. He simply oozed arrogance and seemed to be in love with himself. He reminded me of my former and only boyfriend who, the one time we had boned, spent the entire time looking down admiring his own yoked body and enraptured by the sight of his own cock thrusting in and out of me like he was watching a porn movie. I had been mostly superfluous to the whole business and bored too, so I wasn't the least bit regretful when he dumped me two days later after I refused to do it again.

Thomas assumed a pose, placing his forearm on the doorpost to support him and give him an opportunity to flex those biceps - browning me off big time.

"What do you want?" I growled.

"Nothing much," Thomas beamed a gorgeous smile. "Just came to tell you your grandparents are here."

I shot up and directed a look of utter fury at him.

"There is NO way that is funny," I snarled. "Quit scorching me you bloody skag."

"I'm not trolling you Wendy," Thomas looked hurt. I was about to hurl myself at him and rip his pretty bollocks off when Sharon appeared in the doorway too.

"Thomas isn't parring you, silly douchenoggin," She smiled at Thomas and let him slip his free arm around her waist. "They are downstairs waiting for you."

"Grandparents?" I asked in total confusion but I might as well have been invisible, they were drowning in each other's eyes like they were having a mack moment.

"I am going to miss you babes," Thomas told Sharon.

Grandparents?

"Really? You'll miss me?" Sharon purred.

"I'll be thinking of you every day," Thomas promised and pulled Sharon towards him for a snog. Normally I would have gone into insultive mode but my head was still spinning. *Grandparents?*

I squeezed between them and rushed down the corridor towards the stairs, a host of scenarios playing out in my head. Had they been looking for me all this time? What if I didn't like them? What had prompted this sudden interest? Had something happened to my mum or dad?

None of the scenarios matched what I encountered when I got to the top of the stairs. I heard Hairy Mare's voice first, protesting shrilly.

"This is a very irregular situation. Most irregular." She was speaking to a man and woman who had their backs turned to me. There was something vaguely familiar about their peculiar sense of fashion. Then I heard a male voice I recognised.

"I doant know what be irregular. We have come to collect ourn grandchild for the weekend. According to yern own rules and regulations."

Willick and Joy looked totally out of place in the hallway as if they had stepped in from another century. It took me a few seconds to connect the two totally separate worlds of the Wyrde Woods and Neverland and a few seconds more to digest that these two seemingly honest country folk were lying through their teeth.

"And where is ourn grandchild?" Joy demanded to know in a loud voice. "Wenn'll tell ye, so she will."

Elation literally exploded inside of me, lifting me to a level of utter delight I had never known before in my life.

"GRANDMA!" I hollered at the top of my voice and bounded down the stairs three steps at a time as Joy turned. She spread her arms and I hurled myself into her embrace, starting to sob like a child.

"There, there, sweetie," she comforted me.

"Get me out of this place," I whispered hanging on to her for dear life.

"Jes play the game lass and we shall," she murmured back.

"I didn't know Wendy had grandparents," Hairy Mare looked at me accusingly then withered under the gaze Joy directed at her.

"I find it unaccountable that ye be so poorly informed, ye ought to feel ashamed o' yernself," Joy said sternly. I dug my face in Joy's bosom so Hairy Mare couldn't see me laugh.

"We can't just simply hand over a child in our care to strangers," Hairy Mare squealed.

My heart sank.

"Who does ye be calling a stranger?" Willick sounded offended. "Disyer Wendy be Joy's fambly, Joy be Wenn's own Gammer and all."

"I am afraid our records just don't make any mention of you," Hairy Mare insisted.

"Show this lady the documentation Will," Joy sighed and stroked my hair. I peered under her arm at Hairy Mare who looked as bewildered as I felt.

Willick dug in his coat pockets and produced some aged looking papers.

"Here tis," He said, locking the shrink in the blue candour of his eyes. "Wendy Alice Twyner, born in Brighton on 5 January 1988. Daughter o' Nyle Twyner and Ashley Pilbeame. Good Sussex names, Nyle be mine wife's son, so he be. And that makes me Wendy's Gaffer o' sorts."

My eyes grew large.

"With mine first husband, Will be the second," Joy nodded. "Mine maiden aftername be Whitfield."

J.W. will play Nyle's mum. The text message made sense to me now. But who had sent it? Willick? How did they get my number?

Will handed the papers over to Hairy Mare who took them nervously.

"Just a moment," she said. "I will just check the records again." She walked into the office and logged into one of the computers there.

"You're not really my grandma are you?" I whispered to Joy.

"'O course not sweetie," Joy whispered back. "I'd have never ever left ye here on yern own if I were yern Gammer. And Will aint yern Gaffer either."

"But the computer…"

Joy chuckled.

"Yon lady'll find all in middling order," Willick said confidently. I loosened myself from Joy's embrace.

"How?"

"In awhiles Wenn," he said and then looked at me sternly. "Does ye feel comfortable leaving with me?"

I felt red shame course through me and lowered my eyes.

"Yes I do."

"That be an unaccountable good thing, surelye," Willick responded.

Hairy Mare came out of the office, relief evident in her eyes.

"Well, it does check out, I do apologise. Joy Whitfield is listed as Wendy's paternal grandmother. I am so sorry. I will have to ask you to show me an ID and fill out a form Mrs. Whitfield. And we'll prepare Wendy's medication for the weekend."

"I will does so," Joy nodded her consent and looked at me. "Doant jes stand there child, gwoan fetch yern things."

"Yes grandma!" I ran up the stairs as fast as I could. Thomas and Sharon were entwined on my bed, mouths locked together and legs gyrating around each other. I ignored them and grabbed my Wyrde Woods backpack, pausing long enough to throw in some spare clothes.

"I am going to my grandparents! Lock the door for me Sharon," I shouted joyfully on my way out. Sharon moaned ecstatically and Thomas uttered an obscene groan. On the way down the stairs I slung the backpack on my back. Joy came out of the office, followed by Hairy Mare who was still offering profuse apologies.

Joy ignored her and stretched out her hand. I took it, Willick took my other hand and we walked out of Nowhere Place hand in hand, just as if I was a regular girl on a weekend outing.

Miss Wendy A. Twyner was going home to the Wyrde Woods.

9. The Earl's Barrel

"How? Why? Where? When?" I was bursting with questions.

Willick and Joy had led me to an old battered green Land Rover parked just outside Nowhere Place. Willick had helped Joy into the front passenger seat and then took the driver's seat while I clambered into the back. We were driving out of Neverland and I leant forwards, leaning my arms on the two front seats.

"Are you two really married?"

Willick coughed and Joy laughed.

"Naun lass," Willick said, "Jes part o' the deception, that were all."

"Though disyer Will does gwaon acrawling through mine bedroom window at night oft enow whiles I were yern age Wenn," Joy gave a girlish giggle. "Unaccountably fond o' mine teats him were."

"Ye maun tells that, tis naun o' hern business," Willick frowned and drove down the High Street.

"Pfff." Joy answered.

I was slightly shocked. I knew old people had been young once, they were forever telling me that, but found it hard to envisage none-the-less. Let alone Joy and Willick messing about with each other forever ago.

"Why did you come today? I mean, I'm dead grateful and all."

"Puck told me ye'd planned to visit on Saddaday. I reckoned ye might as well visit longer," Joy sounded mightily pleased with herself.

"I can stay till Sunday?" I asked jubilantly.

"Aye, if ye want." Willick said.

"All that information you know! And you're on the computer files?!"

"Hmm, maid must've thought we be naught but country yokels I reckon." Willick snorted as we crossed the bridge across the canal. I sensed some distance in him still and couldn't blame him. I guessed Joy had coerced him into the deception.

"Ah Will, but we be and ye knows it," Joy said teasingly. "Twere Puck, the lad be mighty handy with computers and that new-fangled internets. I'd say he be middling ingenurious. He…" She frowned. "What be that word Will?"

"Hack," Willick answered promptly, pronouncing the word carefully and stressing the 'H', "Puck say he hackéd the system."

"Aye!" Joy grinned happily again, "Hackéd. Puck found yern information, and he added mine name to yern files, surelye."

"Bloody hell," I said admiringly, and then thought of something else as we turned onto the Nickleby road.

"Nyle and Ashley, that is what my parents are called then?"

Joy looked at me sharply. "Ye mean ye doant know?"

"No, just the name Twyner."

"Geemeny," Joy shook her head sadly. "It be unaccountable."

We drove on in silence for a while, the Wyrde Woods already to our right and farmland to our left.

"You could get into trouble you know," I suggested hesitantly.

"Zackly, I keep telling disyer old woman jes so, surelye." Willick nodded in full agreement.

"We know Wenn," Joy said. "But Puck says folk believes what be on them computers. And they doant appear to be halfway organised, seems a lot o' hugger-mugger to me."

"No, they're a bunch of tossers," I agreed happily.

"Quiddy?" Willick looked puzzled.

"They be chuckle-headed," Joy explained.

"I see," Willick nodded.

"Be a Gent and stop at the Barrel. I reckon ye can treat us to a pint Will, so I does."

Willick grumbled but pulled over in the parking lot of the Earl's Barrel. I followed Willick and Joy into the magnificent old building and was enchanted by the interior. Everything seemed lopsided and crooked; the walls were made of sandstone and interlaced with stout beams that looked to be a thousand years old, even sturdier beams ran across the ceiling. There was a huge fireplace near the bar where a couple of locals were perched on bar stools. An amiable woman in her thirties behind the bar gave us a friendly wave.

"I'll be right with ye!" She smiled brightly.

Willick and Joy waved back and then walked to an alcove near the fireplace. They settled down on the bench behind the table, I sat on a chair opposite them but couldn't keep still, looking around the pub and the various pictures and farming tools displayed on the walls. I still couldn't believe my luck, I had supposed that I'd be listlessly hanging around the common room to watch telly this evening, and here I was. Out in a pub, at liberty with a whole weekend of the Wyrde Woods to look forwards to. I looked at Willick and Joy and gave them my broadest smile.

"Evening Willick, evening Joy," the barwoman came to us. "How do?"

"Middling, bethanks," Willick answered. "How do Joan?"

"Scratching along, tis full house," The woman called Joan laughed and pointed at the three customers by the bar. "Doant knows if ye fit in mine busy schedule and all. Though tis yetner late." She turned to me and looked me up and down. "And who may ye be lass?"

"Hern grandchild," Willick indicated Joy.

"Ah, is it now?"

"I am Wenn, I am very pleased to meet you," I chirped as sweetly as I could.

"Lass doant half talk funny, surelye," Joan frowned.

Willick was about to open his mouth but I beat him to it.

"All-along-o' that I were raised by Sheere-folk," I said quickly. Willick looked at me quizzically, half a smile forming on his face. Joy chortled.

"Ah, poor lass, mine condolences," Joan gave me a pitying look. "What'll it be for ye this evening then?"

"Pint o' Harvey's Dark Mild if ye please Joan," Willick said.

"I'd like a pint o' Pump Bottom Farmhouse," Joy spoke.

Joan looked at me. I was tempted to try for a beer but knew there was no way I'd pass for eighteen. People were forever telling me I was so small, sweet and cute; much to my consternation as I usually felt bloated, sour and repulsive. But I had been playing the small, sweet and cute thing now ever since I had rushed down the stairs of Nowhere Place earlier, terrified that Joy and Willick would change their minds and bring me back. I wanted this more than anything in the world.

"A Diet Coke please," I said.

"Makes that a half pint for Wenn," Joy said with a wink. I was surprised, I hadn't realised Coke was served in half pints or pints but I understood when Joan came back with the drinks and placed half a pint of cider in front of me. I grinned with delight.

"I would've reckoned ye'd broken enow laws today Joy," Willick pulled a face when Joan had gone back to the bar.

"I recollect ye were at it far younger than she be Will," Joy replied. "Some days folk jes needs a dozzle o' drink, aint that so Wenn?"

I nodded happily and took a sip of the cider. It was dry and strong.

"Why is this place called the Earl's Barrel?"

"Ah, there's a tale for telling," Joy smiled. "Will ought to tell it, he be a bettermost tale teller."

I thought Willick might object, he'd been a bit grumpy, but he launched into the story straight away.

"A long time ago in the Wyrde Woods," he said. "Earl Roger lived in Malheur Hall, so he does. He be a giant o' a man, the gurtest man in the wurreld at the time. Over six foot tall and middling fat on top o' that."

I closed my eyes and pictured the huge Earl.

"One day children start to disappear, jes like that. One or two at first, sad to be sure, howsumdever, nary unlikely. It does happen otherwhiles, what with the Farisees, that Knucker at Devil's Tarn and other critters in the woods. Howsumdever, more and more lads and maids went a-missing. First from Roreford, but then chavees from Tuckersham, Nickleby and Wolfden as well, then even those who strayed out o' Odesby. Folk round here became middling afeared and tried to keep their children at home."

I listened wide-eyed.

"The villagers and farmers went to the Earl to axe him to put an end to it. As Lord o' the Wyrde Woods it were his duty to protect the woods and the people in it. Earl Roger consulted dunnamy wise greybeards and then pronounced that it were the fault o' the wodewoses, so 'twere."

"Wodewoses?" I asked curiously.

"Wild men," Joy explained, "They live wild and feral in the woods. Most-in-general ablamed for mishaps, them and Farisees and witches."

I nodded, this fitted in with my earlier mind picture of these wodewoses.

"Justly," Willick continued, "So Earl Roger sends invitations far and wide and all the nobles from the whole o' Sussex come to Malheur Hall for a gurt hunt. For three days and three nights the hunting party rides to and fro in the Wyrde Woods like Herne's Wild Hunt they were, surelye. Hounds abarking, horns a-sounding and the thunder o' horse hooves shook the ground. They hunted down all the wodewoses them found and folk beleft there were naun left afterwards all-along-o' that hunt."

I thought of being hunted by the Owl Man, it must have been terrifying for the wild people of the Wyrde Woods to have all the toffs in Sussex chasing them. I took another swig of cider.

"Folk were middling relieved and let their chavees outdoors again. Howsumdever, the chavees start to disappear again and folk became afeared once again. Then one day a particularly ingenurious chavee that had disappeared came aback, for he had middling well escaped, and he lit a gurt big fire atop Arthur's Fort and all children o' the Wyrde Woods came to hear him speak. And he tells a terrible harrowing tale, so he does. His story was that he were captured by Earl Roger's men, and kept in those dungeons below Malheur Hall. And he says there be more children there, howsumdever, on each day one was taken to the kitchens and cooked, grilled, fried, broiled or roasted and it were Earl Roger himself who were chanking all of every such meal."

"He was a cannibal?"

"Tis unaccountable, but he were. And the children knew something mus be done, afore there be nary a chavee left in the whole o' the Wyrde Woods. So they made a plan. One night they placed atween Malheur Hall and the Carfax Alus…"

"Alehouse," Joy explained. I nodded and waited for Willick to continue. He took a big swig of his ale and then did.

"They placed there the gurtest barrel o' mead ye have ever seen. Earl Roger were keenly fond o' mead so he were. Prensley he comes out Malheur Hall to gark at the barrel and pegs away e'enamost straight aways and soon he were fresh. Howsumdever, he were a greedy bullock and he pegs aways again till he were primed, then he pegs away till he were none-the-better, and finally Earl Roger were totally tossicated and falls down on the ground singing songs."

"Clever kids," I laughed.

"Justly so. Suddent they come running out o' the woods and tied Earl Roger on the gurt barrel. As he came to he bellicks all manner o' threats most abusefully, howsumdever, he were tightly bound up and they get a gurt big wood saw and sawed the fat Earl right in two halves!"

"Ha, his just reward," I said happily and drank more of my cider.

"And the liddle chipper what escaped were given all the silver and gold what were in the Earl's purse and he opened an alus in disyer Nickleby."

"The Earl's Barrel!" I exclaimed.

"Zackly," Willick said, and downed the last of his pint.

"And some folk say," Joy added with a mischievous grin, "That otherwhiles at night there be a spot atween Malheur Hall and Carfex Alus where ye can hear Earl Roger shruck and skreel like a stuck pig and hear chavees laughing."

"Ye maun speak oakum, there be no-ways that can be," Willick frowned. "Let's get ye two back to the Owlery, telling tales makes me hungry, I reckon ye can treat us to something to eat now Missus Whitfield."

§ § § § § § §

Joy warmed up some of her soup for us when we arrived at the Owlery and after the meal showed me a steep wooden stair, a ladder more like, in the small hallway between the kitchen and the main room. It led to the first floor of her cottage: A loft where the only place you could stand upright was where the sloping roof sides met. There were a few chests scattered about in the area above the kitchen, which was partitioned off from the rest of the loft by the stone chimney which rose up from below, leaving two narrow low gaps on either side which led to the rest of the loft. This was a slightly larger area over the main room; there was a boxed bed at the far end, right next to a low window.

"I am afraid I need mine own bed downstairs for meself, lass," Joy explained. "Tis a good day today, so I can climb disyer stairs, but most days I dursn't. Aside o' that, I reckon ye'd like to have yern own room?"

"It's PERFECT!" I was over the moon.

"I dusted and cleaned some for ye. There be candles for light, doant leave them burning please. Dour them when ye leave or gwoan asleep. Ye can smoke here also, if ye want. Puck said ye smoked. The chimney'll give off a snoule o' heat, but there be plenty o' blankets."

"I'll be just fine, oh this is so amazing!"

Joy beamed and went back downstairs. I started unpacking my backpack and in no time the area around the bed was cluttered with my belongings. It was getting dark fast now so I lit a candle and decided to make a rollie. There was an old cracked saucer by the window which I nominated as ashtray and I lay on my belly on the old mattress and let pure happiness course through me as I smoked and peered outside through the window, just able to make out the outlines of the coniferous trees which surrounded the front garden around the Owlery.

This was the place Joy had grown up, I realised, and if her mother had slept downstairs, this might have well been the very window young Willick had climbed through to be with Joy. It was dead romantic really. I smiled. I wondered if my parents had had romantic moments like that.

"Nyle Twyner," I said softly. "Ashley Pilbeame." Google was sure as hell going to work overtime when I got back to Nowhere Place, I decided. But that was a worry for later. I had two days in the Wyrde Woods to enjoy to the max first. I had already dared to hope Willick and Joy would make a habit of this, but had been afraid to ask as of yet, it seemed ungrateful when they had gone to so much effort already. Effort for me! I grinned as I recalled their playacting at Nowhere Place. Ingenious! Puck too, imagine hacking into the OJCH system.

§ § § § § §

I hadn't paid much attention to the voices I could hear downstairs, partially because they had been mixed with an enormous ruckus made by the owls. But the birds had settled down now and it seemed that Joy and Willick had stopped moving about and retired to the fireplace.

"Ye mean well Goody Whitfield," I heard Willick say. "I admire that, so I does. But ye and yern foundlings..."

"I weren't the one what found hern soodling in the woods having a gark abroad Master Maskall, much as I found yernself in the woods long ago,"

Joy answered. "Twere yernself who found her and ye took a liking to Wenn and all."

"Aye, least till I found hern got a lippy gobbet like a Lunnoner or thereaways." Willick said with some bitterness in his voice. "Doant rightly know why I be jiggered, but furriners be nought but plaguey moil."

"Yern be a teddious old grump Will Maskall, surelye." Joy answered.

"Lass be unaccountable shirty, set and stuckish."

I frowned. I could barely follow the conversation but my sudden hostility had clearly left a bad impression on Willick. I couldn't blame him either. I had no idea what he said but he was probably right.

"Jes like I were Will Maskall, and ye used to say ye loved that about me, and ye knows that middling well," Joy chuckled. "Lass be in no-ways timmersome and why should hern be? Wenn be peert and purty, and ye likes that well enow."

"Hern be devourously deedy, that is true," Willick agreed. "Ye maun be tessy, but I knows ye Joy, ye'll take her into yern home but ye barely kens her, surelye."

"I've a feeling about disyer lass," Joy answered.

"What be that?"

There was a long pause, at last Joy spoke, "One for sorrow, two for joy."

"Three for a girl, four for a boy." Willick answered. "Ye're sure? Wenn being outlandish and all?"

"I be middling sure." Joy answered. "Aside o' that hern Mam and Da have good Sussex names as ye said yernself. Ye read the names: Twyner and Pilbeame."

"Aye, I recollect them, so I does," Willick said.

"Wenn aint Sheere-folk, jes cut o' from hern roots that's all. Ye mus've seen how happy the lass were, there be recognition of sorts, and hern jes doant knows what yetner. The Wyrd be at work I tell ye."

"If ye say so, then so be it." Willick answered.

"And now I'll be fixing us some tea and call Wenn down. If ye've anymore to say about her, tell it to hern face, surelye."

§ § § § § §

"Well, I be taking mine leave," Willick announced when he had finished his tea. "Evening all."

When he had shut the front door behind him Joy looked at me pointedly. There was a sudden strictness there which I had only seen when she had cut down Hairy Mare outside the office in Nowhere Place.

"Be there nought ye want to say to Will?" Joy asked me.

"Yes, I do." I jumped up and rushed outside. "Willick!"

Willick was already by the gate in the low set stone wall that marked the boundary of the Owlery grounds.

"Aye lass?" His blue eyes were so bright they outshone the moon, which bordered on full tonight.

"About the other day, erm…" I wanted to look down but forced myself to look into those piercing eyes. "I am sorry. I am really sorry."

He beamed me the broadest smile, the same which had so impressed me on that day I first met him and I knew I had taken a big step towards making amends.

"Bethanks Wenn, I'll be seeing ye one o' these days, surelye." He stepped through the gate and got into the Land Rover.

He drove off slowly, the beams of his headlamps lighting up the myriad of tree trunks along the narrow driveway.

"That were good o' ye Wenn." I hadn't seen Joy come outside but she was next to me now.

"Not really," I mumbled. "It was cruel of me."

"But ye set it right again, come, we gwoan to the bees."

I didn't have a clue what that meant but followed Joy to the side of the Owlery and then towards the corner of the front garden. I could discern two large square objects set on a low table. I guessed they were bee hives, though there was no activity. Joy took a large old fashioned key from her apron pocket and gave each hive a gentle tap with it.

"Bees," Joy said solemnly, "Disyer lass be Wendy Alice Twyner whom we call Wenn and hern will be staying here at the Owlery somewhen. I want ye to know that."

Joy's solemnity stopped me from giggling, it was apparent this was an important moment.

"Why did you do that?" I asked when we walked back to the Owlery.

"Tell the bees?" Joy sounded surprised. "Why, one maun ever forget to tell the bees o' important changes in the home. Weddings, births, deaths and such. It'd be ill fortune to naun tell the bees, surelye."

It sounded like a weird custom to me but I was mostly thrilled to be counted in amongst such important domestic milestones. Might it mean more home leave visits? I was dying to ask but decided not to. It was incredible enough to be here now and I should try to be content with that.

We went back into the Owlery. The owl which had greeted my first awakening here hopped up and down restlessly. Joy released him from his binds and the bird flew to a grand old wardrobe at the far wall, gave a screech and then seemed to doze off.

"Bronwen be the only one to fly free like this. The other owls pick a fight with each other so I need to close the boxes first when I let one o' them fly free. Bronwen also be the only one with enow sense to stay clear o' candles and such, so she can come out in the evenings."

I looked around at the owls as Joy introduced to them to me. Bronwen was a female barn owl though Joy said she called it a scritch owl.

"All-along-o' the scritching sound they makes," she explained.

The other scritch owl was a male called Bran. The small grey one was called Horsa and was a little owl. The fourth, with the surprised look, was a long eared owl which Joy called Aethel.

I found them fascinating; they had a beauty about them that was compelling. On the other hand, Ufmanna still lurked in my subconscious and they reminded me of what was out there in the woods. Though I was delighted to be back the Wyrde Woods weren't all nice.

We settled by the fire.

"You and Willick?" I asked. "It never came to more?"

"Ye've a healthy curiosity," Joy nodded her approval, and then sighed. "There were another ye see."

"Another boy?"

Joy looked at me sharply for an instant. "Naun, twere a grown man."

I pulled a face.

"Different times lass, ye maun forget," Joy shifted to a more comfortable position. "I were fifteen springs and that summer had ta gwoan work in kitchens at Malheur Hall. That meant staying in the servant quarters, so naun more rolling about with Will. Him were devastated so he were, poor lad. And I missed him as well, Will made me feel unaccountable special. Then I does catch the Lordship's eye so I does."

She frowned.

"Was he handsome? Did you fall in love?"

"Mortimer were handsome enow I suppose, but nigh on forty."

"Ugh!"

"So naun, I doant have feelings towards hisn Lordship," Joy stared into the fire. "But him comes to mine room at night anyway."

"OMG! Couldn't you just...?"

"Maids serving in the gurt houses were legitimate prey back then, been like that forever." Joy said wistfully. "If I'd fought him me Mam would have been evicted from the Owlery and the both o' us would have been on the streets o' Stancaster or Brighton."

"It's so unfair," I said thinking of Stubbles and Calcott. I shivered.

"Anyways, Mortimer got me with child afore Yuletide."

"You had a baby?"

"Aye, howsumdever, here at home. When mine belly started to show I were sacked and sent home in disgrace. Tis naun done for a young unmarried maid to be with chance-born child."

"But it wasn't your fault!"

"Doant matter, me Mam were middling good, naun a word o' condemnation, hern jes went to tell the bees o' changes in the house."

"And the baby?"

Joy remained silent for a moment, and I wondered if I had crossed a line. But then she spoke again, her voice suddenly sounded old.

"A fine healthy boy child. I called him Nate."

"Did he grow up here too?"

"Till he were seven, aye. Then Mortimer sent Nate to a Sheere boarding school. Took him away from me."

Joy sounded pained and I felt for her. It must be horrible to have your own child taken away from you; I wondered if my mother had felt the same pain I could now read on Joy's face.

"And Willick?"

"Aye, Will. Him were heartbroken, proper heartbroken. Disappeared for a year or longer, living in the woods alike a wodewose. Folk's tongues wagged aplenty, Will went mad for a whiles I recollects."

"He went cray?"

"Hisn proper name be William," Joy smiled. "Willick means wild person. That was what folk called him, Willick o' the Woods. He kept the name for some reason."

My head spun with all this new information.

"Will came out the woods eventually, and married a lass from Nickleby," Joy rounded off the tale. "Somewhen I does wonder what would have come o' it if he had stayed by mine side."

I nodded, I could well imagine.

"Do you...if he loved you so much..."

"Enow lass, for him to stay with me would have meant acknowledging the chavee as hisn own."

"Would that have been so bad?"

"Twould have been critical o' hisn Lordship, middling publicly critical also. Naun would have seen it otherwise. There would be repercussions, it doant bode well to cross the Malheur family."

"They had so much power," I said, shaking my head.

"Malheur still does Wenn. Howsumdever, this with me have all been a long time ago," Joy came out of her sadness and took my hand in hers and gave me a warm smile. "Jes remember that when ye find someone that loves ye, hang on to them as long as ye can for fate can be a cruel thing."

I nodded.

"Time to put Bronwen back into hern box, and then time for us all to sleep some." Joy decided, and slowly rose to her feet. "I doant think I can manage the stairs again tonight sweetie, so I cannot tuck ye in."

"That's ok," I said, she had done more than enough already. "Good night Joy. Thank you."

"Good night lass, safe dreams."

Part Dinah: Three for a Girl

10. Three for a Girl

The first sunbeams peeked tentatively between the tops of the peaked coniferous trees that lined the stretch of grass at the side of the Owlery and then announced the beginning of a bright day by shining through my bedroom window and enveloping me in pleasant warmth. I threw off my covers and lazily stretched my arms to reach behind my head, content to linger in drowsiness a bit longer. There's nothing like waking up in your own bed in your own room. I knew I was jumping the gun by a hundred thousand miles but that's what it felt like and in all my sixteen years I had never experienced this sensation before. For once I felt at peace with the world, even with myself. My mind produced a bird's eye view of myself, lying there in my knickers and singlet being caressed by the sunlight and I experienced a rare moment of sensuous self-satisfaction, maybe I wasn't all horrible ugliness I figured, maybe even I could be desirable.

Not like Sharon, obviously, my boobs were too small and I wasn't blond, just boring brunette which I tried to make bit more interesting by dying red streaks in it. Sharon drew male attention like nectar draws a bee. I didn't mind that much usually; the sort of attention she drew from boys was driven by a frantic and overeager need to get laid. Pathetic to say the least. They reminded me a little of those neurotic undersize dogs which were forever trying to hump things in the park behind Odesby Castle: The legs of a random passer-by, picnic baskets, footballs or a carelessly mislaid child's teddy bear. Sometimes though, that attention would have been nice. Not from the likes of Biggs but a fit handsome guy. But I couldn't think of a single boy I knew who would be content, had he been here with me right now, to just hold me in his arms and lie still, happy to share this bliss in quiet companionship without starting to grope me. Perhaps though, I considered with unfamiliar smug satisfaction, I couldn't even blame the poor fellow; with a woman like me next to him.

My nose picked up the scent of fresh hot coffee and I yawned one last time. Coffee would be good, I decided. By the time I had pulled a t-shirt over my head, put on my army trousers, socks and boots the smell of sizzling bacon wafted up the stairs too and I hurried downstairs.

I found Joy in the kitchen, busy behind a huge ancient **Rayburn** stove.

"Morning sleepyhead," Joy said cheerfully and in a spontaneous act I walked over to her to give her a kiss on the cheek. I was worried that I might have been too forward but when I saw her beam in response I was glad I did it. Guilty too though, she had no idea what kind of a bitch I really was. Then again, some of her remarks had revealed a shrewd insight into the way of things and she seemed to read me well enough.

I looked around the kitchen. There were open shelves jammed tight with labelled jars and tins and as I had expected bundles of dried herbs. The sink was a surprise; it was the size of a battleship with ancient stains and a maze of cracks but there was no tap.

"You don't have running water?" I asked curiously.

"I draw it from the well out back," Joy answered, then looked at me. "Nary much in ways o' modern convenience here Wenn. Naun electricity, naun gas, naun water mains."

"But you have a flushing toilet," I thought of the little cubicle opposite the stairs in the hallway.

"Rain water," Joy answered. "Will fixed that for me, afore that there were an outhouse in the garden."

She looked at me expectantly. I was momentarily non-plussed, thinking of all the essentials that ran on electricity. Lights mostly, and power for my phone.

"Ye may want to reconsider staying till Sunday lass, I'd understand. I be used to this, doant knows nary better."

"No. NO! I love it here," I answered truthfully.

"Well, that be settled then, time to break bread."

We ate at an ancient wooden table tucked away into one of the corners of the kitchen. The coffee, made from fresh ground beans was every bit as delicious as it smelled and the bread Joy covered with lavish helpings of crispy bacon tasted sumptuous.

"Where did you get his bread?" I asked.

"I bake it meself. Gwoan, have some more."

I ate far more than I usually do for breakfast and helped Joy clear the plates afterwards. She handed me a zinc pail and asked me to fill it from the well, pointing at a door in the far corner of the kitchen. I stepped outside with the empty pail in my hand and gasped.

There was a small courtyard out back, flanked by a wall with a narrow tiled overhang beneath which were stacked piles of firewood. Opposite me ramshackle sheds and a chicken coop lined half of the courtyard, the rest was open to an extensive garden which simply ran riot with the colours of flowers all shapes and sizes. Bees hummed above the flowers and butterflies fluttered about. The garden ended at a low stone wall beyond which was a small orchard where various fruit trees were in full bloom.

"That water lass?" I heard Joy say behind me.

"Yeah, sorry...just that I saw the garden, it's incredible!"

"I'll give ye a proper tour dappens we've cleaned."

"Of course!"

There was a small well a few yards into the garden, a circular stone structure with a wooden beam across it. I had never drawn water from a well before but figured out that the rope tied to the beam and a wooded pail at the other required few operating instructions. In this I was partially wrong, as it was hard to duck the pail into the water, a good 10-foot lower down the well, and bring it up with more than a cupful of water. After two tries I figured out patience was the way to go and waited for the pail to sink. Having filled the zinc pail I returned to the kitchen where Joy heated some of the water on the Rayburn and we did the dishes.

After that Joy accompanied me into the back garden. She explained how she had chosen plants which would flower at different times of the year so that the bees would be happy in spring, summer and autumn. Blue lilacs and forget-me-nots, pink primroses and rosabellas, white fuzzy cherry laurels, potted cheerful daisies, red ruby domes, yellow marigold and cowslips, purple dog violets and lungworts and pansies of all colours bloomed now. I was dazzled by their hues and all the names which Joy rattled off as she also pointed out the plants which would flower in the summer and autumn. Not just for the bees, but also to attract butterflies.

"I love butterflies," I said.

"Aye, a reminder that something that starts out life as a liddle grub a-comes truly beautiful in the end."

The further half of the garden was a vegetable and herb garden. Joy started to explain that the vegetable garden was always a real puzzle to plan.

"Why is that?"

"Plants have theirn own likings and dislikings Wenn. They grow bettermost in good company, so they does. So onions be liking carrots, and carrots be liking beans but beans doant be liking onions, for example."

My mind fought this notion. How could a plant like or dislike another plant? But Joy was entirely serious and looking at her garden, which simply teemed with the abundance of life I decided to believe her.

"Yern wurreld be regimented lass, there be other ways to does things, and Mother Nature now, have rules o' hern own. I garden by the moon."

"You garden at night?" I had mental picture of Joy out in the dead of night gardening in the moonlight.

"Naun," Joy laughed. "But I keep an eye on Mistress Moon. Plants be growing when she waxes, that be the time to sow and plant. Or prune if ye wants more growth. Waning moon, they doant grow much, good time for weeding or cutting things ye doant want back naun too quick. During ascending moon plants be active above ground, and descending moon below, so it be bettermost ta does certain things accordingly, surelye."

"So you have to know what the moon is doing all of the time?" I was flabbergasted; in Neverland I barely even noticed the moon.

"Aye, o'course," she looked surprised. "I could naun imagine that I doant."

"What's the moon tonight?"

"Why, full. It'd be the Hare Moon tonight."

"Likes, dislikes, the moon..." Though I kind of liked the concepts after some initial scepticism I started to reckon Joy was a little cray perhaps.

"There be more to it," Joy smiled. "Ye seen the rowan trees out front?"

"Yes." I had registered a number of trees in the front garden, although I hadn't known they were rowan trees.

"Folk plant them to keep evil away, jes like hazels. Some talk o' the Devil, others jes reckon it be sprites what means naun good."

"Really?"

"Aye, does ye see the rosemary in pots there by the after-door and fore-door?"

I nodded. "What are they for?"

"That keeps those Farisees intent on causing mischief and mayhem away."

"Farisees?"

"Faere Folk. Sheere-folk call them 'faeries'."

"You believe in faeries?" I was incredulous and tried not to laugh, but I must have smirked because Joy's mood changed and she became stern.

"Tis naun a matter o' believing or naun," she said looking me in the eyes. "They be here. Somewhiles they like to lead unwary maidens off theirn paths at night. Dunnamy have been *willed* by Will o' Wisp or Robin Goodfeller, howsumdever, an unaccountable fair shatter surelye."

I had a sudden vivid close-up image of the owl man in my mind, accompanied by the sound of myself screaming. All in response to a creature which was every bit as ludicrous as a faery, probably more so. I felt a shiver running across my back.

"I am sorry, you're right," I said. "It's just that…"

"I understand," Joy smiled again. "Yern wurreld be different from mine."

I nodded but suddenly I felt the icy grip of exclusion, I was just a temporary guest here. But I knew my 'wurreld' all too well and had no liking for it; it was Joy's world I desperately longed to be part of.

Joy suddenly winced and then again and I filled with concern.

"What is the matter Joy?"

"I need…sit down," she inhaled a sharp breath of pain.

I held out my arm and supported her back into the house.

"Best lay me on bed," Joy spoke with difficulty.

"Do you want a blanket?" I felt helpless as I helped her onto the bed.

"Naun. There be a dark blue tin on shelf by sink."

"Yes?"

"It would be middling if ye could boil a snoule o' water, two handfuls o' leaves from the tin when the kettle has boiled. And please bring a tater from the sack by the table."

I rushed to the kitchen and prepared the infusion. When I got back with a steaming mug I helped Joy sit up, propped against the cushions so that she could drink. She put the potato I gave her in a pocket of her apron.

"Tater helps," Joy explained, and then, uncharacteristically down: "I'm sorry lass. I wanted to spend time with ye, but now I'm bethered, I'll doze away for a few hours in awhiles."

"No worries. Really. I'll be fine. What's the matter though?"

"Rheummatics. It comes and gwoan. There be good days and bad days."

"Today is a bad day?"

"Today," Joy paused, "Tis like I'm a prisoner in mine own body."

"Is there anything I can do?"

"Naun, owls need care but they can wait. They aint used to ye yetner."

"I don't mind!"

"They does," Joy grimaced. "And ye'll look a sight less purty with yern eyes clawed out."

I had to concede it wouldn't improve my looks much.

"There's one chore," Joy frowned. "Puck said he'd do it, but he has yetner found the time."

"What is it? Tell me, I'll do it."

§ § § § § § §

"Fax. Shite. Arse. Tit. Fax." I threw down the spade. "Suck on a dingleberry."

There were two large compost heaps at the back of the garden and Joy needed them to be emptied first and then refilled, a task which had seemed entirely pointless to me to begin with but she had explained that it was necessary to mix the more decayed matter at the bottom with the top layers for optimum compost.

"Bettermost for the flowers," she had said.

As I had more or less decided to do whatever would make me useful I agreed to do it, even though she had warned that it was hard work. An understatement if there ever was one.

I had never really appreciated how hard it was to dig. I had started happily enough, glad to be of some use to poor Joy who had moved heaven and earth to set me free from my cage in Neverland. But my back had started to protest after shoving the spade in the compost and lifting it out just a few times and my arms had begun to feel mighty sore shortly thereafter.

The odour wasn't as bad as I had feared but it wasn't pleasant either and drew a host of bugs which all seemed intent on devouring me on the spot. Though I worked in the shade of the trees it was a warm day and I was soon gushing with sweat. I took off my t-shirt to work in my singlet but every now and then I rushed to the well to draw water, drink my fill and sluice the dirt and sweat off my head and shoulders to cool down.

At long last I had moved one of the heaps in its entirety. The great big pile of dirt lay on the grass in front of the place it had occupied and would now have to be moved back.

I sank down on the grass and made a rollie. As I smoked I stared at the compost in despair. A quarter! Just a quarter of the work. I wanted to check my phone for the time but the battery had gone flat.

For a moment I considered refilling the heap I had started and leaving the other one be. I could just say I had done them both. But then I womanned up. Damn it. Had I not told myself that I could leave the deceitful Wendy back in Neverland and become Wenn here? Someone who deserved the affection Joy had apparently decided I was worth? Even though Willick must have warned her that there was a far less pleasant side to me?

I pictured Joy's face for a moment. The love she had bestowed on her bettermost flowers, the impish mischief in her eyes when she had lied my way out of Nowhere Place, her determination not to show how much pain she had been suffering earlier today...

...the compost became my mission, my chance to prove I was capable of bettering myself. Deserving of all the folk of the Wyrde Woods had done for me. Of becoming Wenn. In fairy tales the hero got to rush off to slay dragons and save damsels in distress. Epic glory and all that. In the real world I got to shovel dirt, but damn it, I was going to do it properly.

I attacked the second heap with zeal, willing myself to go on even though every inch of my body protested. Every now and then I'd drink some water or stop for a smoke but I refused to give in to the despair that started to rise every time I saw how much more there was to be done. After these short breaks I'd force myself to rise again and pick up that spade even as my aching muscles begged for relief.

After an eternity -and just a bit longer- I was done at last and stood in front of the two heaps, leaning on my shovel, with a pained lopsided grin on my face. Triumph would be the wrong word to describe how I felt. A victor triumphant would have the energy left to punch the air or raise her arms but my arms felt like I could never move them again. I was too broken to feel elation but the quiet content I felt was good, even though there was practically no visible result to admire, barring the two dark damp circles on the grass where the transferred heaps had been for a while.

I was covered in dirt and filth and stank of musty compost and stale sweat. I managed a laugh. This morning I'd felt so sexy I managed to turn myself on but just look at me now. I might as well grow chest hair and start swaggering around macho style.

I went back inside. Joy was in the rocking chair, bathed in the glow of the small fire she had lit and with a shawl wrapped around her frail shoulders. She looked vulnerable but better than she had earlier in the day.

"Done," I managed to utter. She looked at me and managed a smile.

"Ye be a good lass Wenn, bethanks."

"It was…it was nice to do something."

"Aye, I can imagine that. Ye'll be wanting a wash? Ye smell fouler than a hairy sailor on a three day shore leave in Brighton lass."

I laughed. I would have murdered for a hot shower but I had already figured I'd rinse some of the dirt off by the well.

"If ye walk past the cherry trees caterwise, ye'll find a path, it gwoan down to a brook. There's a bathing place. Naun'll bother ye, jes me what gwoan there. There be a warm towel by the Rayburn and some bio-degredibble soap on the shelf next to the kitchen table."

I nodded gratefully.

§ § § § § § §

I found the path down to the stream easily enough and it wasn't more than a few hundred yards down to the small brook. Someone had used rocks to build a makeshift dam where the stream had widened in one of its turns and there was a small clear pool here with a bed of rounded pebbles which rose gradually to form a broad dry ledge by the brook side. I stepped down onto the ledge and experienced a moment of discomfort when I undressed. It felt weird getting naked out in the open, surrounded by dense undergrowth which could have held a thousand hidden eyes. The only signs of life however came from the cheerful chorus of birds in the surrounding trees and I figured they couldn't care less.

When I had finished stripping standing there starkers felt entirely natural, liberating even and I couldn't really be bothered anymore anyway. I just wanted to get into the water as the congealed dirt and sweat had started to itch. I tested the temperature of the water with a big toe and then stepped in up to my knees. The water was cold enough but it seemed manageable and I let myself fall forwards to plunge in at once.

"SHIIIIIIIIIIIIIITTT!!"

The water was icy cold towards the middle of the brook and my first instinct was to jump out and rush to the Owlery to seek the warmth of that fire. I stayed in though, I was girly enough to appreciate clean hair, and the cold soon became refreshing. I was tingling all over as the dirt washed off and I took my time to shampoo my hair and rinse it properly. Only then did I get out to dry myself vigorously and that warmed me up some.

I had just finished drying myself when I heard rustling in the undergrowth and then a loud bark as something furry sailed through the air and landed in the pool with a big splash. Lady popped her head up above the water and turned, looking idiotically happy as she paddled back to the bank.

"Lady!" I exclaimed.

The dog wagged her tail enthusiastically as she scrambled to me dripping wet and then began to shake herself at great speed, starting with her head and then all the way to the tip of her tail, soaking me all over again.

"Oh Lady!"

Then it struck me that Puck was likely to be nearby if Lady was here and I instinctively clutched the towel in front of me as I tried to peer into the undergrowth. Then I shrugged, if he was hidden somewhere he had probably already had a good long look so I let the towel drop and took my time in dressing, feeling a secret thrill as I did so.

I walked back up the path, Lady wagging her tail at my side. I felt clean and refreshed. My muscles still ached but the worst edge was off. I heard a thud coming from the direction of the Owlery, followed by more.

As I walked through the garden I saw Puck on the courtyard splitting logs with an axe. To judge by the pile of split wood next to him he had been at it for a while and I felt slightly disappointed. I watched him handle the axe deftly and with apparent ease. He had a lot of strength in that absurdly puny body of his. He was dressed entirely in green again.

"Hullo there," Puck's face was somewhat red from the exertion and he took off his glasses to wipe his brow with his sleeve before dutifully greeting Lady who had been waiting for him to rest the axe and now bounded up to him for an exuberant greeting.

"Hey Puck," I said. "In green again?"

"Yes, I haven't got any other colours."

"Why?"

He grinned and thought it over and then answered: "Because I can."

§ § § § § §

Joy had apparently invited Puck for dinner. She was apologetic about the meal. Though she felt better she hadn't had the strength to prepare a proper meal, just warm up some soup added to which was another loaf of that sumptuous bread. Both Puck and I wolfed it down and Joy was amused by our appetites.

"I heard you did the compost heaps today?" Puck asked me.

I just nodded; my mouth was too full to try a verbal answer.

"Wenn worked harder than Master Dobbs she does, a middling duzzick." Joy nodded in approval. "Puck lad, tis full moon tonight. I were planning to take Wenn to the Maidens. Naun better night for it."

"You are not going anywhere with your Fibro acting up like this," Puck said sternly. "You might be feeling somewhat better, but walking all that way will do you no good."

"Justly so," Joy confirmed. "I were hoping ye'd be willing to take hern in mine stead."

Puck chewed on a piece of bread thoughtfully, contemplating me.

"Do I have a say in this?" I asked as cheerfully as I could, for I was somewhat miffed that I seemed to be left out of the decision making process.

"Nope, not really," Puck chuckled. "Once Joy has set her mind to something it'd be easier move Arthur's Fort seven miles than convince her otherwise."

"'O course ye've a say Wenn," Joy looked at me with a sparkle in her eye. "Tis jes that I be thinking ye would likes to see some secret places of the Wyrde Woods."

11. Lover's Lane

We had about an hour-and-a-half to sunset, Puck told me as we set off, so most of the walking would be in the dark but it'd be easy going on a good path, there and back.

"Why did Joy tell you to take the long way round?" I asked.

"Cause she doesn't want us going through Roreford in the dark."

I frowned; I'd heard the name mentioned a couple of times now, though it wasn't on any of the maps I had studied.

"What's Roreford? A village, right?"

"Aye, there used to be five villages in the Wyrde Woods: Nickleby, Wolfden, Mordrove, Roreford and Tuckersham."

"Wolfden and Mordrove?"

"Wolfden is west of here, Mordrove is to the north. Roreford was destroyed and Tuckersham deserted."

"Why is Roreford a bad place at night?"

"It's a long story."

"I like long stories."

"Okay, but don't blame me if you get bored," Puck said.

"Oh but I get bored easily. The story better be good," I answered and drew a laugh from Puck.

"Glad we're clear on that then Wenn. It was back in the 16th century."

I yawned in an exaggerated fashion.

"Oi!" Puck exclaimed and gave me a playful poke in the side.

Lady barked in protest.

"Ho-hum, she doesn't like it when I pay attention to other ladies, do you Lady?" Puck grinned sheepishly and gave Lady a pat on the head.

"She doesn't have to worry if that was your best move," I grinned.

"Ah, I have been wondering why that never works," Puck retorted, and then shifted into serious gear again.

"A bloke called Cecil was the eldest son of Roderick, Lord Malheur, and a right Pratt Cecil was as a child. Spoiled and self-centred. He grew worse when he became an adolescent. By the time Cecil was seventeen he was arrogant, overbearing, egotistical and pig-headed."

"Just like all teenage boys," I joshed.

"No Wenn," Puck sounded serious. "Cecil was dangerous. Being the heir of Malheur Hall, the future Lord of the Wyrde Woods, it gave him power over folk around here and he used that badly."

"How?"

"Roreford was the closest village to Malheur Hall and Cecil rode there often, sometimes alone, sometimes in the company of friends. He would persuade the village girls to sleep with him or the bunch of them. Ply them with gifts or cajole them, but if that didn't work he'd just threaten them."

"Did the villagers know?"

"Everybody knew. But any wrongly-directed word would mean eviction, a family forced on the road as beggars with nothing but inevitable starvation ahead of them."

"So they didn't do anything?" I was appalled.

"They did though. One day someone'd had enough, nobody knew who. A father? A sweetheart? One of the girls?"

"What happened?"

"The gatekeeper of Malheur Hall opened the main gate because a rider approached from the Wyrde Woods and he recognised Cecil's horse. It wasn't till the horse was halfway down the long moat bridge that he realised the rider was headless."

"Headless?"

"Aye, it had been cut off. They knew it was Cecil because the next day they found his head by the base of the Blood Stone, with his severed genitals stuffed in his mouth."

"UGH!"

"Precisely, though not undeserved."

"What is the Blood Stone?"

"A standing stone on Gallows Hill. Traditional place of punishment and execution for those who crossed the Malheur family."

"Was Cecil's father angry?"

"Absolutely livid. They said that he was foaming at the mouth with fury. His steward went to Roreford to question the villagers but nobody had any answers for him. So Roderick formed a militia made up of his own retainers and some nearby aristocrats and he led them to Roreford. There he had the whole village rounded up in the village square. He told them that his son had come to his end by means of witchcraft and that he would not suffer a witch to live on his lands. His own manservants, who knew the village well enough, dragged four girls out of the crowd, the ones they knew for certain Cecil had been spending time with. They were stripped and received 20 lashings each, right there and then."

I felt an icy shiver pass by my spine.

"Didn't the villagers protest? Rebel?"

"Roderick's men were armed with longbows, handguns, pikes, swords…and eager for a fight too; a chance to plunder the village. Besides, aiding accused witches meant being accused yourself and everybody sensed that Roderick was furious enough to summon a Witch Hunter with the orders to see every man, woman and child in the village tortured and strung up. Roderick then had the girls, weeping and bleeding, tied to the great big wheel of the water mill for a water test."

"Water test?"

"Yes, a fool proof way of testing if someone was a witch. If they drowned they were innocent, if they floated and lived they were obviously accomplishes of the devil and would be strung up by the neck."

"But if they drowned they would be dead!" I protested.

"Yes, but their immortal souls would be saved and that was what mattered."

"That's just faxing daft."

"So it is. Anyway, this wasn't an ordinary water test, being tied to the wheel there was no way they could float. Roderick had the wheel turned and turned again and again, speeding it up or slowing it down. They'd be dragged along the rocks just below the wheel's rim too. At the end of it the girls died agonising deaths, their bodies mangled and broken and drowned a little bit at a time. But their immortal souls hadn't been tempered with, so Roderick's soul was in the clear too. He acknowledged their apparent innocence and reimbursed the families with some silver pieces. But he had made his message pretty clear. You don't fax with the Malheur family."

I shuddered, trying to imagine what it would feel like; going under the water slowly and then gasping for breath as you came up again, barely registering the grinning soldiers and horrified villagers as the wheel went into another revolution and you needed all your fading strength to prepare for another dunking, never knowing how long this one would last, or if they would just keep the wheel in place till you expelled your last breath.

"Did he destroy the village after that?"

"No, that was much later, another Malheur. But the girls…"

"Shims?"

"Yes. They haunt the mill. Sometimes they're in the water and it looks like they are drowning and need help. Folk who try to help are *willed* in and drown. Other times they've been heard screaming like banshees."

I shivered and wondered if Puck had experiences like I had with Ufmanna.

"There's more. They say that once a year on the full October moon a headless rider is seen crossing the moat bridge at Malheur Hall."

I thought about Earl Roger who had his cooks prepare the village children as a meal, Cecil Malheur who helped himself to the village girls and his father Roderick who punished them for it, Mortimer Malheur who got Joy with child and then fired her for improper behaviour.

"That's one hell of a psycho family in that hall," I said.

Puck gave me a funny look. "Yeah, you need to be careful with the Malheurs."

The path started broadening and then split into two, the dual paths separated by thirty feet of grass centred by a line of some dozen trees.

"Sirageous!" I exclaimed looking at those trees.

"Lover's Lane," Puck said.

Each tree had short thick boles below the crowns. At first I thought they were two different kinds of trees but then I registered that each crown seemed to consist of two parts. One half consisted of regularly spaced and similarly shaped branches curving upwards and smothered in pretty white cup shaped blossoms. The other half had branches that stretched further and higher in irregular serpentine patterns on which the clusters of blossoms were coloured bright magenta. The white and pink formed a stark contrast and made the hues of green on the surrounding trees seem monotonously dull and it was all made more magnificent by the setting sun which enhanced the colours of the blossoms.

We walked closer and I inhaled the air expectantly, rewarded by a rich sweet fragrance. It was like breathing in honey and almonds. I looked at Puck with utter delight.

"How?"

"It's called grafting. Fluttergrub did this lot years ago, some sort of romantic notion he had."

"Say what?"

"He took a section of a stem with leaf buds from one tree and inserted it into the stock of another tree, kinda complicated to explain, you need to see it done really,"

"The pink ones are amazing!"

"That's Japanese Kanzan cherry, the other one is local wild cherry. In another few weeks or so the petals will start falling, on a breezy day it's like walking through a surreal snow storm. Or kicking your way through the most incredible pile of autumn leaves you have ever seen."

"Spring, autumn and winter rolled into one," I smiled. "You missed the summer."

"A summer breeze causes the snow storm," Puck said happily.

We walked by the trees slowly. The air was thick with the fused perfume of the flowers here, giving me the sensation that if I spread my arms and lifted my feet off the ground I could float on the stuff. I took more deep breaths and I wished I could take a bottle of the stuff back to Nowhere Place with me.

It was with reluctance that I left the trees behind as we continued our journey. The path started to climb gradually though it didn't twist and turn like the paths up Arthur's Fort nor were there roots and rocks to contend with. We came to a junction with a path to the left and right but Puck led us straight on across a small grassy clearing which ended abruptly when the ground fell downwards at a steep angle for a thirty yards to rise again forty yards away. There wasn't much to see in the chasm as most of it was screened by the foliage of abundant trees. I could hear the sound of rushing water though; there was a considerable river down there somewhere.

"Hood's Gorge," Puck said, "These are the upper reaches. The Rore River cuts deeper further on, almost a hundred feet at places; sheer sand rock."

"Can we go climbing there?" I asked eagerly.

"Yes," Puck nodded. "There's good fun in that. But it's too dark now."

He was right; twilight had set in. We walked northwards, spotting the gorge every now and then when the path skirted the edge. The gorge was getting narrower and the rush of Rore River wilder.

"Robin's Cave is somewhere down there," Puck said at one of these points. "Big as a house on the inside."

"Robin's Cave. Hood's Gorge," I said pensively. "I thought that was up north. Around Nottingham."

"You know what England is like," Puck grinned. "There is not an old tree to be found which Robin Hood hasn't climbed and hardly a hill where King Arthur hasn't built his Camelot."

"Arthur's Fort!" I exclaimed and Puck nodded.

"In the times that Arthur rode out of Wales to fight the likes of us this wouldn't have been the best place to build his capital. It was already Suth Seaxna Lond. The Saxons called it sacred land."

He grinned again. "I like that contradiction though, that a hero of the Cymru has become one of our own. It's respectful towards the Welsh I think. There's more accuracy to the cave story though, it's said to be one of the secret bases of Willikin of the Weald."

"Willikin of the Weald?"

"And a band of outlaws dressed in green that fought a French army around here with bows and arrows in 1216."

"The French never invaded England! Not after 1066." I was pleased to show that I did manage to learn a few things at school every now and then.

"Oh but they did, we just don't like to talk about it. Anyhow, it's said Willikin kept stores in the cave and kipped there in between raids on the southern edge of the Weald."

"I wonder if that's where Willick lived," I thought aloud.

"How did you know about that?"

"Joy told me."

The path started bending east and then south and we walked parallel to the other side of the gorge. It was dark now and the path became more irregular, but by keeping an eye on Puck I could predict the trickier bits which he circumnavigated with ease.

"How come you know so much about the Wyrde Woods? You said you hadn't been living here for that long."

"I am a voracious reader and I listen. Folk like Joy and Willick, Rob Hornsby too, and Joan down at the Earl's Barrel. They are full of tales."

"I met Joan! Willick and Joy took me down to Earl's Barrel."

"Did anybody pinch your bottom?"

"Huh, what?" I couldn't place what my bottom had to do with this though I was vaguely pleased it was on his mind.

"Another shim," I could just about hear Puck's grin. "A young lad by all accounts, about twelve and cheerful. He haunts the pub. Likes to mimic voices so he does, it causes much confusion when folk are in their cups."

"Drunk you mean?"

"Ah, locals are never drunk Wenn, they'll swear by high and low they had one pint at the most and all their mates will vow that this is the truth, even if they are found atop of a hill howling at the moon."

"You find them like that often? On top of hills and singing wolf songs?"

"Been there, done that. Have the t-shirt tucked away in my hideout."

"You? No kidding?"

"You look surprised Wenn," Puck said amused. "The Earl's Barrel is warm and dry on a cold night and Willick is good company."

"Never more than a pint though?"

"Oh no, never. Just one pint."

"And that's enough to have you howling at the moon?" I grinned. "Amateur. Tell me more about this pub-shim. He mimics voices?"

"Yes to create confusion which he uses to pinch bottoms. Which causes more confusion and so on. He's a jolly little fellow as ghosts go."

"Well nobody pinched my bottom. They served me cider though."

"Aye, they're not too concerned about Sheere-folk laws here, never have been. 'Sussex wun't be druv,' especially not by Lunnon. Only for locals mind you, half of Nickleby has been gentrified by Sheere-folk and they put up an awful fuss about things so the natives do have to mind where tradition is applied."

I beamed; it was ridiculous but I was pleased the half-pint of cider at the Earl's Barrel marked me as a local. It was like belonging to something.

The path now angled away from the gorge and the Rore's rush of water slowly faded away. We walked on in silence though the now familiar sounds of nocturnal activities in the woods provided enough to listen to. Now and then Puck would break his silence by naming the animals we heard; foxes and birds of prey mostly and once a badger. We came to a steep descent that ran down in a broad curve. At the bottom of the descent we emerged from the tree line in a wide open space, a dramatic spectacle in the silver moonlight.

The end of this clearing was marked by a semi-circular cliff, some twenty foot-high in the middle and gradually decreasing in height towards its ends which curved inwards to us. The low cliff was practically vertical, too steep for growth and the pale ochre stone reflected the moonshine in such a way that it appeared there was a second moon; the full one overhead and the sickle of a new moon in front of us. Within the embrace of this second moon was a circle of standing stones, about twice the height of Puck and just as narrow and slender as he was. The ground around the circle was lit up by hundreds of tiny green lights as if somebody had carelessly left dozens of fairy lights strings unattended and plugged in somehow.

"It's amazing," I sighed, enchanted by the sight. There was something mysterious about the place. Not just the sight of it as I also sensed an ancient sanctity. I didn't need Willick or Joy to tell me this was one of the good places in the Wyrde Woods, surelye.

"A whole bunch of glow worms and the seven Shy Maidens," Puck said.

12. Shy Maidens

I did a quick count.

"But there are only six of them."

We approached the stones; even Lady seemed to be impressed for she stopped rushing to and fro and stayed unbidden at Puck's side. The standing stones towered over us serenely in the moonlight, casting long shadows on the grass.

"Part of their story," Puck said. "See how they are arranged in an almost perfect circle?"

"There's one missing!" I exclaimed, noting the obvious gap now.

"Yes, there used to be seven. The story is that a long time ago, when the Faere Folk used to walk far and wide in the Wyrde Woods seven fair maidens dwelt in their midst."

"Faere Folk? Faeries?"

"Yeah, but not quite like we know them now. Faere Folk applies to a large collection of creatures, from tiny winged pixies, to goblins -of all shapes and sizes- and then the uncommonly tall ones, forever young and extremely beautiful to behold."

We were circling the Shy Maidens now.

"Like Elves!" I pictured Tolkien's descriptions of Rivendell.

"Almost. The Faere Folk know no mortality, no aging and they can't feel pain. Unless it's by magic. They don't really understand humans; not sure if we're just hairy apelike creatures or have started using our full brain potential at last. They have fierce debates about us. Some claim we don't exist."

I laughed at that.

"Anyway, those that do believe we exist like to play tricks on us. The tricks remind them that they are the clever ones, capable of outwitting humans. They like to laugh at commotion they cause; sometimes by good deeds but it depends on their mood. They are just as likely to become dangerous. Locals are wary of the Faere Folk."

Puck paused for a moment and then recited:

> *I met a lady in the meads*
> *Full beautiful – a faery's child*
> *Her hair was long, her foot was light*
> *And her eyes were wild.*

"Where's that from?" I asked.

"A poem, it's much longer. About a young knight who was seduced by one of the Faere Folk by a pool. There's a place," Puck pointed westwards. "Not far from here called the Fey's Pool. It's reputed to be the favourite haunt of a Faere Fey like in the poem."

Puck grinned shyly. "She seduces men there by the sight of her bathing nude in the pool; she lures them in the water with her beauty."

"She fell for hairy apes?" I asked, wondering at the same time if perhaps Puck had seen me bathing in the brook after all.

"You know what women are like, whimsical and unpredictable. They'll demand gentle kindness and then fall for assholes or hairy apes."

"Hey," I protested.

"It's true though," Puck said brusquely and I wondered at this. I decided not to contest his claim.

"Sometimes," I conceded. "Go on with the story please."

"The Fey of the Pool revels in her own beauty and male adoration is the only nourishment she requires. Once under her spell they are her captives for eternity, doomed to behold but never touch the most beautiful woman they have ever seen." Puck shuddered.

"Anyhow," he continued. "These seven fair maidens here were different from the other tall Faere Folk in that they were shy and in no way desired to show off their beauty like the others, though they loved dancing, as all Faere Folk do."

"So every full moon they would come here to dance in secret but one night they were seen by a young mischievous goblin called Powke, who went and told Oberon, the King of the Faere Folk. And the next full moon Powke led Oberon to this place and they spied on the maidens as they danced, unaware of the prying eyes of the lustful king."

I listened; spellbound by the tale as we circled the stones.

"But then Powke told a Queen's handmaiden he fancied the secret to impress her and she told Queen Titania. Titania was proud and felt wounded in her pride so she went to talk to the bees and cast a spell on them so they could hurt the Faere Folk with their stings. That's why they are treated in a special way by locals, because the Faere Folk fear the bees and listen to them. Folk around here believe and hope the bees will intercede with the Faere Folk on their behalf if they treat the bees in their own hives like family."

"Joy spoke to the bees yesterday!"

"Did she? What did she tell them?"

"About me, that I'd be staying over."

"You know what that means then?" Puck smiled broadly.

"No?"

"You only tell bees about family matters, she was asking them to welcome you into her family."

"REALLY?" I was thrilled to bits. "But she barely knows me?"

"If she likes you and set her mind on it, that doesn't matter much to her. She sort of adopts people every now and then. Do you want to hear the rest of the story?"

"Yes please," I said, floating on a cloud as we continued circling the Shy Maidens.

"On the second full moon Oberon and Powke were hidden in the bushes again to watch the Shy Maidens dance when all of a sudden a swarm of bees appeared above them and…"

"I thought bees were inactive at night."

"Hey, I didn't make this up. Fey magic is strong."

"Okay, so the bees attacked?"

"The whole swarm dove down as one being and stung Oberon and Powke on their bottoms again and again. So Oberon and Powke, entirely unused to pain jumped out of the bushes where they had been hiding: Howling and hollering and clutching their arses."

I laughed, seeing the unfortunate Faeries hopping around in pain. We continued walking around the stones.

"But this startled the Shy Maidens in a major way…they froze where they were and changed into stone."

I stopped and lay my head on one of the stones. It felt smooth and cool to the touch.

"Poor maidens."

"Zackly." Puck said.

"Justly and jes so," I replied. "But what about the seventh Shy Maiden?"

"Titania had the seventh stone taken away and hidden, so that Oberon would never be tempted to change the Shy Maidens back into flesh and blood. Folk have searched far and wide but nobody has seen the seventh stone since. It's said that if you come here at a full moon with the fairest maid of the Wyrde Woods and place her there where the seventh stone stood and circle the stones widdershins…"

"Widdershins?"

"Anti-clockwise. If you circle the stones anti-clockwise at midnight and speak certain words the Shy Maidens would turn to flesh and blood again and dance for the whole hour of the witch."

"Has anyone ever tried?"

"Why do you think I brought you here?" Puck laughed. "You'd pass for one of the Faere Folk easily enough."

I grinned. Had he just said he thought I was pretty? Was he chirpsing with me? It beat the usual unimaginative lines. Probably he just thought I was like a small goblin, he'd just said they weren't all fit.

"No one dares," Puck continued. "For who knows what would happen? The poor girl might turn to stone, or be taken into Pook Hall. For the girl her stay there might seem like a few hours at most, but when she'd return every one she knew could be dead or grey, old and incontinent. It's better not to mess with the Faere Folk, even in jest."

He sounded as serious as Joy had sounded and I suddenly wondered why even today's city kids knew you should never accept food and drink from faeries. I had always thought it was a cautionary tale but maybe the warning had much earlier roots than that, surviving the march of time against all odds. And perhaps for good reason.

"Do you know the words?"

Puck nodded and spoke:

> *Come in the stillness*
> *Come in the night*
> *Come now and bring delight*
> *Moon shadows long, moonlight bright*
> *Stones still and tall, left and right*
> *Let heart beat and blood flow*
> *Come now, come tonight.*

"That poor seventh Shy Maiden," I said. "As if being turned to stone for eternity isn't enough she'll be on her own as well, these have each other for company and someone might just show up one day to let them dance again."

Puck smiled.

"Come on, let's head back to Joy," he said and we departed.

§ § § § § § §

Lover's Lane was just as enchanting in the moonlight as it had been in the sunshine, the white blossoms ghostly pale in the moonshine while the pink seemed to have turned deep red. Once again I inhaled a breath of honey.

"Puck?"

"Yes?"

"The story…Powke. Puck. Powke? Pook Hall? Puck?"

"From 'Puca'. It's Anglo-Saxon for a mischievous goblin."

Much as I liked his stories, I wasn't after an old story this time.

"What is your real name?"

"Puck," Puck insisted.

"What is your old name?" I persisted.

Puck stopped and looked at me. I could see his lenses shine in the moonlight, a halo of ghostly white and dark red flowers around his head. He looked almost alien.

"Peter," he said at last.

§ § § § § § §

Lady barked in alarm as we approached the Owlery and we rushed through the garden. Joy was a dark figure piled on the ground by the well, an upturned pail by her side. My heart skipped a beat, for a moment I thought she was unconscious or even dead. When we got to her however, she moaned and then whispered.

"Fell. Cannot get up."

"It's okay grandma," Puck said. He slid his arms around her and then lifted her in his arms as gently and tenderly as if she was a new born child. She leaned her head against his chest like a little girl and he carried her inside, laying her down on the bed.

"Wenn…" he spoke.

"Blue tin? Infusion?" I answered, already on my way to the kitchen.

"Yes please, I'll stoke the fire."

Sometime later Joy leaned against the cushions sipping from her infusion and we sat by her. Puck on a stool near Joy and myself on the edge of the foot end of the bed.

"Puck?" Joy said.

"Yes?"

"A song if ye please. The one with the sea."

Puck nodded and took a deep breath before launching into a soft melodious song. This was totally different from the bawdy ditty I heard him sing on Arthur's Fort. That had been done well enough for a bloke but this was plain sirageous. He really had a golden voice. Joy sighed and hummed along.

> *Child of the Ocean, young Siren of the Sea,*
> *knee-deep in the surf, still as a rock you stand*
> *overlooking the vastness, your back to me,*
> *loneliness ahead, behind you the land.*
> *Hand in hand we stand, like soldiers in the ranks,*
> *now's the moment, the magic flows fast and strong:*
> *Fire in the sky, water, breeze and the sand banks.*
> *All is whole, so whole, here and now we belong.*
> *Mermaids in the surf, sand, shells, salt spray.*
> *Seize joy, seize love, seize life, fight now to be free,*
> *like a child splash, dive, swim, in the Blue Sea play,*
> *like Ocean's child, like Siren of the Sea.*

Joy had fallen asleep and we moved to the fire. I felt tired; it had been a day of intense physical exertion and emotional contrasts. But there was one more thing I needed to know or I would not sleep at all.

"Puck," I said softly.

"Hmm?" Puck looked tired too, drained of energy but I could be as merciless as that femme fatale by the Fey's Pool.

"Grandma," I looked at him pointedly. "GRANDMA?"

§ § § § § § §

"My name was Peter Nathaniel Mortimer Malheur-Whitfield." Puck stared into the fire.

"So your father is...?"

"Nathaniel Malheur, the offspring of Mortimer Malheur and Joy Whitfield."

"She said your father was taken away," I said softly.

"He was seven; Lord Malheur had only fathered one other child. A girl."

"Lady Malheur."

"Yes, Aunt Catt is the legitimate one but I understand that my grandfather wanted a back-up in case anything happened to his daughter. In such a case a bastard would do nicely too. So my father was taken away and raised as one of 'them'."

"Did Joy see him often?" I cast a glance at Joy, she looked frail and vulnerable.

"He dropped by during the summers when he was allowed to stay at Malheur Hall. Only twice after he left for university. The first time after he completed his degree at Cambridge. They quarrelled. The second time was three years ago when I was fourteen. He took me along, it was the first time I met her."

"What happened?"

"They quarrelled again. He wanted to place her in a care home for the elderly. She refused point blank."

I hesitated, thinking of Joy's 'rheummatics', the heavy work in the garden, the tub I had seen with an old-fashioned washing board and wringer, drawing water from the well, feeding chickens and owls...

Puck must have guessed my thoughts.

"I know it isn't always easy for her to be here Wenn. But a care home? You live in one, do you like it?"

"I hate every minute of it, but surely it's different for the elderly, I mean, your father can afford private care right?"

"Even if the care was okay, think of her, she's a child of the woods, lived here all her life. How long do you think she'd last stashed away in a stuffy room somewhere?"

I thought of a leopard I had once seen in a zoo. Pacing endlessly from one side of its cage to the other, eyes focused on a faraway place, a home where it had never been. I remembered thinking that I understood exactly what it felt like, my cage being only a bit bigger. Joy would be like that too if she was taken out of the Wyrde Woods.

"Not long," I admitted softly.

"My father is an arsehole," Puck hissed vehemently.

"Maybe he cared, maybe he was worried."

I realised immediately that this was unlikely if he barely ever visited.

"No!" Puck said viciously. I winced.

"Sorry Wenn," He laid a hand on my forearm and looked mortified. "Didn't mean that...I didn't want to take it out on you."

"That's okay," I said quickly.

"When Mortimer died ten years ago he left Malheur Hall to his daughter. My father inherited a corner of the Wyrde Woods. From Roreford to the road north of here, from Hood's Gorge to Willikin's Drove."

"Wow."

"He's got enough decency not to forcibly remove her, but that is about it. He doesn't care for her, for anyone really, and is waiting for her to die."

"Why?"

"He has planning permission and building plans for a holiday park."

"Here?" I was shocked.

"Neat rows of bungalows, tennis courts, indoor swimming pool, restaurant etcetera."

"That's horrible." I was appalled.

"It's one heck of a motivation for grandma to live well past a hundred." Puck grinned. "I can see her do it too."

"Does that mean…you stand to inherit all this?"

"My father disowned me, so no." Puck said curtly.

"How? Why?"

Puck raised his hands to ward off my next hundred questions.

"It's late Wenn, another time okay?"

"Okay, I said, trying to hide my disappointment.

My mind turned to sleeping arrangements.

"Do you want to sleep upstairs?" I asked, and then blushed when I realised the question might be misunderstood. I hastily added: "I'll sit by Joy, I don't mind."

"It's okay Wenn," Puck yawned. "She's my grandmother, we've been through this before, she'll be much better in the morning. Should be her old self again in a few days. I'll keep an eye on her and kip by the fire with Lady."

Lady had been dozing off on the sheepskin rugs by the fire. At the sound of her name she raised a sleepy head and thumped her tail on the ground.

"Okay then." I said wearily, suddenly feeling excluded again. It was selfish of me, I knew, but I liked having Joy to myself, she was my secret of the Wyrde Woods and my haven, but she was Puck's too, much more than she was mine. And Willick's. I went upstairs and even though I was tired I had a restless sleep that night, not helped much by the owls downstairs who made a fuss all night.

§ § § § § §

I woke up early on Sunday and for a moment experienced that contented feeling of waking up in my own space again but then I recalled the previous day's events and quickly dressed to go downstairs. I went into the living room.

"Morning Wenn," Puck greeted me just before Lady avalanched me in joyous greetings. "There's coffee on the Rayburn."

Puck was feeding the owls, Joy appeared to be asleep. I petted Lady and then went to pour myself a cup of coffee. When I returned Puck had finished with the owls and came over as I sat down on the edge of Joy's bed.

"I've given her another draught," he explained. "She'll come to this afternoon."

"Okay, will she be all right?" I asked anxiously.

"She should be, these spells never last long if she gets enough rest. She'll be sorely disappointed though, she had planned to take you to Roreford and maybe Willikin's Drove today."

"That's fine, really. Just being here with you all is enough already. You simply have no idea. I just wish there was something I could do for her."

"There is, help me weed the garden," Puck said.

I was happy to be of use. We spent the afternoon in the garden, Puck taught me how to recognise the weeds that needed to be removed and we set to it. Apart from having to bend over a lot the work was peanuts compared to the compost heaps and it was grand to be surrounded by all the plants and flowers in a flurry of butterflies. The bees didn't mind me as long as I minded my own business and that was okay by me.

"So," I said after a while, "You were telling me last night…"

"Oh no Wenn," Puck said cheerfully. "It's my turn now."

He proceeded to ask me about Nowhere Place and when he gathered it was just the last in a long list of institutions he wanted to know about the other places as well. I spoke hesitantly at first; giving only short answers because I was kind of annoyed about dragging those places into my activities at the Owlery. Puck seemed genuinely interested though and it became easier for me to talk. It even felt good offloading some of my frustrations.

I left out a number of details of course, like Calcott for one, and Stubbles. I spoke about Lifers and Snooties. About the camaraderie of the Forlorn Hope, where we didn't always have much in common but we all shared being hopelessly messed up and viewed as being irreparable outcasts. I talked about the system, how you could sabotage it in small ways but never challenge it in any major way. I talked about what it was like to grow up knowing you had been taken away from your parents and having only the vaguest memories of them. The inherent and continual fear that I could pass my parents on a street and not even recognise them because I had no pictures and couldn't recall their faces. I ended with my sullen mood every home leave Friday and what it had meant to me that Willick and Joy had shown up, that Puck had helped them do so. How much it meant to me that the seemingly hopeless dream of feeling at home somewhere had unexpectedly come true a little bit.

Puck was an attentive listener and asked pointed questions, though he ended it all on a lighter note.

"Soooo," he said contemplatively. "You're nuts?"

We had finished in the garden and had moved to the kitchen where I helped Puck cut vegetables for soup. I hesitated, I was pleased that he didn't start to say how sorry he was and such. I hadn't told him because I wanted pity. I had told him because it was surprisingly easy to talk to him about it in an objective manner, something I could rarely do. I had swapped the misery list with Sharon and Biggs and the like, but that was always subjective with a collective final chorus of: Fax 'em all.

But to admit to being off the hinge? Would it change his mind about me? He seemed to like me. I liked him too; I had never met such a wonderfully weird person before. Well, Joy and Willick excepted of course, but Puck was young and spoke my language. Best to be honest though, I decided, if it weren't obvious enough anyway.

"Yup, certifiably."

"Mad as a hatter?"

"Off my rockers."

"There's a few marbles missing then?"

"The wheel is spinning, but there's no sign of the hamster," I nodded.

"Porch light is on but there is nobody home."

We both laughed and it felt good.

"What're ye two chavees smirking about?" Joy made an appearance in the kitchen, looking and sounding remarkably better. "Planning mischief?"

"A wheelbarrow full of mischief," Puck confirmed.

"Good!" Joy smiled and came to inspect the soup. She tasted it critically, closing her eyes for a moment.

"Aint half bad," she conceded. "Puck, be a dear and fetch me some o' that Vietnamese coriander from the garden. It'll give it jes a dash o' sharp freshness."

Puck left and Joy looked at me, scrutinising my face.

"I am sorry Wenn, surelye," she said, downcast. "I were hoping to give ye a fine weekend, this darn wornout body o' mine, tis naun always much o' a help."

"Joy please, I've had a wonderful weekend, honestly." I said, my voice starting to tremble lightly. "You don't know what it is like...I have never known…people making an effort for me. I don't even know how to thank you. I don't even deserve this."

"I'll be judge o' that," Joy said. "Come here sweetie."

She spread out her arms and I sank into her embrace, cautiously at first because I did not want to hurt her but her grip was tight and I placed my forehead on her shoulder, letting a few girly tears flow. It felt so good, like being a kid again, but then one who had a place to hide, warm and safe protection against the world.

"When is yern next home leave time Wenn?" Joy asked.

"In three weeks Gammer," Puck said as he entered the kitchen again.

"Oi, are you stalking me?" I loosened myself from Joy's embrace and quickly wiped my eyes.

"You bet," Puck said sounding proud of himself and I laughed.

"Does ye want us to fetch ye again?" Joy wanted to know.

I nodded, my heart soared but I did not dare to say anything in case I'd go totally emo.

"Well then, we shall," Joy said, clearly pleased. "Now, I be wanting to try some o' this soup o' yern Puck."

§ § § § § § §

Puck had left on some errand when Willick came to collect me at about eight. Joy wanted to come with us but we convinced her to not exert herself too much just yet. I sat next to Willick as we drove off. The road to Nickleby was practically dark already, the trees blocking the day's last sunlight and it symbolised my gloomy mood. Willick stayed silent and I didn't mind, my mind fighting the dread as every second brought me closer to Neverland.

When we passed the Earl's Barrel in Nickleby Willick began to talk.

"Ye does puzzle me lass," he said in a tone that was friendly enough. "I doant know what to make o' ye."

"That makes two of us," I sighed. "I don't know either Willick."

"Joy and Puck have taken a liking to ye."

"And I to them. I thought…I hoped…you did too."

I didn't want to admit it but in my most secret mind the four of us formed a little family. It was incredibly far-fetched and based on little at all but to someone like me that little was a hundred thousand times more than I had ever known and a straw to clutch on to, something to tell the bees about. Hell, serenade the bees about with an epic ballad.

"Yern reaction to me, back at the Giant's Grove."

"I don't know how to explain," I said miserably. "I apologised. I meant that."

"And I appreciate that to be middling sure," Willick said thoughtfully. "Tis something unaccountable ye somewhen doant control?"

"Yes, exactly like that, it just happens."

"I like ye well enow lass," Willick spoke slowly, choosing his words carefully. "Mine fear be that ye gwoan does that to Joy."

"I would never do anything to hurt Joy," I protested vehemently.

"Can ye be absolutely sure o' that?" Willick looked at me, those remarkable eyes demanding the truth.

"No," I whispered.

"That be what I thought and be unaccountable afeared for," he said, turning his eyes back to the road. "I'll give ye a chance Wenn, but I'll naun stand for it if ye hurt Joy. Or young Puck for that matter."

I nodded, feeling miserable. I felt a little angry too because for the third time I felt exclusion, a reminder that I was the outsider. Then again, Willick had loved Joy with his heart and soul ever since he had been a boy. Love had literally driven him insane when he lost her, it sounded wildly poetic. I could hardly blame him for being protective of her, could I? These people had a connection reaching back over whole decades, well before I ever even existed. Or a connection forged by blood. Family. I should be glad Joy had people she could count on to stand by her side. Would anybody ever love me like that? I doubted it, Joy was special, I was just a mistake.

Willlick walked into Nowhere Place with me to sign my return form. Outside the office we said our goodbyes.

"Thank you so much," I said.

"Ye be taking care now lass," He gave me a warm smile and then started leaving.

"Wait!" I shouted when he opened it. He turned and raised an eyebrow and I ran to him to give him a hug. He was uncertain at first but then hugged me back, a great big bear hug. When I stepped back he looked pleased.

"Ye'll does alright lass, ye be a Brighton lass, they breed 'em tough in Brighton I recollects," he said. "Jes does yern best, will ye?"

"I will," I promised. Then Willick left, closing the front door behind him, sealing my return to Nowhere Place in Neverland.

13. Skirting the Edge

I was in a foul mood for the next four days. Being back in Nowhere Place was surreal, it was like swimming under water where everything was slightly distorted and the sounds of everyday life muted. I seemed to be living somebody else's life to pass the time till I could get back to my own.

The Wyrde Woods sometimes seemed like a distant but persistent memory like one of those really intensive dreams that hangs on in your mind for a day or more, seemingly more real than every day mundane routine. At other times I could almost hear the branches sway in the breeze, feel it in my heart. The Wyrde Woods were calling me and were so enticingly close and so frustratingly out of reach.

I spent hours behind the computer in the common room scrolling through webpages on local history, trees, plants and flowers; much to the irritation of Forlorn Hopers who needed it for more important things like posting pictures of kittens.

The mixture of chagrin and nostalgia wasn't helped by the fact that I was having my period, never a good time for me, I felt bloated and was hampered by cramps.

"I didn't know you had grandparents," Stubbles said when he cornered me in the Common Room on Wednesday afternoon.

"That is because they spent a long time looking before they found me," I answered as lightly as I could.

"Funny that," Stubbles looked thoughtful. "It's policy to encourage any rapprochement between the children in our care and their families. Had they made inquiries, we would have arranged a supervised visit as soon as possible."

"They're country folk, simple in their ways." This felt like a dreadful betrayal, but I needed to get Stubbles off this particular scent. "Not used to how things work here. They do really like me though; they make me feel like I am part of a family."

I offered this personal confession to Stubbles as a sacrifice. Michael would have seized on it; it was one heck of an opening. I didn't like handing it to Stubbles but I wanted to turn his mind elsewhere.

Stubbles didn't seem to recognise this though; he just nodded and said, "Well, it takes all sorts I suppose."

He walked away. I wondered what he had meant by that but then decided it didn't sound encouraging at any rate. I wanted to shout after him if his thick skull could comprehend what it meant when I said that someone made me feel like part of a family.

I tried to talk to Sharon about my weekend, though it took a long time to change the subject as she talked incessantly about Thomas. They were an official item now and she seemed intent on sharing every graphic detail of every shag they had, which was quite a lot as it formed just about the only base of their relationship, apart from the fascination both of them had with Thomas's six-pack. But that just led back to shagging.

"I met a boy in the woods Sharon," I managed at last.

"Did you shag him?" Sharon asked immediately.

"No, but..." I paused. How could I tell her how tender and gentle he had been when he had picked up Joy by the well? That I kept on asking myself if he had been just as considerate when he had found a strange girl in the woods, shivering, bleeding and crazed by fear? Lifted her up like she was precious, rather than a bag of potatoes. How he was totally not my type, not fit at all, but had a connection with me on a mental level that was hard to explain. It was all very remote from shagging.

"Oh you poor thing," Sharon cooed, misunderstanding my silence. "He didn't want to."

She held me and comforted me and I let her. The truth was complex with faked and real family connections. I might have told her a few months back but now I could be certain that she'd tell Thomas whose lack of discretion was famed in Nowhere Place.

I was upset with her though -even became angry- for removing herself as my confidante and leaving me to my own devices as most of her time was now devoted to Thomas. I was angry with Thomas for taking Sharon away from me. I even became unreasonably angry with Joy and Willick for giving me a taste of a different life and then shoving me back into Nowhere Place.

That would be followed by anger at myself for being so unlike my true self when I had been in the Wyrde Woods, so eager to please by being polite and considerate, to be that sweet little girl people liked to see rather than a mutated monstrosity who lugged a 150 faxing years of emotional baggage on her bloody back in a twisted imitation of Atlas.

§ § § § § § §

One evening I started being angry at Biggs too, as he knocked on my door and entered my bedroom shaking with nervousness even before I was given the chance to tell him to bugger off.

Oh bloody hell, here we go again.

We had been through this before a few times, his anxiety ridden confession of love for me. Or else an awkward attempt at flirtation, a game he couldn't really play well.

"What is it Biggs?" I said.

"I need to talk Wendy," he stammered.

"Okay," I answered. I didn't want to but to his credit he always helped me out, I could rely on him for that. It'd be too cruel and heartless for me not to even lend him my ear.

The news was good and bad. The good thing was that Biggs had finally accepted that he and I would never get together and was starting to graft Jasmin, a fancy which seemed pretty harmless. This pretty much let me off the hook and I encouraged him to pursue her with vigour, assuring him he wasn't a bad catch. The bad news was that he was worried that Stubbles seemed to be developing an interest in Jasmin too.

I talked to Sharon about this and she told me Thomas had known Stubbles from another institution where it was well-known he had 'special interests' and chose them carefully, picking ones without much support from a home front. Perhaps this is why he had inquired about my grandparents, for he seemed to be keeping a more careful distance since he had asked me about them. This week's session had been mild, he had followed the book and stuck to casual blunt digging in my fragile past, filled with all sorts of conclusions he drew, none of them positive.

Though I was pleased he seemed to be off my back I was furious about Jasmin. She wasn't a friend of mine but she was a rare specimen; innocent, wandering about with her beautiful black hair in a ponytail and clutching a stuffed teddy, totally oblivious to most of the world around her. Poor Jasmin lived in a bubble and I, like the others on my corridor, felt protective of her. Sharon suggested organising some sort of do where we could give Biggs and Jasmin a chance to hook up. She said she would talk to Thomas about it. I doubted she would though; they hardly had time to have conversations when they spent time together but I encouraged her to look into it.

My mind turned to my parents; a recurring and particularly painful obsession but worse this time as it wasn't longing that dominated this particular spell but bitterness. If what Stubbles had said about encouraging contact with family was true that meant they had gone to little or no effort to get me back. Somewhere deep inside I had always thought they were desperately looking for me and would appear on the doorstep of Nowhere Place one day to take me home. How the fax can you bring a child into the world and then totally abandon it? How could the both of them be so indifferent? What if I resembled them so much I too was incapable of even the most basic form of love? I googled them anyway, just in case, but found nothing. Once again my heart was crushed in an uncompromising steel grip, crunched a fraction of an inch at a time.

I knew I was torturing myself and I knew that being angry at the whole world was a projection of the struggle my inner self was having with a hang-up the size of Jupiter but I couldn't stop it. This was so frustrating I now directed the full blast of my fury at myself. I had felt so bloody wonderful that Saturday morning and most of the rest of the weekend. Why was I incapable of holding on to that feeling, being content with what I had been given?

All considered Joy and Willick had already done more for me than my parents ever had. It wasn't much of a life they had gifted me with. It had seemed impossible that I would ever escape from the vicious circle of morose gloom they had condemned me to. Now people were making an effort and I just wanted more of it, wanted to be with them the whole time instead of appreciating that I already had more than I had ever dared hope for not all that long ago.

The pressure increased and there wasn't much I could do to vent it without risking repercussions, Stubbles might have set his sights elsewhere but I doubted that would mean he would become lenient. On Thursday night I sat at my desk, shaking almost uncontrollably and contemplating an old fashioned razor blade which I kept at the back of my desk drawer.

Control. It was all about control. I needed to get a hold, release the pressure before I ended up in the reflection room and housebound forever and longer. But where would it stop? The emergency room of the hospital again? One led to two, two to four, four to sixteen thousand and somewhere in that last lot would be a cut too deep. The emergency room would mean punishment anyway, they'd kindly wait till I got out of hospital and then serve their judgment.

If I felt this bad about being away from the Wyrde Woods for only a few days, what would happen if I lost the privileges of day passes and home leave? I'd be crawling up the walls drooling like a rabid dog and then be so doped up I'd become like Jasmin on home leave weekends. It was a fool proof way of keeping a trouble kid nice and quiet and I had seen it happen far more often than I cared to.

Sometimes it was a tempting thought, just drug me and let me wander around with an idiotic smile on my face, enthralled by door knobs and light switches, frustrated at most by the complex operation of using toilet paper. My cruel mind disabled forever. But my fear was that underneath that outer vegetative state my mind would just carry on and it would be my ability to respond in action that was disabled. That was a hell which made my current down a picnic in the park.

Drugs: Just say no or take them all at once and be done with it.

I wanted to sob and shout and yell and cut and curse and punish and cry and die and scream and bleed. I wanted control but I also wanted the bliss of losing all my self-restraint in the thrall of a complete rage. I felt like a pressure cooker which was fast reaching boiling point.

My phone beeped the arrival of a text message. I picked up the phone immediately out of habit, considered throwing it against the wall with all my strength just to see it shatter into pieces for a moment but then looked at the screen anyway. There was no name, just a number that seemed vaguely familiar. I opened the message.

> *Faery Child. Get day pass if U can/want.*
> *Meet me SAT, 9am, bus stop Carfax. Puck.*

He must have lifted my number off my OJCH files and I read the message over and over again, and slowly, ever so slowly, my anger melted away, like an icicle under a wintry sun. It was time to go back to the Wyrde Woods. The Wyrde Woods and Puck.

Part Doe: Four for a Boy

14. Curse of the Blood Stone

I leaned my head against the bus window and watched the streets of Odesby pass by. I had put on my woods gear that morning and brought my backpack, enriched this time with a thermos of coffee. I began to breathe easier as the bus left the confines of the town. The week had been bad but I had skirted the edge and pulled away in the nick of time. Looking back there was just one major cause I could find for the severity of my downturn and that was the Wyrde Woods, much as I didn't like to admit it.

The bus was heading north-east now on the A267. The industrial estate was to my right and on my left the woods began. Not far from here was St. Lewinna's and beyond that the Giant's Grove, Tuckersham Church, the Owlery, the Shy Maidens, Lover's Lane and other places which filled my dreams at night. It felt as the Wyrde Woods were calling me home.

"I'm on my way," I whispered.

It was simultaneously hard and easy to explain the power the Wyrde Woods exerted over me. Easy, because my world had been suffocatingly small. Nowhere Place, Neverland, school, the supermarket, the High Street and occasional sojourns to Stancaster. My flight into the Wyrde Woods had opened a whole new world to explore, filled with people who had captured my usually sealed heart with remarkable ease and rich in stories which added living character to this new green world. It was so completely different that it felt as if I had been bewitched.

The woods now turned northwards and in the distance ahead east again, folding around a patchwork of fields around a farm. I saw the distant figure of a farmer walking across a field where sheep grazed.

Difficult to explain because the Wyrde Woods had definitely messed with my perceptions in some strange way. In the beginning, the woods had seemed surreal, a different world altogether as if it wasn't even geographically joined to my own. It was the same with the people there: Willick, Joy and Puck. They had seemed unworldly, far too kind and easy-going to belong in mine and the whole thing had been a miraculous place of escape. Now however, it was the Wyrde Woods which had begun to resemble the real world for me, I just felt so much more alive there. Being back in Nowhere Place and Neverland was like struggling through a bad dream that threatened to become a nightmare before I could find a way out.

I had thought I learned to cope with Nowhere Place and Neverland years ago, I now realised I would have to learn how to do so all over again. I simply couldn't afford to derail every time I came back from the Wyrde Woods because I knew exactly what would happen. Sooner or later I wouldn't be able to back off from that edge and the whole thing would blow up in my face, meaning I'd be confined to Nowhere Place or some such exile, with the Wyrde Woods out of my reach forever. I resolved that, no matter how much I wanted to be at the Owlery, I would have to force myself to accept precious moments, rather than wanting it all. I pulled a face, knowing how hard it was for me to stick to the firm resolutions. But damn it, I had to try. I felt like I really had something to lose now.

The bus started slowing down and I looked around, eager to spot Puck. I wondered if I should give him a hug as greeting. Or was that too soon?

I could see the Carfax Inn to my right, another large structure looking suitably aged though it wasn't timbered like the Earl's Barrel. It bore all the hallmarks of a country pub, signs advertising a beer garden, pub dinners and live music on Friday nights. There were only a few cars parked on the car park in front of it but it was early yet, nine in the morning as Puck had suggested. There were road signs at the crossroads where the Carfax was situated and one caught my eye; indicating the left turn it read: MALHEUR HALL.

The bus pulled to a halt 50 yards past the intersection and I got off, lugging my backpack. The bus drove away and I stood at the bus stop sign, feeling awkward as there was no sign of Puck. Immediately cracks began to appear in my carefully reconstructed sanity and there were howls of triumphant delight from the deep chasm at my frayed edges.

"No," I whispered anxiously.

Then I heard a sharp whistle and saw a movement at the edge of the woods. Puck and Lady were there and I slung my backpack on my back and walked towards them. Lady launched into her exuberant greeting mode and I dropped on my knees to indulge her in attention, saving me worry about how to greet Puck.

"Would it have killed you to have walked to the middling road?" I said somewhat curtly.

"Possibly," he answered cheerfully. "Dursn't try it."

"I thought you had stood me up for a moment," I pouted to make it a joke, but that fear had been icily real.

"A Faery's Child?" Puck looked shocked. "I told you, it's a bad idea to mess with the Faere Folk."

"Don't you take anything seriously?" I was irritated. Inwardly I cringed, I recognised that he was just trying to make light of the situation.

"Wenn," Puck looked down at his boots for a moment, then up again, honest sincerity on his face, "I take you very seriously, okay? I wouldn't dream of standing you up."

Well that shut me up for a moment. There'd be a myriad of possible interpretations of those words to contemplate later, but the primary effect was that I relaxed somewhat.

"Sorry. I've been a bit tense."

"Bad week?"

If only he knew, he'd run a hundred miles.

"Something like that, how is Joy?"

"Let's walk," Puck said, picked up a green satchel and we set off into the woods, Lady scouting ahead. "She recovered, for now."

"It comes back?"

"She has Fibromyalgia." Puck said.

"She said 'rheumattics'."

"They haven't really made up their minds yet what Fibro is. I can tell you what it does; it causes bad chronic pain at different points of the body. Knees, hip bones, lower back, upper back, neck…basically the joints. In Joy's case the locations keep changing. On what she calls a good day, it may be just one or two places."

"And bad days?"

"Everywhere at once."

"Can it be helped?" I asked.

"Not by a great deal. She's coping pretty well you know, some people let the disease get them down."

"She seems a tough one," I said.

"She's a fighter," Puck said with pride in his voice. "A real warrior."

We came to a road and crossed it, logic told me it was the road to Malheur Hall, and there had been no other side roads.

"Can we go see her?" I asked hopefully.

"The Owlery is on the other side of the woods, quite a way," Puck said. "And Willick is taking her to town today for shopping."

"Really? I thought she just about grew or made everything herself."

"Almost, there are a few things she still needs from town though. So I am afraid you're stuck with me today." Puck stopped walking and peered at me through his glasses, suddenly looking a little anxious: "Do you mind?"

"No, it's cool," I answered. "This place…" I swept my arm through the air indicating the woods around us.

"Gets to you doesn't it?" Puck smiled. "It'll get worse, I promise. It should have a health warning stuck to it."

"Warning: The Wyrde Woods are highly addictive." I said and wondered if I should tell him the Wyrde Woods weren't the only thing I had been looking forwards to. I decided not to, there was already a nagging shard of sharp guilt which accused me of being dishonest to him in presenting myself as a nice person. Far better, perhaps, for me to not expose others - especially not someone weirdly wonderful like Puck- to something as torn and twisted as myself. But selfishness surfaced, I really wanted to spend the day in his company exploring the Wyrde Woods, relishing in his boundless enthusiasm and spreading my wings in freedom.

"Must be awful for a smoker like you, all that fresh air," Puck commiserated.

"It's bloody torture. So where are we going today?"

"How do you feel about fighting dragons?" Puck's eyes sparkled.

"Are they an endangered species?"

"Definitely not on any of the lists of protected animals."

"Sounds good to me."

With that the mood had been wholly redefined, aided by the appearance of the sun as the cloud cover began to break.

The woods around us were changing, thinning out and then gradually becoming dominated by birch trees as the path started climbing, a gentle but continuous slope. I was pleased to encounter trees of which I knew the names and I liked the slender silver grey trunks of the birch trees. I stopped to run my hand along one of the trees, the slightly protruding bulges made it look and feel like the trunk was slightly muscled and the thin bark felt silkily smooth to the touch.

"The Lady of the Woods," Puck had stopped as well.

Lady came running back at the sound of her name.

"Huh? Who? Me?" I was slightly confused.

"I meant the birches; it's what a poet called them."

"Hear that Lady?" I looked down at the dog, "Between the three of us Puck identifies the tree as the lady."

Lady wagged her tail.

"I didn't…that is not to say that you…" Puck stumbled over his words. It seemed unlike him to be rattled and I laughed.

"It's okay; I'm just pulling your leg."

"Very funny. Can you help me pick a handful of leaves?" Puck produced a carrier bag from a pocket.

"For Joy?"

"Yup. She makes tea with them when they are dried, helps against inflamed joints she says."

We started harvesting the leaves, taking a few from each branch that we could reach in order not to strip one or two branches in their entirety.

"I came here a lot a while back, just before the leaves began to grow to collect birch sap."

"Really? For Joy again?"

"You can drink it, it's quite nice. Good for Joy too, but she also makes really nice wine with it, you should ask for some on your next visit."

"Oh look!" I exclaimed. The tree I was walking to had a limb growing outwards eight feet up the trunk and in the fork between trunk and limb there was a bird nest. It looked deep and seemed to be decorated with lichen. A small bird flew towards the nest with an insect in its beak and perched on top of the nest for a moment. It was a colourful little thing, blue, red, brown and a flash of white on the wings and tail. It leaned down into the nest and then flew off again.

"She's feeding her young!" I exclaimed, touched by the image.

"He, the colourful one is the male, it's a chaffinch. It's usually the female who does most of the feeding. Locals call it 'caffincher'."

"Well she's a lucky girl then, if he pitches in."

"He's lucky too; most of his ilk are still trying to find a mate. Listen."

I listened but wasn't sure what I had to focus on. The birdsong was pretty rampant here; it seemed to be coming from just about every tree.

"There are a lot of insects in birch woods," Puck told me. "Which means a lot of birds, especially the chaffinches and willow warblers. Do you hear the repetitive whistle?"

Puck imitated the call, emitting a quick succession of whistles which descended in scale

I listened again and this time I could discern that particular sound amidst all the birdcalls. I nodded.

"That's the warbler. They have grey-green backs and a yellow chest; you'll probably see a few."

"And the finch?"

"The males sing a little song," Puck canted his head to listen. "Yup, there it is. Four slow notes, then four more a bit faster and higher, then another four fast and low. Then you get the wheee-oo fink-fink."

I listened and then thought I recognized the call.

"So the 'wheee-oo fink-fink' gets him a date?" I asked amused.

"Yup, chicks love it."

"You sing well."

"I was in a choir for a while," Puck said in the curt tone he used when his previous life as Peter came up.

"Have you tried sitting on a branch and singing 'wheee-oo fink-fink'? You might get lucky."

Puck looked puzzled and scratched his head. Then he brightened.

"I shall try it at once!" He walked to the nearest tree.

"No, not there you idiot, that's got the bird nest."

"Well spotted Wenn." He backed off grinning.

We had filled about half of the carrier bag with leaves and Puck carefully rolled the bag up and stuck it in his satchel. We walked on the path which ascended at a steeper angle now and the birches thinned out further till we reached the summit of the hill we had been climbing and there was just grass and, on the highest point of the rounded top; a single large standing stone. In contrast to the Shy Maidens this stone was far bulkier. It was slightly canted to the side and the bottom third was about twice as broad as the upper third, with the middle forming the angled diagonal transition. It made the stone resemble a hand with an outstretched finger which pointed resolutely at the heavens in silent accusation. Large parts of the stone were covered in a rusty-red coloured moss like blood stains.

"The Blood Stone," I said in wonder.

"Yes," Puck confirmed.

"So this is where they found Cecil Malheur's head?" I said as we approached the stone. It had an ominous feel to it, sullen and malicious.

"And other bits and pieces of him. A fitting place really. This place was used for executions and ritual sacrifice thousands of years ago but the Malheurs had a gallows built here and they used this spot to punish locals for centuries. Plenty of poachers and highwaymen ended up swinging from the ropes on Gallows Hill. I think they hung a few witches here as well."

"Joy said not to come here at night," I curled my nose. "But even without the warning this place doesn't feel good."

I walked up to the stone and saw that a circular pattern had been carved into it; it reminded me of one of those Celtic designs.

"Don't touch the stone," Puck said sharply. "It's cursed."

I turned.

"Cursed how?"

"Just that an awful lot of bad things happen to those who touch the stone. They also say you can curse an enemy by laying your hand on that pattern you were looking at. It always works, apparently, but there is also always a high price to pay."

I backed away from the stone, all powers of logical reasoning muted by the immobile menace exuded by the Blood Stone. I re-joined Puck and we stood there, gravely contemplating the stone.

"Must be a host of shims here," I said warily, not even sure if I wanted to know.

"It's reputed to be haunted, but nobody in his or her right mind has ever come up here at night as far as I know," Puck said.

I didn't answer, the stone was creepy but it was hard to take my eyes off it, it seemed to command my attention.

"It's a very symbolic place for the Wyrde Woods," Puck continued. "It represents centuries of oppression. Sure, the Saxons who lived here used it as a place of execution too, but then a man could only be punished after he was brought before his peers and all sides of the story were considered at length. When the Normans came…"

He was silent for a moment.

"When the Malheurs came, they distributed so-called justice as they pleased. Folk who had been used to hunting in the woods to put food on the table now broke laws in doing that because all belonged to the new lord. Men were hanged here for catching a rabbit to feed their children. Women and children too, it didn't matter to the Normans."

"Place gives me the creeps," I answered, tearing my eyes away from the stone.

"Let's walk on then." Puck suggested and we left the Blood Stone somewhat subdued to see what other adventures the day would bring.

15. The Dragon Slayers

We entered the woods again but these were different kinds of trees. I recognised the serrated leaves at once.

"Oak trees," I said, happy to be able to identify yet another tree.

"Yes, it's mostly oak forest between here and the Shy Maidens. Some really old parts of the woods."

The oaks had branches along the entire length of their trunks and these spread out above to form wide uneven crowns. As we progressed the trees got older and bigger and some of the lower limbs were easily three or four times as thick as most of the birch trees.

"I'd like to climb one of these," I ventured.

"Just a few minutes more and we'll be at the Halfhollow Oak, that's a stunner to climb."

"It has a name?"

"Most of the really old ones do, the Halfhollow Oak is about 800 years old."

"Amazing, that's like 12 times a human life?' I was impressed.

I was even more wowed when we got to the Halfhollow Oak. It seemed big enough to form a forest by itself. The trunk was immensely broad and as the name suggested had a cave like cavity at its base which broadened into a space large enough for some six to eight people to stand in. The lower boughs were trees in their own right. The crown seemed to span a vast area and towered into the sky. Not as spectacularly high as the redwoods, but it was elevated above its neighbour's topmost reaches by at least 40 feet. I looked at it longingly.

"Better take off your pack," Puck said looking pleased with himself and taking off his glasses which he put in his satchel.

"Will you be able to see?"

"Not in the distance, but well enow close up, don't want to risk it slipping off," he answered, and then said, "Stay. Lady, Stay."

Lady whined a protest and then sank down to the ground by our bags.

The climb was exhilarating, easy going at first as there were multiple options spaced closely together, but, just as had been the case with my chestnut, the higher we climbed the more thought had to be put into where to go next. This included thinking three or four steps ahead, it was useless clambering up a branch to find there was no further way up. As usual the climb required all my focus, though I had time to note that Puck was an accomplished tree climber as well.

I reached the highest branch that seemed sturdy enough to hold me, about ten feet below the topmost part of the tree, and sat down on it, leaning on the trunk with my torso. Puck elected to stay one branch lower; he stood on it and rested his arms on the branch I sat upon. I was aware of his elbow nudging my flank and stayed dead still, I didn't want movement that might alert him to it and make him shift his elbow away. I liked it; there was both a sense of trust and of intimacy about it.

The view was amazing from up here. We looked over a broad valley in which the continuous tree coverage was broken in the centre where a patchwork of open grassy clearings showed. The largest such stretch was bordered by a single long row of trees whose tall crowns were only just overreached by the castle's towers. The tallest tower consisted of a crenelated platform flanked by two round spired watchtowers from which flew a Union Jack and a red flag with some sort of yellow heraldic symbol on it.

"Malheur Hall," Puck said. "Ever been there?"

"Of course not. I've never had the 20 quid for entry." I shook my head.

"Those chestnuts in front of the castle," Puck pointed at them, "they're magnificent."

"What happened to not seeing the distance?" I hoped I wasn't poking him, but sometimes I just needed to know something and I would blurt out a question.

"I can see a broad green blur," Puck said, then added with a grin, "All around me."

"The Wyrde Woods. Do I get a point for guessing?"

"Sure. I just know what I am pointing at, because I've seen it close up. I've snuck in quite a lot. Can't help the fascination."

I was immediately intrigued. 'Snuck' in sounded like it wasn't allowed.

"Puck, let's sneak into Malheur Hall," I urged.

"Just the castle grounds," he said.

"That would be amazing. Let's go," I lowered myself onto his branch.

"Whoa, hold your horses," Puck laughed. "It closes at five."

"And then what happens?"

"Most of the staff go home, just the three security guards who stay and two of the household staff. But that last lot stay in their quarters in the hall and the security guys hang around in their own place by the front entrance. Nothing much to steal from the gardens they reckon."

"No CCTV?"

"Only place with alarm systems is the castle proper, the outside doors and windows are wired. Aunt Catt is too stingy for much more, that's why she doesn't like her caretakers to spend too much time in the woods; she wants the gardens in order for when she comes in from London to host a dinner party for business partners. That's all she uses the castle for, about one weekend every month. She doesn't care about the woods at all."

"Is she here now?"

Puck shook his head.

"The biggest threat is Fluttergrub; he takes to wandering around the grounds sometimes."

"Who is this Fluttergrub? Is it his real name?"

"No, local name for someone who likes digging around in the dirt. He's the groundskeeper, in charge of the gardeners and the like, wood maintenance too, though they're too understaffed to do more than the absolute essentials."

"What if we run into this Fluttergrub guy?"

"We run like hell," Puck said happily and I smiled. The prospect of sneaking in was tempting. Running like hell sounded like fun too.

"How do we get in?"

"What time do you have to be back at the Home tonight?"

"Terry is on duty tonight, which means well late for a change. He said nine pm, meaning ten is fine with him too. There's only a minimum of staff in the weekend and Terry is just about the easiest going of them all. And in charge tonight."

"Good," Puck said. "So you're up for it? After five that is?"

"Deffo."

"In the meantime," Puck said, "I'm hungry, let's climb down, grab something to eat and then see about slaying that dragon. I have some bread and cheese with me."

"I brought warm coffee!" I remembered.

"Splendid," Puck said.

I nodded happily and we started climbing down again.

§ § § § § §

We shared the bread, cheese and coffee. Puck had brought a handful of dry dog food for Lady and poured her some water in a bowl. After lunch Puck put his glasses back on, we packed up and then we walked on through the oak woods. Some of it was younger, trees crowding each other for space. Other areas were much older and here there was hardly any undergrowth, just broad trunks rising like old Greek temple pillars. We didn't speak much, each of us happy to enjoy the woods in silent contemplation.

After about an hour we heard a rapping, more than a score of rhythmic taps in quick succession. It was almost like somebody was tapping on a drum. This was followed by a similar sound from a different direction.

"Woodpeckers?" I asked Puck.

He nodded and left the path in search of the sound. About thirty feet into the woods he put a hand on my shoulder to stop me and pointed at a large oak with the other. About two thirds of the way up was a bird; strikingly colourful with a beige belly, black and white wings, and a bright red cap and bottom. We saw it rapping the trunk so rapidly that it became a blur, and then it flew off.

"That was the Great Spotted Woodpecker," Puck said with a satisfied smile.

"Why the knocking?"

"Territory, other birds sing, this one drums."

"All we need now is for one to play the fiddle," I grinned. "Then we can teach them Raggle Taggle Gypsy."

The drumming sound resumed as we found our path again.

"How much wood would a woodchuck chuck?" I demanded to know.

"A woodchuck is a groundhog," Puck shrugged.

"Not today it isn't, today it's a spotted pecker," I joshed him. "So how much wood would a woodchuck chuck..." I started tapping out a rhythm on my thighs "...if a woodchuck could chuck wood?"

"As much wood as a woodchuck could," Puck replied, beating his own rhythm. "If a woodchuck could chuck wood."

"Faster now!" I demanded.

"Why not the song of the woodpecker?" Puck asked.

"Never heard of it."

"Kinda old," Puck said and started whistling a jazzy tune before he began
to sing.

> Caught this bird in the neighbourhood
> Peckin' away on a piece of wood
> He pecked and pecked on my front door
> He pecked till he made his pecker sore
>
> Peck-a-peck peck-a-peck peck peck
>
> He's the loveliest little bird you ever did see
> He'll take a chance on any old tree
> The other day he was peckin' in an oak
> Making his strokes and his pecker broke
>
> Peck-a-peck peck-a-peck peck peck

"Peck-a-peck peck peck," I said happily.

I liked Puck for not giving a hoot, if he felt like singing he just did. All the
green stuff he wore sometimes seemed a bit pretentious, like he was trying
to make a statement, but the ease with which he let himself go without
abandon was brill. Most Forlorn Hopers would consider Puck a great deal
more cray than they themselves were and I grinned at that insight.

Our path intersected a dirt road wide enough to accommodate a vehicle. As
we crossed this byway I saw the roof and chimneys of a cottage to my left. I
stopped and looked at Puck questioningly.

"That's where Willick lives with his Allison, it's called The Cottage," Puck
said.

I was about to suggest that we drop by but then I remembered Willick had
taken Joy to town.

"That's where I get internet access," Puck added. "Willick's place is
modernised, running water, electricity, internet and all."

"What is Allison like?"

"Allison is nice enough."

"Do you think Willick still fancies Joy?"

"He says not, but I don't think a love like that ever really goes away, do you?"

I shook my head, though I didn't really know much of that kind of love from personal experience. Not the ground-shaking world-upside-down madness I had read about in books anyway.

We continued on the smaller path, heading into a younger area of oak forest again.

Puck stopped.

"See this?"

I shook my head, not sure what I was supposed to be looking at. He pointed at a narrow trail which dissected our path.

"One of the routes followed by deer, the woods are crisscrossed by them."

I saw it now, though I would have walked right past it without giving it any notice if Puck hadn't pointed it out.

"What kind of deer?"

"Roe Deer," Puck said. "Look," He pointed at a branch which hung low to the ground. The tip had been broken and hung on by a strip of bark and there was a little reddish fur attached to it. "Traces of bigger deer like Fallow and Red would have been higher up."

I was impressed by Puck's forestry skills; he was a fount of knowledge on the woods and their history. I thought about the few times I had been in other woods before, and how it had just been a mass of green where it was pleasant to walk. Puck made it all come alive.

"It's your turn now Puck," I said resolutely. "How did you end up in the woods?"

Puck sighed. For a moment I thought he was going to be evasive again but he wasn't.

"I was a late child. My mother died giving birth to me," Puck said slowly. "My father remarried, but just for the looks. My stepmother had all of two brain cells to rub together. She was half his age and a former model. She married him for the money. It was like living in a cliché."

"But you had a family," I said softly.

Puck looked at me sharply.

"A loveless one. My father blamed me for my mother's death I think. No actually, I know. He told me twice. I think my mother is the only one he ever truly loved. He was cold and distant to me. The step-bimbo couldn't wait to get me out of the house, and like my father I was sent to boarding school when I was seven."

"You're a toff then?" I was impressed; I had never met a real life toff before. I thought they were all haughty and arrogant. I supposed Puck was like that at times but in an okay manner, with him it was about all that knowledge he seemed to have soaked up like a sponge. He was dead smart really and wasn't a wazzock in an irritating way. To me anyway, I don't know what the other Forlorn Hopers would have made of him.

"Privileged," Puck conceded.

"What was boarding school like?" I pictured a kind of Hogwarts with young Peter immersed in books like Hermione and honing his intelligence.

"Faxing awful," Puck said. "With the Masters it was all about academic results and I get distracted easily. I can tell you a bird is a spotted woodpecker and I learn the sounds. I like sounds; I guess I collect them in a way. But they have a special name for the feet of a woodpecker, and that kind of information, Pfff."

"Passed you by?" I guessed he probably didn't have Wyrde Woods wildlife classes at school but I understood the comparison.

"The other boys cared mostly about sports; can you imagine me playing rugby?"

The image came to me pretty vividly and I bit my lip so I wouldn't laugh too loud.

"Well, I had to," Puck pulled a face. "My father combined the academics and sports when I saw him in the holidays. I always looked forward to those visits, hoping that one day we would find some sort of connection. He'd just ask about test results and sporting achievements. That was his indication of well-being. I was forever disappointing him."

At least you had a father, I thought, but didn't say it out loud.

What we shared would be the inevitable questions about our mothers. What was she like? What if…? I wondered if Puck blamed himself for her death. That was one hell of a demon to struggle with at night. He must have been pretty miserable growing up. He wouldn't have lasted a minute in Neverland though, far too clever and soft.

"We quarrelled like hell after we visited Joy. I was fascinated by her and soon after ran away from boarding school. Stayed with her for a year, camped out in the woods mostly, and then went up north where I got involved in local politics. Then I came back here."

"And your father?"

"Disowned me, officially. His lawyer sent me a letter which said that would only be reversed if I went back to school."

I looked at Puck. There was sadness about him now; it wasn't all cheer and fun. I wanted to reach out and touch him, just to comfort him. I admired him as well and changed my mind about him being soft. He had been fourteen when he made the decision to just drop out. Fax the system, follow his own rules. Just about everybody I knew at school talked about it, but no one ever dared unless they lost themselves on drugs, topped themselves or got knocked up. It must have taken some courage. I mean adults talked about it too, but few had the courage to carry it through. I supposed the Wyrde Woods were a pretty good place to hide too, I couldn't see Social Services people running about on the muddy paths in their neat suits or high heels and skirts trying to trace one lost boy. A thought occurred to me.

"Does your aunt have children?"

"Her? No. She never married."

"Sooo, if you went back to school, and your aunty died and your father relented you'd become the Lord of the Wyrde Woods?"

"Lord of the Wyrde Woods," Puck said pensively and I was glad that his grin returned.

"Family tradition after all," I suggested. "Sir Peter, Lord Malheur."

I made a curtsey.

"My father and the step-bimbo had a child not long ago, the way things are now I'm not in line for the job. I think I prefer living like an outlaw anyway," he said with powerful conviction. "Puck of the Greenwoods."

"Yes Milord," I made another curtsey and Puck laughed.

§ § § § § §

As we approached our destination the oaks were replaced by alders and willows and the pervasive bird song lessened significantly. I was stuck by the profusion of anemones which grew some ten inches high, the white star shaped flowers rising above the greenery. It wasn't like the almost continuous haze of the bluebells, here the haze was dark green and broken up by whole constellations of celestial white dots.

"Devil's Tarn," Puck pointed in front of us. The anemone carpet continued right to the edge of a small lake some fifty feet wide but much longer as it snaked its way around a corner. The banks were lined with anemone beaches and clusters of weeping willows, the pendulated slender branches of which hung serenely over the surface of the lake. The water in the lake was perfectly still and clear, it reflected every detail of its surroundings with the sharp clarity of a mirror so that clouds seemed to sail in its blue centre surrounded by the inverted domes of the weeping willows which doubled them in visual size.

"It's bloody incredible," I said with admiration.

"Isn't it just?" Puck said, pleased that I liked it. "You should see it in the winter; it's fed by a spring down there so the water never freezes and if there is frost vapours rise from the water like smoke."

"As if something lived in it?"

"Yup," Puck nodded. "There are a lot of lakes like this in Sussex and they used to believe that they were bottomless, leading all the way to the Underworld from which an occasional serpent-like monster would make its way up. Two of them were killed here."

"Dragons?" I looked around me for traces of epic combat but everything looked serenely peaceful.

"They call them Knuckers here." Puck switched to a creepy movie voiceover mode: "A nine footer with a tapered elongated neck and tail. Ebony black scales on its back and a red underbelly with large feet, cold lizard eyes and jaws a foot long filled with a double row of razor sharp ivory teeth. Coming to a woods near you, soon."

"I don't suppose they called them 'Fluffy' then?"

"The first Wyrde Woods Knucker was called Heolstor. It terrorised the countryside, twere middling terrible. It would devour cows, pigs and stray children whole. This was before there were Malheurs here and the villagers of Roreford armed themselves with farming tools and picked a fight with the beast."

"Who won?"

"The villagers lost a few men altogether, the survivors a number of arms and legs."

"So how was it killed?" I thought of a heroic knight in shining armour.

"By a woman," Puck grinned.

"REALLY? Awesome, good for her. Tell me!"

Folk around here were mostly pagan, but a few of the Christians who were here went to the priory and spoke to the prioress, Lewinna."

"Saint Lewinna?"

"Yup, but then she was just a prioress. She said she would rid the Wyrde Woods of Heolstor if folk would convert afterwards for it would be the power of her God who would drive the Devil's creature from the woods. They agreed and she set out on her own, dressed in chainmail and on horseback. Apparently she was quite handy with a sword. She probably had some kind of martial past before she devoted herself to her God. It wasn't uncommon back then for women to be warriors."

"Girl power," I noted with satisfaction.

"Girl power indeed," Puck nodded. "They say that for a whole day and night the woods echoed with the sound of combat, the clash of sword and claw, the roaring and bellowing of Heolstor and the strong clear voice of St Lewinna as she recited prayer after prayer. She returned with the creature's head and the pagans duly converted to Christianity. They were baptised at St Lewinna's Pool, I'll show you where that is one day if you want."

I nodded; I wanted to see the whole of the Wyrde Woods.

"And the second drag…Knucker?"

"Back in the Middle Ages, that's where I got the description from. They said it was a punishment for people staying pagan on the sly even though their forebears promised St Lewinna otherwise."

"An armoured knight," I said, "Sir Lancelot came to slay the beast."

"Bugger the knights, they were mostly Malheurs around here, not a family with a track record of chivalry I am afraid."

I nodded and thought about how weird it was that Puck was part Malheur too. His blood was bound to these woods by centuries but also contained traces of a long line of amoral men steeped in evil. I wondered if he ever thought about that, and decided he probably did, his thoughts seemed to reach far and wide like the branches of the Halfhollow Oak.

"Though one of the good ones did try, in armour too, so you're not far off, his name was Richard Malheur, the younger brother of the Lord at the time. Richard carried on the family line though when his brother died without living heirs. The Knucker observed traditions too; you'll be pleased to know he insisted on eating only virgins as dragons ought to."

"Humbug, why always virgins?"

"Maybe they taste better?" Puck laughed. "Possibly because it meant young children, the Knuckers weren't the size of Smaug, most of the local Knuckers were even smaller than Heolstor and Drefan. Overgrown lizards really. Kids would have been an easier prey."

"I still think it's because the writers were men and men are obsessed with virgins," I said. "But who killed Drefan?"

"Well Sir Richard tried, but he was grievously wounded and found by the Farisee who nursed him back to health. Folk despaired, if a trained and armoured knight couldn't slay the beast, who could?"

"Please tell me it was another woman!"

"It was," Puck beamed. "Local farm lass, called Ellette Hornsby. Though there was mention that she might be a changeling."

"Changeling?"

"A Faere Folk joke, they'd switch one of their own for a human baby right after birth."

"Maybe I am a changeling," I said dreamingly.

"I wouldn't be surprised," Puck conceded. "Anyway, Ellette means 'little elf' in Saxon and she was about twelve years old at the time and clever. She decided to tackle Drefan on her own and in secret. First she snuck into the grounds around the old castle and visited the Poison Garden."

"Malheur Hall had a Poison Garden?"

"It still does. Ellette snuck in during a full moon so she could see what she was doing and because the plants are at the height of their power then. And there, most carefully and wearing gloves she picked foxgloves, belladonna, poppies, laburnum and hemlock. Ellette took her deadly bounty back home and made a huge pie, filling it with the most savoury meats but also adding all of the poisons she had prepared from the plants."

"Clever girl!"

"Indeed, and then Ellette loaded the pie on her father's two wheeled cart, harnessed his horse to the cart and drove to the Devil's Tarn singing a particular song to let Drefan know a virgin approached and he duly rose from the Tarn to investigate. Now she was lucky, because first Drefan ate the horse, and then the pie and then the cart and by then he was too full to eat another bite. Ellette waited only a little while before the Knucker began to twist and turn and suffered the most horrible convulsions as the poison began to melt his organs. Drefan bellowed one last time and then fell down dead. Ellette cut off its head and returned home a heroine."

"I can imagine!"

"Sad to say, it did not last long. Ellette had been too careless with the poison, probably when she prepared the pie. Sometimes just touching it with a bare hand is enough and she fell ill and died within a week. She was buried by the side of Tuckersham Church, the grave is still there, covered by a great big sheet of stone they call the 'Slayer's Slab'."

"Poor Ellette," I said. "What was the song, do you know it?"

Puck smiled.

"Should I perch on a tree branch for you? Or just sing it here?"

"Sing it here," I decreed. Puck drew a deep breath and started singing.

> *A Master of Musick came with an intent,*
> *To give me a lesson on my instrument*
> *I thank'd him for nothing, but bid him be gone*
> *For my little fiddle should not be played on*
> *My thing is my own, and I'll keep it so still*
> *Yet other young lasses may do what they will.*

I laughed, Puck grinned but continued singing.

"Hush young maiden!" I laid my hand on Puck's arm and he ceased singing. "I do think the Knucker has heard you. Listen!"

Puck tilted his head and listened intently, Lady looked around in some confusion.

I started speaking softly in a low voice.

"Beware the Jabberwock, my son! The jaws that bite, the claws that catch! Beware the Jubjub bird, and shun the frumious Bandersnatch."

Lady growled.

Puck grinned and was about to say something when I hushed him again.

"LOOK!" I said in alarm and pointed at the water. Lady growled again. "See there, those yellow eyes with black slits, the Knucker has surfaced!"

"Hell's Bells, it's seen us!" Puck said in alarm. We started backing up to the tree line.

"It's swimming to the shore now, there, it's climbing on land by those willows!"

"Quick, arm yourself!" Puck shouted. Lady barked as Puck picked up a long fallen branch and I found a shorter stick.

"There it comes!" I shouted. "Whiffling through the tulgey wood with eyes of flame!"

"And burbling, that's a bad sign, it's about to attack," Puck hissed.

"Attack is the best defence," I replied. Then I shouted "GERONIMO!!" and rushed forwards, beginning to hack at the Knucker with my sword, it growled ferociously and lunged at me with its powerful jaws, I smelt a wave of foul decomposition as it snapped its jaws shut just inches from my face and fell backwards.

"Help!" I shouted.

"HOKAH HEY!" Puck dashed forwards, yielding his branch in both hands and thrusting it forwards like a spear.

"Take that foul beast!" He shouted and started driving the Knucker back. I jumped up and rushed to his side, piercing the eye of the monster. It roared and reared upwards, Puck drove his spear through its chest and bellowing it fell, slithering back to the nearby willows.

"He's trying to get away!" I shouted. "Stop him!"

We hacked and slashed our way forwards into the hollow of the willow's dome, the Knucker ineffectively trying to ward off our blows.

"It's done for!" I yelled triumphantly, "Finish him off." We fell upon the creature, stabbing and piercing its scaly armour until it bled from a hundred wounds and bellowed its death cry.

Puck dropped his branch and let himself fall to the ground, laughing all the way. I dropped my stick and sat down next to him, grinning like mad. Lady came over cautiously and gave us a worried look, causing renewed laughter on our behalf.

"Well that was FUN," I said joyfully when the laughter subsided. Puck looked up at me and smiled his agreement.

We looked each other in the eyes and I suddenly felt the urge to lean over, bring my lips to his. This was definitely one of those moments and I thought I sensed an air of expectancy from Puck too.

But I didn't dare, what if he was shocked or explained why it was better to friend-zone me? Worse, he might just laugh me in my face and tell Joy it would be better not to invite me again. There was far too much at risk. I couldn't stand to lose the Wyrde Woods like that. A few minutes of awkward silence followed, the air laden with potency.

I broke the spell and stood up, brushing leaves off my legs.

"Maybe we ought to go?" I suggested.

Puck nodded silently and stood up too. We were on our way again.

16. Malheur Hall

Getting into the grounds of Malheur Hall was a piece of piss. Puck lifted a loose corner of the chain link fence and the three of us crawled through after we had concealed our bags underneath a nearby bush. The next obstacle was a tall hedge row but Puck pointed out where he had discovered a low gap and had burrowed into the earth beneath to make it deeper and more accessible, though it was barely visible for anybody walking by. It was a tighter fit than I thought but I managed to scrape through, followed by Puck and Lady.

The excitement of doing something that wasn't allowed sent a pleasant low dose of adrenaline coursing through me and I felt bright with glee. We were outlaws of the Greenwood sneaking into a castle to steal silver and gold and release a few imprisoned comrades. I wished I had a bow and arrows to complete the act.

We had to cross a moat next, some eight feet wide, the last barrier before the gardens began. Puck walked along the hedge for a minute or so and then knelt down. With some effort he pulled loose a long narrow beam from a hiding place and he placed this across the moat.

"A Sword Bridge," he said softly with exaggerated reverence. "Only a true Knight of the Round Table can cross it without plummeting into the depths of the waters which, of course, are simply teeming with voracious water monsters."

"After you Sir Knight," I answered.

"No, I must insist. Beauty before brawn Elf Changeling," Puck said, and then added in a more serious tone: "It's best to cross fast, before your mind registers there's not much foothold."

I nodded and took a deep breath, this shouldn't be hard, I had about four inches and that was more than enough for me. I placed a foot on the beam and tested it. It seemed lodged securely enough and I stepped on it altogether and walked quickly across, turning to give Puck a grinning thumbs-up when I reached the other side safely. Puck followed next. Lady looked indecisive for a moment and opted to jump into the water instead; braving the many-teethed water monsters she made it safely to the other side.

Having negotiated the obstacles we now entered the grounds. The gardens on this side of the castle were divided into separate compartments by tall hedges and walls as well as strategically planted groves of trees. I occasionally caught a glimpse of the castle, a few windows here, a tower there or a set of chimneys rising up from the roof tiles elsewhere. The compartmented gardens were fascinating; each had a theme of sorts and were connected by gaps in the hedges or open arched doorways in walls. There was a herb garden where the air was thick with familiar and unfamiliar aromas. Puck handed me a mint leaf.

"Just let it rest on your tongue," he said popping one into his own mouth too. I did and after a while it was like having a peppermint melting slowly in my mouth. Next was a butterfly garden with neat rectangles of flowering plants which were favoured by the delicate creatures, though there were few butterflies about. I had been surrounded by clouds of them in Joy's garden. There was a magic garden, shaded by the foliage of red leafed trees. It sported a small maze of footpaths through ferns and weirdly shaped tree stumps. A little sign warned about not scaring or stepping on the faeries.

"I could imagine them living here too," I quipped.

Puck shrugged.

"The Farisees live much deeper into the woods," he said dismissively.

We walked on into a large rectangular space with statuettes and bowered benches. The centre of the garden was a long rectangle of various plants and flowers with a small wrought iron cupola in the middle and two low trees to either side of it.

"This is the Shakespeare Garden," Puck said, "with all of the plants and flowers mentioned in the plays. Those are medlar trees, people used to eat the fruit a lot."

The medlar trees had long glossy leaves and a sparse bloom, not clusters but individual white flowers. We walked there and Puck pointed at a small information sign which showed pictures of the blooms and fruits.

"Medlar fruit, have a good look," Puck grinned.

I examined the picture of the fruit more closely. About two thirds towards the end of the bulb four spiky leaves emerged and folded out a bit. The fruit curved inwards at the tip of the bulb, forming creases as it swept into a little pit surrounded by strands of stiff filaments that looked like hair. I laughed as I suddenly realised it looked like a puckered dog's arse.

"Common folk name it 'Open-Arse Fruit," Puck said. "Shakespeare used it in *Romeo and Juliet*."

"Bollocks, *Romeo and Juliet* is a love story." I was vaguely offended by the notion that the country's greatest poet would demean his most beautiful love story with anal matters.

Puck grinned and recited:

> *Now will he sit under a medlar tree*
> *And wish his mistress were that kind of fruit*
> *As maids call medlars when they laugh alone. —*
> *O Romeo, that she were! Oh, that she were*
> *An open arse, and thou a pop-er-in pear.*

"A pop-er-in pear?" I was incredulous. "Open arse? Shakespeare?"

"He was a dirty bugger really," Puck conceded.

"Pfff."

Puck seemed to have a filthy mind as well, I decided. Most of the songs I had heard him sing were either bawdy or pretty suggestive. Mostly funny though.

Puck laughed.

"Righto," he said. "See that gate in the far wall?"

We walked to the gate. It was shut and secured with an oversized chain and lock.

"The Poison Garden?" I guessed and peered between the wrought-iron bars into a walled courtyard lined with stout tables on top of which stood pots large and small with various plants and flowers. Most seemed harmless enough; I had expected something more sinister looking.

"Yup, not open to the public, some of the stuff you need to prepare in special ways, or is harmless except for a particular part of it. Others, just touching the leaves can be bad news."

I looked around and wondered how Ellette had sneaked in. Maybe she had found a ladder. We walked away to another archway that was gateless and through a rosarium where paths were neatly laid out between regiments of rose bushes; most of them were not flowering yet though the multitudes of buds were pregnant with promise. We left the rosarium through another gate and then stepped into a whole different world altogether.

We stood at the edge of a huge open space, bordered by tall ivy clad walls on two sides and Malheur Hall at the far end. Adjacent to the walls were flowerbeds. They weren't arranged in a riot like Joy's flowers at the Owlery but there were more hues and shades of colour in the rectangular patterns than I even knew existed.

The flowerbeds surrounded a huge stretch of meticulously kept lawn broken only by low ornamental hedges which bordered neatly laid out pathways. Malheur Hall dominated it all; the brick grandeur seemed like something out of a fairy tale with rectangular towers set at regular intervals and two round ones in the centre to either side of an imposing gatehouse. The whole exuded an ambiance of exclusive luxury and I envisaged some of my favourite Jane Austen characters strolling daintily up and down the pathways in their fineries, shading their pale skin from the sun with parasols while they discussed what to wear to the next ball.

"Imposing isn't it?" Puck asked. I just nodded breathlessly and wondered what I'd look like in a ball gown. Ridiculous probably.

"Remember though," Puck said with a hard edge in his voice. "That all of this grace and elegance was purchased at the cost of the sweat and blood of the common people."

For a moment I was peeved that Puck made my ambling ladies appear parasitical rather than harmless fools. I wanted to say that it was kind of odd hearing him of all people speak for the common people, but then I remembered who his grandmother was; his father had only been half a Malheur. Joy's kin had probably lived here forever and longer.

"The gardens are beautiful," I said, thinking about the magic garden. "But also a poor imitation of the Wyrde Woods and what is in them."

"Very true. All structured and regimented, maximum control over nature. Lots of shims though."

"Tell me!" I demanded.

"At your service M'Lady," He bowed elegantly. "You know about Cecil already of course. Have you heard about Earl Roger?"

"Yes, the fat Earl." I smiled. "Willick told me."

"Ah, and the Drummer? The White, Grey and Red ladies? The Kitchen Boy? The Malheur Twins?"

"That many?" My eyes grew wide.

"While we walk. The permanent staff stay on the left side of the castle, so we'll go to the right. Lady. Heel."

Puck started to amble down the gravel path which led past the flowerbeds by the wall to the right of the lawn. We walked slowly now, Lady obediently by Puck's side. I listened to Puck whilst looking around continuously, not knowing whether to admire the magnificent castle or let my eyes be drawn by the flower beds. Some flowers looked familiar; others had almost alien shapes and the weirdest pistils ranging from the exquisitely beautiful to the outrageously obscene.

"There's a room in the castle called the Drummer's Vault. They lock it up at night because sometimes they can hear somebody beating a tattoo on a drum in there. The drummer has been seen on the parapets as well."

"That's all he does, beat a drum?"

"Yes," Puck shrugged. "But I'll be honest with you, it would freak me out if I heard that going on in the dead of night."

"True," I nodded.

"The kitchen boy makes noise as well. He was literally overworked and harried to death by and sometimes, in the place where the old kitchens used to be, you can hear him banging about invisible pots."

"Doing the dishes for eternity. Now that is horrifying."

"The twins are not really castle ghosts, but they belong to it none-the-less. The Malheur family had fallen out of favour with bad King John and the whole family tried to escape to their lands in Normandy. They were caught and King John demanded the two eldest children, twins, a boy and a girl, as hostages. He had them imprisoned in Windsor Castle and had them deliberately starved."

"Kids? That's cruel."

"John was cruel. He had his niece, your age, locked up and her brother, who was fourteen, blinded and castrated before he threw him off a castle wall. It is said he did all that himself when his knights refused to do it."

It struck me again how much cruelty was interwoven into the history of the Wyrde Woods. Cruelty, abuse and oppression. No wonder there were places which were fairly saturated in negative energy.

"Anyhow, on the road between Malheur Hall and Carfax folk have seen an emaciated boy and girl, dressed in rags and holding out their hands as if begging for food. They'll follow anybody walking on the road, staring at them with big imploring eyes until they are spoken to or reach Carfax Alus or Malheur Hall. Then they vanish again."

I felt goose bumps. These stories were deliciously creepy.

"How about the ladies?"

"Ah, see that corner tower there?" Puck pointed at the corner tower we were slowly approaching.

I nodded.

"Herne's Tower they call it. Young girl, one of the maids, jumped down that in the eighteenth century."

"Let me guess, she got pregnant?"

"Yup, another one of my ancestors. The Grey Lady is actually really scary. She has been seen in broad daylight and looks like she's real, made of flesh and blood. She'll climb up one of the embrasures, stand there for a moment, looking indecisive and then jump and plummet down giving onlookers a real fright. She disappears just before she hits the ground."

I folded my arms and shivered. In a way the stories were getting tedious, so much abuse going on, more or less the same tale told over and over again. I liked the ones where the women stood up and fought best. The enforced passivity in the other tales was just sad. I thought of No-Tooth and Broken Nose in Neverland, did this stuff never stop?

"The White Lady is a similar story, one of the maids with an illegitimate Malheur baby in her belly. The father, I think it was Gregory Malheur, somewhere in the 1550s, had her locked up in the castle. He wanted the bastard, his first wife was barren. She escaped by jumping from a window on the other side of the castle. The moat is much broader there, almost a lake. It's where the main gate is. Anyhow, she tried to swim across but drowned when she almost reached the other side of the moat. Folk have seen her floundering in the water at times."

"What is it with you Malheur men and maids?

"They used to select the prettiest girls in the Wyrde Woods for jobs in the castle," Puck said grimly.

"Worse than a Knucker then. The villagers having to offer up their daughters to whatever Ogre was ruling the roost in the castle."

Puck nodded thoughtfully.

"I haven't thought about it like that," he said. "But it is almost like a sacrifice isn't it?"

"So what am I to conclude from the fact that you haven't ravished me yet?" I said in jest, a poor one perhaps considering where we were. "Not pretty enough?"

"I am trying to break the habit," Puck jested back and winked. "Seriously though, I hope I take after Richard and Foster and Oscar Malheur. They weren't all bad."

"How about the Red Lady? Another village girl?"

"No actually, she was a Malheur, Emily Malheur. She died around the 1860s I think."

"How?"

"She starved herself."

"Anorexia? You're kidding me."

"Sort of, she was desperate to fit into the tightest corsets and went too far. She haunts the courtyard inside the castle. Sickly looking, moaning and wringing her hands."

"I dunno if I could live here, with all of that going on." We had come to Herne Tower now and I looked to the top of the tower with a vague feeling of anxiety, but there was no apparition by the battlements.

"You shouldn't anyway Wenn," Puck decided. "You belong in the woods with…us."

"You really think so?" I was pleased.

"Of course."

"It's just, sometimes when I hear of all the connections between you all and my complete ignorance of the woods, I feel…"

"Left out?"

I nodded.

"Joy spoke to the bees and that is that," Puck shrugged. "You need some time, that's all. I came here new too." He suddenly looked shy. "Provided you want to of course."

"Hell yes," I beamed and Puck brightened up at that.

"This is what I wanted to show you, planted in the 1600s."

He pointed at a row of chestnuts which lined the entire side of the castle here. They were huge, their trunks massive in circumference and marked by bulbous growths surrounded by fissures and furrows which swirled to form odd shapes. One was hollow on the inside though it still towered high with lush foliage above. The gnarled trees spoke of age, weary and wise they must have been witness to untold antics of the Malheur family and they invoked a sense of resigned poignancy.

"They're beautiful," I whispered, laying my hand on one of the trees, weathered rugged bark greeting my touch.

"We better head back, the front side is too risky," Puck said after a while.

"Sure," I said and we headed back to the lawns.

"Have you ever met your aunt? Lady Malheur?"

"Naun, she'll have nothing to do with bastards, I think my father met her once or twice, but he didn't say much about it, just that Aunt Catt was openly hostile."

"Joy said she was brab...bro..."

"Brabagious?" Puck chuckled.

"Middling brabagious," I confirmed.

"That's just about the worst a woman can call another woman around here. She is though. Just because we're in the twenty-first century doesn't mean the family has given up their habits of destruction. Lady Malheur is planning mayhem and havoc on a massive scale."

"Huh? What do you mean?"

"Nobody told you about the M33 Wenn?"

"M33?"

Puck sighed, and suddenly seemed weary with sadness.

"Puck?"

"Where do you live? It's been big news in the Weald for ages." There was an accusation in his tone that made me frown.

"Neverland. We don't do news," I answered curtly.

"Just seems incredible to me," Puck shrugged. "They plan to build a motorway, to link up Brighton and Hastings with London. From the M25 straight through the Weald to Stancaster and Hailsham, where it will split to Brighton and Hastings."

"Not through the Wyrde Woods, surely?" I was appalled.

"Right through the middle of the Wyrde Woods. Between the Lusty Giant's Hills and Arthur's Fort, then past Tuckersham Church and straight through the Giant's Grove."

"Faxing hell. They can't cut the Giant's Grove down, can they?"

"None of it is protected."

"What do you mean it's not protected? The woods are amazing!"

"It's private property. Aunt Catt is eager to sell the land; she has some expensive habits, like her town house in London."

"But…but isn't there anything anybody can do about it?" I could still only half believe the bombshell Puck had dropped. A bloody motorway!?!

"One last appeal in Odesby, but it's a foregone conclusion really," Puck said softly.

"We have to fight!"

Puck gave me one of his mysterious looks and was about to say something when a loud voice hollered in the distance.

"BLOODY KIDS!"

"SHIT! It's Fluttergrub!"

We were about halfway down the gravel path on the lawns. Behind us, at the very beginning of the row of chestnuts, a man in green overalls was making his way towards us, waving his arms and bellowing at the top of his voice.

"OI, YE BE TRESPASSING!"

"RUN!" Puck shouted and we launched into a frantic run towards the arched gate which led to the themed gardens.

"STOP. COME HERE."

Not likely, we were flying across the lawn now, ignoring the gravel paths, Lady still heeling. We rushed through the gate just as Fluttergrub reached the lawns. There was a loud bang behind us. I looked back to see Fluttergrub surrounded by a puff of smoke.

"Hells Bells," Puck laughed. "He brought his shotgun."

We dashed through the rosarium and into Shakespeare's Garden, still pursued by Fluttergrub's angry voice.

Onwards we ran through the magic garden, the butterfly garden and the herb garden. We could still hear Fluttergrub in the distance but his voice was fading somewhat, we were far faster. We pounded over the beam bridge and I paused for a moment, hands on my knees and gasping for breath as Puck lifted the beam off the moat and hid it again.

"...if I get mine hands on ye...scallywags..." Fluttergrub was still fuming in the distance.

"We have to go," Puck said. "I don't want him to see where we got in. And the shotgun will have brought security out."

We scrambled underneath the hedge and then underneath the chain linked fence, grabbing our bags on the way and then, somewhat slower, through the woods until we reached the Halfhollow Oak. There we collapsed by the oak's trunk, chests heaving and panting, too blown to speak for a few minutes. Lady circled us, wagging her tail, eyes bright with excitement.

When we recovered our breath Puck and I looked at each other and then simultaneously burst out into peals of laughter. That happy mood marked our walk back to the Carfax Inn.

When we reached the spot where Puck had been waiting for me that morning we stopped. I stared at the Carfax Inn, the parking lot was full now and it was busy in there.

"I'd kill for a cold beer," I said longingly.

"I've got something even better," Puck responded brightly and rummaged around in his satchel, bringing up two brown bottles. "Langham Sundowner. Local ale."

I let myself fall onto the ground in happy response, and we sat there, at the edge of the Wyrde Woods, drinking our ale and looking at the road and farmlands beyond in silence. The ale had a hint of tropical fruit and citrus which was odd but I decided I liked it. Slowly the enjoyment of a brew after a hard day's work gave way to a morose sense that the long day was ending. I didn't want to go, I wanted to stay but I had little choice in the matter. In a short while, I knew, the bus would come and I would head back to Nowhere Place. Even though it seemed we had been talking all day, there was so much more I wanted to say to Puck but I simply couldn't find the words.

17. FUBAR

"Guess what?" Sharon promenaded into my room at Nowhere Place, dragging Thomas behind her.

I was on my bed reading a book. Sharon seemed bursting to share her news with me and I sat up making space on the bed. Sharon sat down next to me. Thomas grabbed my desk chair and assumed a suitable pose. I hoped that Sharon hadn't come in to tell me she was pregnant. With her eagerness to accomplish that it seemed only a matter of time now.

"So tell me," I commanded.

"We talked to Terry," Thomas flashed us his gorgeous smile.

Quiddy? He expected a response but I didn't have a clue.

"Terry's cool on it, it'll be legend Wendy," Sharon tried to clarify.

"Start at the beginning Sharon," I smiled to hide my confusion. "Please."

"You know," Sharon said. "Biggs and Jasmin."

It began to dawn on me again. Some kind of a matchmaker do.

"I've been thinking about that," I said. "Maybe a House Party in the common room?"

We were allowed about five of these a year so that we could imitate normal teenage life. The tenements were off limits by definition and Forlorn Hopers were seldom invited to parties elsewhere in town.

"House Parties are moist," Thomas said.

He was right: Alcohol wasn't allowed, we were supervised by adults and basically in the same common room we saw each other in every day anyway. The main difference was that the lights were dimmed, music was allowed to be played louder than normal and lights-out was extended to 1 AM. Usually most Forlorn Hopers sat around staring at each other till midnight when we were allowed to drift off to our rooms.

"We have a better plan Wendy, a real beast innit." Sharon said, her eyes bright. "Well, Tommy thought of it." She threw him an adoring look.

"Do tell," I was curious. "How is Terry involved?"

"He said that the rules actually state that we're allowed to attend social events five weekend nights a year and stay out late," Thomas gleefully.

"Wow. Just...wow." I laughed.

"They sort of changed that to House Parties because we never get invited anywhere anyway," Sharon explained. "But that is an informal system. Terry read the official Nowhere Place rules, he showed us."

"So we can go out on a Friday or Saturday night and stay out till one? That's sirageous," I said.

"Only if we've been invited to a party as a group," Sharon answered.

"Well there's the hard bit," I shrugged. "Nobody at school is going to invite us and I'll be damned if I go begging those faxing princesses."

"We go on Saturday, this Saturday," Thomas grinned. "Cause Terry is on duty, and he'll give us permission based on the rules."

"Terry is cool," Sharon shot Thomas another adoring look.

"Brill," I began to get enthusiastic. Without adult supervision we could get some alcohol and then party true Forlorn Hope style. "But...location?"

Sharon and Thomas exchanged a meaningful look.

"Remember you told me about your nature ramble the day Michael left?" Sharon asked.

I nodded carefully.

"You told me about this priory, not far from the Make-out Corner," Sharon continued.

"Now that would be a chill place," Thomas contributed enthusiastically.

"Bun that," I shook my head resolutely. "It's not going to happen."

"Come on Wendy," Sharon said. "It'd be a good place."

"It'll be warm enough on Saturday, no rain. I checked the weather forecast," Thomas added.

"You're so clever Tommy," Sharon beamed at him. He raised his eyebrows in wannabe James Bond fashion.

"Well then we can have it anywhere outside," I suggested.

"We need it out of town, and some place with a few walls would be brilliant, plus I found it on a map, there's nothing at all out there, we won't disturb no-one." Thomas said.

"It's not a good idea," I said. "It's a monument, we'd be trespassing."

Even as I said this I realised what a silly argument this was. A bit of trespassing out in the open was not something any of us would lose a night's sleep about. The truth was that my eagerness to share the Wyrde Woods with Sharon had long passed. The woods had changed from a refuge to a home of sorts. I was getting to know them, learning how the singular word 'wood' harboured a hundred different worlds, a thousand stories and ten thousands of lives, from the smallest field mouse to the oldest oak. I didn't want three dozen intoxicated Forlorn Hopers rampaging through that world.

"We'll clear up and all," Thomas promised. "No one will even know we've been there."

"Come on Wendy," Sharon persisted, "We wouldn't even be there long; we'd have to leave well before midnight to get back in time."

"You're up in those woods every free minute you have," Thomas said, "Can't keep it all to yourself, don't be selfish."

I pictured the faces of Joy and Willick, imagined their disappointment.

"Nope," I said, and shook my head again. "It's not going to happen."

"Well it bloody well is," Thomas said angrily. "I've been making the faxing arrangements already and we can find the bloody place without your negatons."

"Fine, then you can faxing well go have your party," I snarled back.

"Guys, come on," Sharon was in half a panic. "Wendy, I want you to be there too, wouldn't be the same without you." She gave Thomas a pointed look. He gave some ground.

"It'd be sic to have you there, real peng," he grumbled. "Do it for Biggs and Jasmin at least."

"We stick together, remember?" Sharon gave me a pointed look now.

"Look, I'll think about it, okay?" I pleaded.

"Sure thing Wendy," Thomas got up. "But there's going to be a party. Come on babes."

He beckoned Sharon and walked towards the door. Sharon followed, turning her head towards me and mouthing the word 'please'.

§ § § § § § §

I got permission to spend a few evenings at the library, ostensibly for homework assignments at school but the homework I did was of a different nature. I only had the word 'M33' to go on but one of the librarians helped set me up and I spent hours poring over local newspapers and got an impression of what had been happening in Odesby.

Plans for the M33 had been revealed around the time I had arrived in Nowhere Place and stirred up a great deal of fuss. Locals had set up a campaign group almost straight away: Friends of the Wyrde Woods. They had launched a campaign with leaflets, posters and stickers, as well as organising a petition that was destined for the local M.P. and the Wealden District Council.

Their actions were countered by the founding of the Odesby Concerned Citizens group which was a pro-M33 campaign lobby supported by the British Road Federation and the Odesby Chamber of Commerce. That in turn had been countered by another anti-M33 group called Weard Hunt, and after that the anti and pro groups had seemed on the verge of war, using the local media to cross their swords.

Friends of the Wyrde Woods seemed the most civilised of the bunch, they continued their campaign by opening a website, holding fund-raisers, selling t-shirts on market days and organising route walks in the Wyrde Woods so people could see what was at stake.

Weard Hunt seemed much more aggressive, stuff like gathering something called bulldozer pledges which were promises by people to come stop the bulldozers when these would arrive to wreak havoc in the woods.

How the fax do you stop a bulldozer? Steal a tank from the army?

Things had come to a head at a public debate organised by the City Council. The Concerned Citizens had accused the Weard Hunt crowd of being supported by the radical Earth First movement and threatened dire consequences for any 'eco-terrorists' who dared show their faces in town (terrorists in Odesby!). The Weard Hunt group, in turn, had revealed what connections there were between local businesses, landowners, construction companies and local politicians; all of whom stood to gain a great deal at the expense of the Wyrde Woods. The name 'Malheur' surfaced several times. The exposure of the vested interests of all these people laid bare a structural level of fishiness which was even picked up by national media.

I was intrigued, I always thought local politics was dull to the extreme and more or less a fixed deal between the head honchos, but they seemed to face some determined opposition now. I liked the style of Weard Hunt, going down with a bang and fighting for the Wyrde Woods appealed to me. I pictured myself taking on a bulldozer. If I was in the right mood the odds were just about even I figured.

It also reminded me how isolated Neverland really was in Odesby. I'd never heard a whisper of the M33 there and none of the groups had leafleted on the estate or gone from door to door as far as I knew.

Around the time that I had first gone into the Wyrde Woods the Highway Agency had invited contractors to start placing their tenders for the roadwork that was to be carried out in the Wealden District. The most recent reports speculated that the winner would soon be officially announced as the first people who owned land along the route -bought under Compulsory Purchase laws- had begun to receive something called Notice to Treat to inform them that work could start as early as September.

I wondered how much Puck knew about all of this. It seemed unlikely that he didn't know. But still, he had chosen to talk a lot about things that happened hundreds of years ago rather than a current impending crisis which was about to hit his beloved woods with destructive vengeance. I resolved to subject him to a little grilling next time I saw him. First though, I had a more immediate problem to deal with.

§ § § § § § §

Nowhere Place was abuzz with the prospect of the party. Biggs had been briefed thoroughly by Thomas and was practically dancing through the corridors. Expeditions were sent to the supermarket to start acquiring necessities in small quantities, some of which was actually paid for too; Biggs had offered to spend some of his illicit earnings.

I passed the time in desperate internal debate. Stopping the whole thing by informing someone about the plans was not an option, I was a Forlorn Hoper, we did not rat on each other. Distancing myself from the project and not showing up was an option but I knew full well it could easily be misunderstood. The Forlorn Hope may have been united against the rats of the world but internally it was just as fragmented into politics as just about any other large group of people. To be seen as aloof would be followed by distrust and then increased exclusion. I'd seen it happen before. It was fine to pick a fight, stand your ground and if necessary slap someone around to show you were strong, but not to pretend you were above the rest.

I despaired when I thought of Joy and Willick, but knew they lived far away from the Priory and the party was at night. They'd never know. There was a nagging thought too concerning the negativity Willick claimed there was at the priory and I recalled Ufmanna's red eyes, but I figured there was safety in numbers. Besides, Tuckersham Church and the Blood Stone oozed negativity, I hadn't felt it at all at the priory.

The party was going to happen anyway and I had to admit it sounded like it was going to be a great deal of fun. Plus Sharon had been right, we needed to be back at Nowhere Place by one, though probably that would become two, Terry wouldn't mind the extra hour but even he could not ignore an all-nighter, so it wouldn't be a drawn out affair. In the end I decided to go simply to be able to keep an eye on things, make sure it didn't get out of hand.

§ § § § § §

I entered the consultancy room warily, another session with Stubbles and I didn't know what to expect. I certainly didn't expect to find Hairy Mare there, sitting next to Stubbles and looking particularly smug.

"You will recall, perhaps, Wendy, an incident not long ago," Stubbles started. "When I reached out to stop you tapping your fingers on the table and you made certain remarks which could be interpreted as accusations."

I looked from one to the other carefully, trying to figure out their game.

"Wendy, please answer Mr. Dagle," Hairy Mare piped pedantically.

"I recall the incident," I conceded.

"I must admit that it was wrong of me to reach out and establish physical contact. I was irritated as it interfered with a serious conversation I was trying to have with you vis-à-vis your behaviour, but it was a lapse of professionalism." Stubbles sounded jovially contrite. "So I would like to offer you my apologies."

I nodded and had to admit to myself that his phrasing was extremely clever. Inwardly I started to fume because of the way he twisted what had happened and I fought to control myself. Blowing my fuse wouldn't help.

"Which is why I have asked Mrs. Hare to be present at our meetings from now on," Stubbles concluded with one of his fake smiles.

For a moment I dared to believe that his game was up, that he had been reprimanded and was no longer allowed unchaperoned access to the likes of me. My heart started to soar but I cautioned myself to retain clarity of focus. At the very least, it would mean I'd be safe from a repetition of what happened during that particular session. Michael's absence suddenly hurt again. It had been so relaxed with him, every minute with Stubbles was like a boxing match, warding off blows while keeping a good footing and keeping an eye out on the sucker-punch.

Stubbles delivered that punch straight away.

"I hope you understand that it is in both our interest if I take measures to protect myself," the gobshite said in a tone of utter reasonableness.

My mouth nearly fell open. To protect *himself*?

"Something has come to light Wendy," Hairy Mare shrilled accusingly.

"I am really not following this," I spoke tersely.

"I was at a regional conference this weekend," Stubbles declared self-importantly. "And I met one of your previous caretakers."

He allowed for a significant pause. I still didn't have a clue, I knew it was a small world and those people met each other all the time. Half the Forlorn Hopers knew half the Lifers from previous places and most of the Lifers had worked with each other elsewhere before too.

"Michael?" I ventured hopefully, knowing the answer would be no. Stubbles was way too pleased with himself, he was up to something.

"No Wendy, not Mr. Hassock," Hairy Mare contributed prissily. "Somebody else. It seems you make a habit of making false accusations."

The world went black for an instant. When it came back tiny pixel sized dots danced before me and my belly flipped over in rapid succession in anticipation of a deep plunge of some hundred thousand miles.

"I think today would be a good time to talk about..." Stubbles' smile radiated emphatic concern but his eyes were triumphant. "...your attempts to ruin the career of John Calcott."

I cringed, my mind screamed, stopping only in surprise when I heard someone roaring incessantly with bloodthirsty fury. It sounded far away at first, but it wasn't.

It was me.

§ § § § § § §

I peered stupidly into the vodka bottle, holding it up to my eye. Definitely empty I decided, which was probably good as I would have got an eyeful of vodka otherwise. I giggled stupidly and then looked around in a daze to see if I could spot any other beverage. Loud beats shook the air around me and battered my eardrums. The convoluted walls of the priory seemed to coil and twist under the assault of the decibels and vague unfocused shapes moved about: Dancing, snogging, drinking, and vomiting.

Looking for a drink wasn't necessary. Yet another Forlorn Hoper approached me as they had all night, this one proffered me a joint.

"Shtoned, immaclate," I greeted the jay and took a few puffs after which I stretched out my hand to the tin of beer another Forlorn Hoper handed me.

My physical assault of Stubbles had lent me a temporary state of infamy and I was much admired by the Forlorn Hopers. I didn't recall much of it. One moment the world had gone black before my eyes, the next I woke up in my bed this morning feeling grotty beyond belief. But as the Forlorn Hopers brought me their offerings in the priory this evening they dropped enough bits and pieces for me to piece together a picture of what happened. They thought my decision to murder Stubbles by trying to strangle him was a fine idea. They regretted the fact that he had punched me in the face in self-defence but assured me that the swollen black bruise around my left eye would be gone in no time. They were full of admiration that it had taken all of seven staff members to subdue me, which explained the lesser bruises I had on my arms and legs. They commiserated with my 36 hour sojourn in the Reflection Room but reckoned this was somewhat compensated by the heavy sedatives I had been given.

In this they were right; I couldn't recall being in the Reflection Room at all. But somehow, not knowing what had happened over the course of 36 hours was far worse than experiencing it. I had been given house arrest again but sneaking out in the evening to come to the Forlorn Hope's party at the priory had been a simple affair.

Now I sought new oblivion and I took another swig from a bottle. I didn't even know what was in it, but it stung my mouth and went down my throat in a warm wave. The world began spinning around me and I wanted to hang on to something so I wouldn't fall over.

I raised my hand and shook my head when a new offering was brought. The movement of my head was enough to set off a wave of nausea and my stomach gave two or three gentle heaves.

"Good thing…I can hold my liquor," I told nobody at all and then turned around and threw up on the grass behind me.

Though leaving a foul aftertaste in my mouth it cleared my head just a bit. I felt miserable. I looked around for a friendly face. Biggs was some twenty yards to my left and I was about to demand his attention when I saw that he was in animated conversation with Jasmin. The two sat against a wall and had their heads close together in a world of their own.

"Aww, schweet," I mumbled and decided to let Biggs be. Where was Sharon? I looked around in vain for my friend but couldn't see her amidst the many bodies sitting, standing, walking, dancing, exchanging saliva or unconscious already. I became dizzy again and told myself to move my head and eyes slowly to keep renewed nausea at bay.

Then I saw her. Sharon appeared from behind one of the taller walls wiping her mouth. Thomas followed closely behind and, unseen by Sharon, brought his fist to his mouth and moved it back and forth rapidly. His mates for whom he performed this mimicry laughed and hollered in response. Arseholes. They started throwing empty beer tins at Thomas when he made a little bow for them.

I shook my head.

"Don't bloody litter," I scolded them. Then, looking around, I registered that the ground was covered in empty tins, bottles, shards of broken bottles, open bags of crisps with their contents crushed into the grass, pools of vomit, crushed empty cigarette packs and other unidentifiable objects.

Someone had even requisitioned a tube of lipstick to draw erect cocks spurting cum on tits on some of the remnants of the priory walls.

I closed my eyes and felt despair. It wasn't supposed to go this way. Thomas had promised.

I opened my eyes again and saw the shims.

I wasn't even surprised; the priory was one of those places after all. There were four of them; vague shapes by a gap in the wall to my right, dressed like nuns though their habits vaguely resembled short skirts for nothing showed beneath the knees, not even legs. The visible parts of them were as clear as daylight though.

I wasn't even scared, I thought, but then a horrible realisation struck me when I perceived it was the shims who were scared; frightened and confused, bordering on being downright terrified. My whole being suddenly reverberated with the immense folly this party really was. We weren't trespassing on Lady Malheur's property as much as we were intruding on something much larger and more important than that. We didn't belong here. We shouldn't be here. The collective intoxication of the Forlorn Hope was a brute penetration of the sanctity of the Wyrde Woods. I had made a colossal blunder, repaying the only place which had ever seemed like home with the careless ingratitude of violation.

I freaked, I panicked, I wanted to get away. I didn't want to be part of this anymore and I scrambled to my feet.

"Wendy!" I heard Sharon shout. I shook my head.

"No, no, no, no, no." I increased my speed, half running and half stumbling away from the corner of the Priory which the Forlorn Hope had invaded. The whole world began spinning frantically again and a new wave of nausea threatened to overcome me.

I careened over the moat bridge and instinctively took a left turn, deeper into the Wyrde Woods. The woods didn't bring the solace I so desperately wanted though; the trees were cold and distant as if they had turned their back on me. I floundered on, sometimes stumbling and falling. But always I rose again and lurched on with the incoordination of the walking dead, driven only by my need to get away from myself. The best thing that ever happened to me and I had gone and destroyed it. I hated myself.

The trees I could register in the dark of night became a blur, the path endless and time ceased to exist. It wasn't until I heard the sound of burbling water that I faltered, peering vainly in front of me searching for the source till I realised I had just passed it. There was a bridge behind me and I tottered to the riverbank, falling on my belly to stick my head in the refreshingly cold water. I came up for air, took a deep breath and then drank from the river. The water had a cleansing effect and I stuck my face in the water two more times before getting to my feet again.

In front of me, to my right, I saw a shape which looked familiar and realised it was the chestnut I had climbed on my first day in the Wyrde Woods. I walked towards it hesitantly but felt no disapproval. I pressed myself against the rough bark and I felt a little comforted now I had a friend to lean on.

I don't know how long I stood there till I was struck by the realisation that whatever else I did, I had better not head straight on. I knew what awaited me down the path to the ruined church. What then? The river, I decided, follow it north. Follow it to Hood's Gorge and I would be nearer to Joy. I followed the river upstream, aided by a grassy riverbank that was only occasionally broken by a bush or young tree and these I negotiated as well as I could in the dark.

My mind was dulled again for a while but then predictably became a red raw wound as I contemplated my betrayal, this time from a wider perspective. I had professed to love the Wyrde Woods but the love I had given was one of careless indifference. Like my parents had given me.

I began to weep. Three years beyond my memory's recall had been followed by three years of bewilderment as the world I grew up in somehow did not make sense and those had been followed by a decade of being tough and strong. Never must a crack show, never a weakness. Sometimes I failed in this, like now, and then it would be like a dam had burst and there was no end to the tears. Eventually the exertion of my nocturnal activities got to me and I sank to the ground, ceasing to cry now, it was as if I had no more tears left to spill.

§ § § § § § §

Dogs can pick up on moods and act accordingly. So Lady didn't greet me in her usual happy manner, she announced her presence by pressing her moist snout into my neck and uttering the softest of whines. I petted her absentmindedly.

"Good girl," I said to ease her worry. Slowly it dawned on me that Puck might be near. I stood up. Lady wagged her tail and then slowly ambled down a dark narrow path, looking back to see if I was following. Obediently I let Lady guide me, using the white flash on her tail as my beacon.

We didn't walk all that long, half a mile maybe, when Lady stopped. I slowed to a halt, confused. All I could discern were the dark shapes of bushes and trees. I looked down at Lady for further clarification and then noted a thin line of soft light by her front paws. It seemed set in a large clump of undergrowth but upon exploring the area over the light with my hands I felt the planks of a door.

I swung it open and was greeted by the light of a LED lantern which hung from a sloping roof. There were three steps down into a rectangular pit lined with a wall of loose rocks. Chests and a low bookcase lined one wall; there was a small woodstove at the far end and a pile of blankets on two low stacks of pallets by the other wall. I could see Puck's head, half his face concealed by the book he had been reading when he had fallen asleep. Lady slipped in and I closed the door. Lady barked softly and Puck grumbled, and then leaned up, groggy with sleep.

"Wenn?!?" He shook his head to clear the sleep.

I must have been awful to behold, one eye disappearing into a dark bruise the other red-rimmed and cheeks moist from my tears.

"I messed up."

"Wenn, what happened?"

"I messed up Puck. Big time. It's FUBAR."

Puck lifted the covers.

"Come here Elfin."

"But I faxed up."

"We'll sort it out in the morning, okay?"

I nodded and crawled into the bed. Puck winced at the smell of alcohol and vomit on my breath but wrapped an arm around me anyway and I rested my head on his chest.

"FUBAR." I whispered.

"Ssshhh, it'll be alright Elfin." Puck answered. "Everything will be alright."

18. Four for a Boy

I woke slowly in a disorientated daze, an aching pressure in my skull and limbs of lead which wouldn't move at first. I stared up at the ceiling and was befuddled by the sight of neat sloping rows of tree stems against a blue tarpaulin. I had no idea where I was till I heard Puck fidgeting with a small kettle on the woodstove.

"Morning Elfin," he said cheerfully when he perceived that I was back in the land of the living.

"What happened?" My voice sounded cracked and wobbly and my breath tasted foul.

"I have no idea," Puck responded. "You showed up here, my top secret whereabouts which nobody knows about, in the dead of the night, totally wasted." He gave my face a thoughtful look over. "And pretty battered too. Who did that to you?"

"Stubbles," I groaned.

Puck raised an eyebrow.

"Therapist, Nowhere Place, the home," I explained as briefly as possible. My mouth was dry and felt filthy like I had eaten the contents of an ashtray.

"Interesting therapy," Puck nodded. "I am making you some coffee, but you really need to drink lots of water."

He handed me a water bottle and I took a small sip. It was good and I raised the bottle higher, letting the water flow into my mouth, spilling some on my chin.

"Whoa, take it easy," Puck grinned.

"Woozy," I clarified.

"Your very own fault. No sympathy," Puck shook his head. "You smell like a vodka distillery."

"Dishevelled," I mumbled thinking of the morning after Ufmanna and my muddy state atop Arthur's Fort.

"Quiddy?"

"You don't see me at my best very often." I struggled to an upright position carefully, still feeling queasy.

Puck laughed, and then beamed at me.

"I think I do Wenn, I think I do. You live life to the full, up and down. Better than a vain poppet worrying about the state of her nails."

I nodded; my nails were, as usual, ruggedly chewed back as far as possible.

"There was a party," I confessed hesitantly. "Kids from Nowhere Place."

"In the woods?"

I recalled last night's shame and guilt and coloured red.

"Priory."

"Good place for a party I reckon," Puck shrugged.

"They…we thrashed the place," my lower lip trembled. My assumption was that the Forlorn Hopers hadn't bothered to clear up behind them.

"I hate to break it to you Wenn," Puck's eyes shined with mirth. "But I think you'll find Rolf Ragnarsson the Dane beat you to that by some twelve centuries. Took the silver, buggered the nuns senseless and set fire to the place." He handed me a cracked mug of steaming coffee and I accepted it gratefully.

"The nuns…"

"What about the nuns Wenn?"

"I saw them," I said hesitantly.

Puck didn't show any incredulity, he just nodded.

"They were frightened. It was wrong, we shouldn't have been there." I bowed my head, there, it was out. My trespass confessed.

Puck was silent for a while and I waited for him to pass judgment. Inwardly I growled at myself, nobody judged me, no one had the right. But I found that I wanted to know his mind on this.

"Look," he said at last. "I am not saying it was a good idea of you to bring those people out to the priory."

I nodded.

"But what I hear most of all is that you were, even in the state you were in, in tune with the Wyrde Woods." He gave me a gentle smile. "There's a bit of good in everything Wenn."

"But if Joy and Willick find out…"

"I really don't think you have ever managed to do anything Joy hasn't. She remembers what it's like to be young and yearn for freedom and talks about it openly."

I smiled, that was true and Joy was different from most adults I knew in that.

"Willick is a different matter. If he finds the priory in a state he'll happily drag you to the Blood Stone and sacrifice your innards to the Old Gods."

I pouted.

"But he's away for the day, so we are lucky."

I noted the 'we' with interest.

"So what do I…what do we do?"

"Make amends," Puck said. "I gotta go fetch some water and wood, will you be okay?"

I nodded and he opened the door of the hut and left, followed by Lady.

I finished my coffee and set the mug down. I looked around the hut. It was small but neatly organised. The chest closest to the woodstove was open and I saw pots, kitchen utensils and tinned food. I noted a longbow and a quiver of feathered arrows hanging on the opposite wall. He really did live the life of a Greenwoods outlaw. There was also an acoustic guitar propped up against the bookshelf.

I checked my phone. To my surprise I had reception. But the volume had been turned off and I had missed a host of messages. A few from Biggs and many from Sharon; concerned inquiries as to my whereabouts. I sent a short text back to say I was okay. Sharon texted back immediately to say I was in trouble at Nowhere Place, they knew I hadn't come back and she urged me to return as quickly as possible. I sent her a reply saying that I needed to clear up the mess at the priory first.

I put the phone away again. My eye fell on the book Puck had been reading last night. The words *Fierce Dancing* were on the cover of the well-thumbed paperback. I took it and opened it at a random page. For a moment the words danced on the page as the title suggested but then they settled down and grabbed my full attention. It was about jackboots, jackboots in Britain marching in a manner the whole nation had resisted back in the 1940s but seemed to accept when it concerned a minority subculture a few years before I had been born. The injustice touched me, injustice sucks big time.

I flipped the pages till the words 'road protest' caught my eye. I was intrigued and started reading more thoroughly about a road protest in a place called Whitstable in Kent back in the early 90s. I continued reading and was in the middle of a description of destructive group politics in the road protest camp at a farmhouse when Puck returned with a jerry can of water and an arm full of fire wood. He threw a glance at the book.

"Stone is brilliant I think," he said. "Today's George Orwell really. He's a good writer; he doesn't just present a list of everything that is wrong with this country till you get dead tired of the moral outrage. Nor does he make up your mind for you, he just sort of tells you tongue-in-cheek how he stumbled across things and then let's his closer scrutiny set your blood boiling. Or not, that he leaves up to you."

I nodded; my interest was in the road protest.

"The road protest…" I said.

Puck suddenly became wary.

"Oh yeah, that," he tried as nonchalantly as he could, but he didn't fool me. He was on his guard, there was a secret here.

"I went to the library. Looked up the M33," I told him.

"Did you?"

"Read about Friends of the Wyrde Woods, the Weard Hunt, Concerned Citizens, your aunt…"

"Yes, if there is mischief to be made the Malheurs will be in it up to their eyeballs." Puck sighed.

"Are you a member of this Weard Hunt?"

That wariness again.

"No, not quite."

"Is something like this going to happen here?" I indicated the copy of *Fierce Dancing.*

"I don't know," he said looking away.

"I think you're lying Puck. I can't see you giving up the Wyrde Woods without a fight." I insisted stubbornly.

"It's complicated Wenn."

"Puck, please don't lie to me. Not you." I looked him straight into his eyes. He didn't look away this time. "Please Puck."

"Not without a fight, you're right," Puck admitted. "But these things can get pretty dicey, so there's a lot of cloak-and-dagger stuff going on that I can't tell you about."

"I want in."

"You sure?" It was his turn to scrutinise my eyes now. "It can get violent, the police aren't the worst. You can get arrested, taken to court for criminal damage, real or not. Prison even."

I hesitated. Like all Forlorn Hopers I had been in juvenile detention already and had a record. Any further serious brushes with the law could spell young offenders institution. Then again, the way I was going, that might just be a matter of time anyway.

"I am sure," I said.

"I'll have to talk to some people first," Puck nodded.

"I need a leak," I got up and walked out of the hut, finding a suitable bush some 30 yards away where I unbuttoned my trousers, squatted and took a piss.

Walking back I admired Puck's hut. Though the door was reasonably visible the fact that the hut was set partially in the ground meant that it was low and I couldn't even see the blue tarpaulin beneath the piles of branches and moss which camouflaged the hut's roof effectively. A casual passer-by would have to get real close to recognise it for what it was. I saw some traces of smoke from the metal chimney pipe that protruded through the roof and finally placed the odd smell Puck had, it was the smell of wood smoke that permeated the entire hut as well.

"You do archery?" I asked Puck when I was back inside. I indicated the longbow.

"Yes, Hornsby taught me. An old tradition in the Wyrde Woods. Joy and Willick used to shoot when they were kids."

The first name sounded familiar.

"Ellette the little elf!" I exclaimed.

"Not Ellette no," Puck chuckled. "Rob Hornsby, local farmer. Same family and same farm. Most of the locals trace their roots back a long way around here. Others, like Willick, they come and never leave again."

"I have always wanted to fire a bow," I said longingly. It was a partial untruth, the wish had started when I had seen the massed archery at the Battle of Helm's Deep in Peter Jackson's *The Two Towers*.

"Shoot a bow," Puck corrected me. "You don't fire a bow."

"Can you teach me?"

"Rob is a far better teacher, but not now," he gave me a meaningful look.

"Oh yeah, amends," I mumbled.

"And, as I am an honest Puck, if we have unearned luck, now to escape the serpent's tongue, we will make amends ere long," Puck smiled.

"You're a bit daft Puck, but I like it," I told him.

He reached out his hand.

"Give me your hands if we be friends, and Robin shall restore amends."

I looked at the bow and arrows. Robin indeed.

I let him pull me up.

"You better. Do you have a toothbrush I can borrow?"

§ § § § § §

We walked to the river and then followed the bank south. Both of us carried a pail filled with rolls of bin bags.

We came to the bridge and my eyes greeted my chestnut tree.

"Nan Malone's bridge," Puck said. "Tuckersham Church is that way." He pointed towards the path that led to Ufmanna's haunt.

"The ruined church?"

"Aye, a thriving village once. There was an old woman who lived there, Nan Malone. Wise in the ways of the forest, folk came to her for cures and the like."

"Like Joy?"

"Very much so. And Joy's mother Sarah. But there were also jealous spiteful people in the village. Just a handful, but they can often set the general mood."

I thought about how Stubbles had changed Nowhere Place and the few crappy protesters in *Fierce Dancing* who had turned a well-intentioned enterprise into something sour.

"There was a spate of…sightings."

"Ufmanna." I ground my teeth.

Puck looked surprised.

"Yes, Ufmanna. So you did run into him that night when I found you in the woods the next morning?"

I nodded.

"Thought so, that's why I took you to the Owlery. If it had just been a cup of regular tea you needed the hut was much closer by. But Ufmanna…leaves an impression Joy knows how to heal."

"The charm-stuff!"

"Yes, the charm-stuff. Nan Malone concocted brews like that as well, but the jealous ones blamed Nan Malone and sparked off a campaign of tongue wagging that led to Nan Malone being chased out of the village by an angry mob. She made it to the bridge…"

"And then?" I asked softly, dreading the answer.

"They lynched her, on that Chestnut tree there." Puck pointed at my tree and my eyes grew wide. "There's something nasty that happens to people when they group up on one other person. It's haunted, most locals stay well away from the tree, I get a bad feeling from it myself."

I stayed silent, I didn't want to tell him that the Chestnut had sheltered and protected me. Even now, when I looked at it, I still perceived it as a friend. To think though, that Nan Malone had been strung up from the very branches I had climbed…

"What happened to the village?"

"Ah, shortly thereafter a plague of some sorts broke out and there was not a single survivor. They said it was the Devil's revenge for taking one of his own."

"Or the Wyrde Woods," I said.

I looked at the chestnut. In my mind Nan Malone looked like Joy. How could you even begin to describe how she must have felt when she got to the bridge? Devoted her life to the health matters of her neighbours. Then one sour apple starts the gossip and more tongues start wagging, ever faster and then so vicious that hate takes seed in the collective mind and there is no more room for reason. It is only the view of the majority that can be the truth. There is no way to fight that. She must have been devastated by that realisation.

When she got here exhausted from the run -unable to carry herself any further- and looked around at the circle of spiteful faces: How many faces did she see which she had once looked upon with the warmth of friendship?

It wasn't the chestnut which was to blame. A tree which had given me so much pleasure in climbing it and sheltered me from my fears could have hardly been eager for a bit of sadistic action.

I walked to the tree.

"Wenn, maybe…" Puck called out.

I turned.

"It's okay Puck. I'm fine."

I continued my short pilgrimage and laid my hand on the bark, then pressed my side against it and laid my ear on the trunk. There wasn't anything to hear of course, I was just struck by the silly notion I could comfort it the way it had comforted me.

§ § § § § § §

When we got to the Priory I saw that my assumption about the Forlorn Hope had been correct, parts of the ruins looked like a rubbish tip. We set to work straight away and I was glad Puck had come along, after about half-an-hour of work it still looked like we had barely made an impact on the party debris.

We took a short break, I used some of my last baccy to make a rollie and had just lit it when a pleasant surprise arrived in the form of Sharon, Biggs and Jasmin; all looking slightly embarrassed as they looked around and saw the state of the place. My heart leapt, I jumped up and ran to them to give them all a hug.

"I hadn't expected this, sirageous!" I beamed as I led Sharon towards Puck, Biggs and Jasmin trailing us.

"Sometimes Wendy," Sharon said, slightly irritated, "You forget that I am more than just a bimbo. I am also your mate you know."

I felt embarrassed.

"Thanks," I mumbled.

"It's okay darling," Sharon laughed at the look on my battered face and then cast an inquisitive look at Puck. I introduced them all. Puck was just his jocular self but my fellow Forlorn Hopers were cautious, to them the boy dressed entirely in green was something of an alien from another planet.

We set to work again and it went much faster with the five of us. We collected all the rubbish and separated the empty tins, bottles and glass and plastic rubbish. We probably wouldn't have bothered to do that if Puck hadn't been here, but he insisted.

The pails were used to sluice the worst congealed piles of vomit away and we cleaned the lipstick graffiti off the walls as best as we could. After another hour or so we were done; flattened grass and faint red smudges on walls being the most tell-tale sign that the Forlorn Hope had come and gone.

We carried the filled rubbish bags out of the priory and headed south. Puck had said he'd come as far as the railway bridge, there was a skip there where we could dump most of the rubbish and after that the Forlorn Hopers would carry the plastic and glass to the recycling containers by the supermarket on the way back to Nowhere Place.

Puck walked ahead with Jasmin and Biggs. The three were joking and laughing like they had been the best of mates for ages and I was pleased that everybody was making an effort to be friendly.

"Sooo…?" I asked Sharon.

"I like him," she declared to my surprise. I had expected her to be dismissive because of his outlandish clothes and lack of cool swagger. Sharon and Puck were just about extreme opposites to my mind.

"Why?" I wanted to know.

"Because of the way he looks at you Wendy," Sharon said. "He really cares about you."

"Really?" I was astonished.

Sharon poked me in the side, laughing.

"For someone as brainy as you, you can be pretty stupid sometimes Wendy. He fancies you, trust me." She laughed some more and I felt sheepish but at the same time uplifted. Putting all the puzzle pieces together now I realised he probably did. I felt elated and beamed.

Puck and I lingered by the skip under the bridges where we had deposited a good half of our rubbish collection. Sharon, Biggs and Jasmin were already heading further into the industrial estate.

"Thank you, a hundred thousand thanks," I said.

"It was no big deal Wenn," Puck answered, shrugging.

"It was too though. I…you set my mind at ease about the whole thing. I felt so bad about it."

"Okay, you're welcome Elfin. I was glad to help." Puck suddenly looked awkward. "Wenn, I…"

"Ssshhh," I said and took his face in my hands. I leant forwards and we kissed, briefly the first time but much longer the second time.

This was Make-out Corner after all.

19. Confessions

"I was at the party and fell asleep. Sharon, Biggs and Jasmin came to find me the next day," I repeated stubbornly.

Hairy Mare's hands fluttered over her notepad in frustration. Watson stood by the door for security. Stubbles was still on sick-leave recovering from the shock of my supposed assault. I say 'supposed' because my hands had come nowhere near his neck as I had found out from one of the Snooties on Monday. My hands were aimed for his neck alright but he had delivered his punch before anything else happened.

"It won't do Wendy, it just won't do," Hairy Mare piped and looked to Watson for support. Watson just shrugged.

I stared at Hairy Mare's moustache, feeling reasonably confident. The shrink was clearly in confusion as what to do with me without Stubbles to back her up. I knew there would be punishment, but at least this time I wouldn't be twisted by clever talk. If it was too severe, I'd see if I could stir up a fuss about the punch, being restrained was one thing, I was sure punching kids in the face wasn't entirely kosher. Stubbles had actually given me a trump card to play, and I felt cheekily confident.

"You fell asleep. Had you been drinking?" Hairy Mare looked at me sternly.

I had thought about this before the meeting. To deny it altogether would be unrealistic. To admit I had been shitfaced would imply there had been a lot of booze there and get the rest of the Forlorn Hope into trouble. In the end I settled for that local tradition Puck had told me about. Nobody in the whole history of Sussex had ever drunk more than a pint on any given occasion. It would be a shame to be the one to break with that tradition and I felt increasingly connected with Sussex, something I had never given much thought to before. I guess because Joy and Willick had said that Twyner and Pilbeame were good Sussex names. When you know absolutely nothing about your parents, just knowing where they came from is like finding a treasure. Maybe that is what Hairy Mare should have been talking to me about.

"I had one pint, sneaked it in before I went to the party."

Hairy Mare shook her head sadly.

"Now Wendy, you must be so careful with alcohol, there is a reason you know, why there is an age restriction. You are still growing and alcohol can cause lasting damage. To your brain for starters."

I stared at her. Here I was, a veritable fruitcake who short circuited on an ever more frequent basis. Only a few days ago I had been manhandled into an isolation cell and calmed down only after I had been given enough sedatives to knock out a horse and she was worried that I might damage my mind.

"I am sorry," I looked down guiltily. "I have learned my lesson I think. I don't want to be damaged."

Hairy Mare rewarded me with an approving smile but Watson snorted. Not in a hostile manner, I noted with interest, there was an air of amusement about her.

"Where did you get your 'single' pint Wendy?" Watson asked, a little sparkle in her eyes.

I shot her a frown.

"Excuse me Miss Watson," Hairy Mare shrilled reprovingly. "If you don't mind, I'll be asking the questions here."

The shrink looked back at me and didn't see Watson roll her eyes. I giggled and to my surprise Watson gave me a wink.

"Now Wendy," Hairy Mare peered at me through her glasses. "Where did you get that pint?"

"My mate in the tenements."

"You have been spending more time with this…?"

"Yes." I answered. "Don't worry, we use condoms."

Hairy Mare's mouth dropped open.

"All three of us," I couldn't help adding, I was on a roll now. And this is what they wanted to hear last time. "Well, the two of them do, I obviously don't wear one."

The shrink was well flustered now, a blush spreading on her cheeks.

"I can't say I approve," Hairy Mare uttered.

"You mean we shouldn't use them?" I asked innocently. "I know I can't get pregnant up the…you know. But I thought…"

"No! You should. Yes. No."

"I'll tell them you approve." I was owning this conversation and I could swear I saw a hint of a smile on Watson's face.

"I don't." The shrink was beginning to lose it so much now that I actually felt sorry for her.

"I am sorry I came back so late on Sunday," I changed the subject and saw relief on Hairy Mare's face.

 "Yes, why is that Wendy?" She asked.

"I was scared to come back," I said in a little voice.

"Why Wendy?" Hairy Mare sounded concerned. "You can tell me."

"I meant to come back on time. Honest. I mean, I am in enough trouble as is innit?" I let my lower lip tremble. "I know I deserve…consequences but I was so ashamed of letting you all down. And afraid that I would be put in the…put in the Reflection Room again." I lowered my face and covered it with my hands.

"Well, I don't think that will be necessary Wendy," Hairy Mare reassured me. "But I will extend your house arrest by a week and then…I will consult the others as to further consequences."

That meant she would ask Stubbles. Bugger.

§ § § § § §

Stubbles was back on the Wednesday, looking none-the-worse for his traumatic experience, all amiable smile and dark inscrutable eyes. He knocked on my bedroom door late in the afternoon while I was staring despondently at a pile of overdue homework. I was wary but he had the sense to stay in the door opening where he beamingly told me that he had extended my house arrest by another two weeks for the time being.

I was determined not to show him how much this upset me, since home leave was coming up this Friday followed by a week of mid-term during which I had hoped to get at least one day pass if not two. Then again, I had already figured out that the more immediate prospects of freedom would probably be cancelled on account of my new homicidal tendencies.

Failing to get much response from me did not faze Stubbles. Next he announced that Mrs. Hare had come to a decision regarding the further outcome of my second unauthorised absence in a short space of time.

Yeah right, cause she is ever so decisive.

Stubbles said that there would be a Broad Situational Conference the next day at noon. He had already informed school that I would be absent for the day. I just shrugged, I didn't mind missing a day of school and Stubbles was obviously going to have to get payback somehow.

When Stubbles had left I went over to Biggs's room to ask him if he knew what a Broad Situational Conference was. He explained that it was a meeting with everybody who was involved with the kid in question. Something occurred to me.

"Does that include family?"

"Yes, it definitely includes family." Biggs said. "Usually they use it to justify a change in treatment, get the family to agree and all. Be careful Wendy, Mr. Perv will probably try to paint you black."

I thanked him and rushed back to my room. I was full of questions. Would they have invited Joy and Willick over? I wished Joy had a telephone so I could call her; sometimes the whole primitive countryside thing could be bloody inconvenient. Then I remembered that Puck had sent me a text forever ago, it would be on my mobile's logbook. I spent a long time composing a message. I had been thinking about him a lot of course, replaying our kisses by the railway bridge in my head extensively. But neither he nor I were the type for a long exchange of soppily sweet text messages, I decided. It wasn't even clear if there was some kind of a relationship, it's not like a couple of kisses bound us together till death do us part or anything. In the end I settled for:

> *I miss you. Do you know if Joy and Willick are*
> *coming to Nowhere Place tomorrow?*

I spent the next hour monitoring my phone to no avail. I reminded myself that Puck didn't seem to carry his phone on him all the time, in actual fact; I had never even seen him with one, meaning that if he was out and about a response might take some time. I lost myself in a book till Puck's response finally came, just before midnight.

> *I miss you too Elfin. Confirm J+W have been invited.*
> *Break a leg. Love Puck.*

§ § § § § §

I found myself back in the consulting room the next day at noon, quietly confident because this time I would not be alone.

Watson and Terry stood at the door as back-up in case I went ballistic. The Head Supervisor was there at the head of the table, which was a miracle, the man barely ever ventured outside of his office. Hairy Mare was there, she had broken out a brand-new note pad for the occasion. Stubbles sat next to her. I sat on the other side of the table, flanked by Joy and Willick.

Stubbles wasn't his usual self, he seemed disconcerted by the presence of Joy. I am not sure what he had been expecting. Probably a nice old granny with silver-blue hair in a flower dress who would easily be intimidated by the expertise of professionals. Instead Joy, already conspicuous because of her facial tattoos, had made spectacular entrance into Nowhere Place simply by bringing Bronwen. The scritch owl sat perched on her shoulder, peering at her new surroundings with suspicious eyes.

"Well," Stubbles began hesitantly. "I would like to start this meeting by…"

"CCCCCCCHHHHHWWWWWAAA" Bronwen gave an almighty screech and pretty much everyone was startled except for Joy and Willick.

"That's why we calls it a middling scritch owl, surelye." Willick nodded grinning.

I smiled.

"Now that this meeting have started," Joy spoke loud and clear, looking not at Stubbles but at the Head Supervisor. "I'd very much like to know how mine grandchild came to get disyer blue eye o' hern."

I had to make an effort not to grin as Joy took the initiative and went on the offensive straight away.

"It's one of the reasons we have asked you to come today," the Head Supervisor answered. "There has been an unfortunate incident last week during which Miss Twyner assaulted a member of staff and had to be restrained."

"This be true?" Joy directed a sharp look at me.

"Yes Gammer," I said softly.

"Did ye hurt someone?"

"No! It's true that I tried to, but he…" I pointed at Stubbles "…punched me before I could lay a finger on him."

"Punched?" Joy redirected her imposing gaze at Stubbles.

"In self-defence only," Stubbles replied.

Joy looked him up and down. Such was her presence that all waited for her to speak. I realised Joy was like me and the Wyrde Woods, someone with many faces. Mostly I associated her with the kindly soul who took me into her home, nursed me, fed me, tucked me in at night and spoke with pride about her owls and flowers or playfully teased Willick. Then there was Joy during one of her bad days, aging before my eyes, frail and vulnerable. The woman who sat next to me now barely resembled either of those two. This wasn't like the last time she had been in Nowhere Place when she had simply been enjoying her con with almost childish glee. This third Joy exuded self-confidence and determination in a most convincing manner. This was power like I had never witnessed before, not based on the threats of punishment but on pure contagious conviction.

What's more, she had come to break a lance for me, I could barely believe it. It was the very first time and I had been through a great many numbers of meetings such as this one, whatever name they attached to it. Always alone. At the ones with Michael he had done his best to radiate empathy but that was the most public support he would give. Not like this; Joy was in a fighting mood.

"Ye mean to tell me that a big man alikes yernself cannot restrain disyer slight lass in any other way?" she asked quietly.

Stubbles cringed under her gaze and Hairy Mare came to his rescue.

"Wendy…Miss Twyner was very much out of control Mrs. Whitfield," she piped nervously but with surprising determination. "I was present at the incident myself."

"Ye were? Out o' control?" Joy looked at me again.

I nodded meekly."Yes gammer."

"And what caused this?"

I shook my head softly. I just couldn't.

"We were trying to discuss an incident at the previous institution Miss Twyner was in," Stubbles spoke up. "Concerning a member of staff there, a Mr. John Calcott."

He looked at me expectantly when he spoke the name. I tensed immediately, sucked in a deep breath and clenched my hands into fists under the table. Joy ignored me but I felt Willick reach for one of my hands, easily enveloping it in his own and giving me a gentle squeeze with it.

"Easy Wenn, easy does't lass." Willick murmured softly. I unclenched my hand and clutched back at his hand. He gave another squeeze and I took a deep breath, calming down.

"EEEEEEEECCCCCHHHHHH." Bronwen hissed at Stubbles who looked at the owl uncomfortably.

"And what does this have to do with the home here in Odesby?" Joy asked.

"There seems to be a pattern of baseless accusations that Miss Twyner makes against members of staff," Stubbles said.

"I would have expected," Joy turned to the Head Supervisor, "that any such incident would've been dealt with at that institution."

"I've looked into that this morning. There was an inquiry," the Head Supervisor nodded. "It was inconclusive. Neither Miss Twyner or Mr. Calcott were found to be in violation of any rules."

I practically crushed Willick's hand in mine but he didn't flinch, just gave me another gentle squeeze, even though he must have inwardly cringed when the word 'accusation' fell. I know I did, for my treatment of him that first time I met him must have seemed supportive of Stubbles' claim. I was unworthy of the support Willick was giving me, yet his hand was there, warm around mine and clutching to it kept me from plunging into that chasm.

"Then that rules out a pattern, does it naun?" Willick asked.

"It seems to be the case," the Head Supervisor admitted.

"There is still the accusation she made here," Stubbles insisted.

"I am very sorry Mr. Dagle," I said, surprising myself, "but I did not 'make' an accusation. At the most you could say there was an *implied* accusation. Which there wasn't at any rate."

There was a particular stress to institutional communication like this with which I coped badly. That stress could turn into various levels of belligerence when I was left to my own devices. Now that I was being genuinely supported I managed to retain my cool. With difficulty, true, but I was doing it. Stubbles had once again worded things in a manner which brought on beginning outrage because of the injustice of it: That somebody whom I was supposed to be able to trust, who was charged with responsibility over *my* well-being sought only to seek advantage for himself. He could do so because he had the power of his status but that didn't make it right. Knowing I wasn't alone however, had made a big difference.

"*Implied* accusation Mr. Dagle?" The Head Supervisor enquired pointedly. I suspected that Stubbles had told him something different.

Stubbles turned to me.

"Perhaps Wendy, you would like to tell us what precisely I might have seen as an implication?"

That smile was back, and his eyes were shrouded again. He was up to something. I swallowed my first answer: That I had shouted 'hands off' when he had reached out to touch me.

"In doing so Mr. Dagle," I said instead, "I might appear to be making an accusation in the very attempt to deny that I made an accusation."

Stubbles' eyes flashed in alarm, I noted with satisfaction.

Gotcha.

"I have thought about it since," I continued, "and I am pretty convinced it was an unfortunate case of mutual misunderstanding. Don't you think so Mr. Dagle?"

I had him cornered for a moment. For *him* to say that I had shouted 'hands off' after he had touched me was far more damning to his credibility than mine, even if he added the lie that he was just trying to get me to stop drumming the table. Had I said it, it would have sounded as if I were making the very accusations he accused me of making.

A cornered rat is not to be underestimated though, Stubbles struck back.

"There is also the time you accused Miss Watson of manhandling you."

The Head Supervisor raised an eyebrow.

I could not contest this one, that had been an accusation with witnesses to boot.

"I did. She hurt me. Physically." I admitted.

"Ahum," Watson scraped her throat.

"Yes Miss Watson?" The Head Supervisor asked.

Oh shit.

"I may have inadvertently applied too much strength." Watson said.

WTF? I was amazed.

So was Stubbles.

"Miss Twyner struggled," Watson explained. "And I had to tighten my grip on her arm."

"I did struggle," I added. "I was…I was being unreasonable."

The Head Supervisor nodded.

"It seems to mine eyes that making baseless accusations be naun o' a habit then." Joy said.

"There are other behavioural issues," there was an edge of anxiety in Stubbles' voice now.

"Yes indeed," Hairy Mare peered into her notebook, forgetting perhaps that it was new and she hadn't written anything in it yet.

"On Monday Miss Twyner admitted to me that she had used alcohol over the weekend," she said.

"That be middling silly o' ye Wenn," Joy admonished me. "Ye know I doant want ye to touch a drop o' that."

I lowered my head to hide a smile.

"This happened under yern supervision, doant it be so?" Willick looked at the Head Supervisor.

"She also admitted to engaging in sexual activities," Hairy Mare squeaked.

"To which I be lamentable opposed at hern age," Joy said. "And so be Will."

I had to put my hands in front of my face now because I was literally grinning from ear to ear.

"Aint ye Will?" Joy nagged him.

"Erm, aye, tis unaccountable," Willick mumbled.

"But naun illegal I does believe. Lass be sixteen," Joy continued.

"And, again, this under yern supervision." Willick added.

"Was mine grandchild supervised at all this past weekend?" Joy asked.

"I assure you Mrs. Whitfield," The Head Supervisor raised his hands. "We do our utmost to supervise the children as much as we can. It is simply not possible though, to do so around the clock. There is still the undisputable fact that Miss Twyner has gone missing twice over the last two months, possibly in attempts to run away. I do believe, Miss Hare, that you have a recommendation with regard to the way we can best ensure Miss Twyner's safety over a trial period of three months."

I raised my head; we were getting to the crux of the matter now.

Hairy Mare scraped her throat, and then looked at Stubbles for confirmation. He gave a barely perceptible nod.

"We…I think it is in the best interest of Miss Twyner to revoke her right to day passes and home leave weekends for the time being."

"Three months," Stubbles added.

Inwardly I groaned. That included the summer holiday. The worst time of year. It was like being stuck here at home leave weekends but then for five continuous weeks. Most Forlorn Hopers went on some kind of holiday and would come back with stories about their adventures. I had never been on a holiday in my life. I had expected to lose the next home leave weekend, maybe two. But those horrible summer months had a total of three of them and spending those at the Owlery would have given me the determination to cope with an almost empty Nowhere Place for the rest of the time.

"I'd like to make clear that I think there be everything o' something and something o' everything in that argumentation," Willick said, mystifying everybody, including Joy.

"There be a different proposal we'd like to make." Joy looked at the Head Supervisor.

He nodded.

"I have heard of unsupervised drinking and more," Joy began.

The Head Supervisor wanted to say something but Joy cut him off.

"I understand ye cannot mind Wenn all the time," she said. "But I come here and hears o' this and see a blued eye on mine lass all-along-o' hern being punched. *Punched*, not restrained but punched. And I cannot help but to think tis bettermost for Wenn to spend time with us. Hern fambly."

"We understand you would prefer to have Miss Twyner visit on home leave weekends Mrs. Whitfield," Stubbles began. "But…"

"Ye naun understand, naun at all," Joy shook her head. Then she looked at the Head Supervisor. "We want more than that. We think mayhap twill make a gurt difference for Wendy. Hern behaviour too. Next week be midterm holidays, aint that so? Starting tomorrow after school is out? And summer holiday in awhiles."

My eyes grew wide.

"We want Wenn to spend hern holidays at ourn place," Willick clarified. "Starting tomorrow after school."

I inhaled such a deep breath that I nearly choked on it.

"Well that," Stubbles pronounced, "is totally out of the question."

"Wait a minute George," the Head Supervisor raised his hand. "On the insistence of one of our colleagues…"

He flashed a look at Watson, as he said this. It was only for a fraction of a second but I saw it.

"…I have had a long telephone conversation with Michael Hassock."

My heart lifted. Stubbles took a deep breath and I saw his face harden.

"Mr. Hassock had quite a lot to say about Miss Twyner. It appears you two got along well?" The Head Supervisor directed this question at me.

I nodded. It sounded like Michael had come through for me. Like he still believed in me even after I had given him an earful.

The Head Supervisor looked in the direction of Joy and Willick.

"Seeing as to the…clarifications we have been able to reach here this afternoon, as well as a new perspective supplied by Mr. Hassock and your own kind offer; I was wondering if you would mind leaving us alone for fifteen minutes so that I can discuss this matter with my colleagues."

Joy and Willick nodded, and all three of us got up. We were followed into the hallway by Watson and Terry.

I turned to give Watson a questioning look. She looked around and then leaned over to me.

"Michael sends you his regards," she said in a low tone. Then her face transformed completely, it softened faster than candlewax in a bonfire, becoming feminine and aglow. I was looking at a woman in love. A woman whose love was being returned. Watson, of all people, simply radiated with beauty and happiness.

"Please say hello," I responded timidly, inwardly happy for them. "And thank you."

Watson straightened again, instantly changing back into the stern prison warden I had one time assumed her to be.

"You're doing well kiddo," Terry winked at me. "I'm proud of you."

I beamed.

§ § § § § §

Joy walked to the front door. Willick opted to stay inside -having started talking to Terry- and I followed Joy.

"Some fresh air," Joy explained and walked onto the pavement where she stood looking at the tenement flats and shaking her head. "I'd go hare-brained in there."

"Kleak-kleak." Bronwen seemed to agree with Joy.

"Ye be a good owl Bronwen," Joy told the bird, and then to me: "I was afeared she'd squirt poo on me, ruin the effect o' bringing her."

"Do you really mean it? The holidays too?"

This time I didn't feel the exhilaration I had when Joy and Willick had talked me out of Nowhere Place the first time. This was much bigger and I was hesitant to allow myself to fully grasp the notion.

"I regret I doant a have chance to talk with ye first," Joy answered. "To find out if ye were willing. But I does hear a thing or two from Puck. He said ye would want to."

"He's right. I want to!"

"That be middling, but..." Joy looked at me, stern and commanding, "...yernself and I'll have to have a good talk. All-along-o' that I doant want ye to get into too much bother."

"Okay," I nodded my agreement.

"Ye maun lie to me neither," Joy did not let her strength waver; there was none of the usual emphatic kindness in her eyes.

"I won't," I promised. "I never have, not to you."

"Naun, but ye have kept quiet on matters, like how the meeting with Will ended."

I nodded, feeling the shame again.

"I'll test that promise o' yern here and now," Joy said. "What be this about Mister John Calcott?"

I froze.

"Trust or naun trust Wendy Alice Twyner?"

"He worked at the last place I was at," I ventured hesitantly, looking at a piece of flattened chewing gum on the sidewalk by my boot.

"Aye?"

"I…I was thirteen. He did what Mortimer Malheur did to you…in my room there."

I shuddered, recalling the smothering weight on me.

"And ye accused him?"

"No! That's just it. I didn't dare. He made all sorts of threats. That nobody would believe me, that he would make my life a living hell…"

"That he were already doing," Joy said quietly.

"My behaviour though, it got bad. Anxiety attacks, aggression. I became unmanageable. It ended in the isolation cell. I got sedated and I must have talked about stuff when I was off my head. Someone heard and talked and next thing Calcott is running around telling people I was trying to ruin his career."

"That be when ye got transferred to Odesby?"

I nodded, suddenly feeling utterly exhausted. It was the first time I had ever spoken to anybody about it.

"After the enquiry," I said quietly.

"Well, now I know," Joy said simply, sensing perhaps that this would have been a bad moment to offer comfort. If she had I would have broken down and they could have taken me straight to the Reflection Room.

"Joy? Honesty right?"

"Aye lass. That be bettermost I finds."

"Last time you came to get me, on that first evening I overheard you and Willick talking. I didn't mean to eavesdrop or anything."

"I does know that, voices carry in the Owlery. It used to be mine room, a long time ago."

"You mentioned my parents' names. To Willick."

"I recollect that, aye."

"But the way you said it, it was like he was supposed to recognise the names. Like he had encountered them before," I continued, looking into Joy's green eyes. "And he said he recalled them, and it sounded like he remembered *them*."

"Ye doant miss much Wenn," Joy said slowly.

"Did you know my parents?"

"Aye," Joy said simply.

I closed my eyes for a moment. I didn't know whether to be angry because she had not told me before or ask a hundred million questions.

"Were you going to tell me?" I asked.

"Aye, that I was," Joy nodded. "But I only learned about the names jes afore the weekend you stayed, and there weren't much time then all-along-o' the rheummatics. And I doant think ye were ready. I doant know them well. I met them in the Raven's Roost, in Wolfden. They came to the Owlery once and that was the last time I sees them."

"What were they like?" My eyes were wide. They had been at the Owlery?

"Young and in love," Joy's eyes were focused on a far horizon now. "Twould have been eighteen years ago I think. Afore ye were born."

"Why did they come to the Owlery?"

"Yern mam was a troubled soul Wenn. There were problems in the Wyrde Woods. Yern mam helped to set them right."

"Problems with what?

"Shims," Joy said and looked at me holding my gaze. "Trouble with shims. Gurt trouble."

"Is that why you didn't tell me?" I nodded, recalling my reactions to mention of the Faere Folk. Had she been testing me? Probably, I decided.

"Ye were alike Will," Joy nodded. "Naun ready to accept a wider wurreld than the one ye sees for yernself."

I remembered the shims I had seen at the Priory and shivered briefly. I was beginning to realise the world held far more than I had figured.

"Do you know what happened to them?"

"I heard later that hern had...Ashley had problems. With hern mind."

I nodded. Like mother like daughter I guessed.

"Hern disappeared. Yern Da kept ye with him but hern leaving like that, it broke him up. He turned to drink. In a bad way."

"Was that why I was taken away?"

"I reckon so, surelye. But I naun heard anything but that Ashley disappeared and Nyle went back to Brighton with their chavee and things turned sour for him there. When Will read out their names at disyer place," she indicated the OJCH, "I realised who ye be."

"Back to Brighton?"

"It's where him were born. Jes alikes yernself and Will."

"Willick isn't from the Wyrde Woods?"

"Naun," Joy had that faraway look again. "Will came here during the war when he were but a lad. Never left."

"And my mother?"

Joy looked at me. "Ashley were born on a small farm, in the Edgelands atween Nickleby and Odesby. She be a local Wenn."

My mind reeled with a hundred thousand questions, insights and realisations.

"Ye have dunnamy questions no doubt Wenn," Joy said gently. "I doant know them well, but there'll be time for axing and answering. Tis time now to go back inside and find out what they decided."

"I hope they will agree," my spirit lifted somewhat. "I hope they'll say yes."

"Doant worry Wenn, they'll say yes, surelye."

I stared at the Neverland flats for a moment. There was a cottage in the woods where I had my own room and friends. Maybe even a proper boyfriend. If weekends already seemed to last an eternity in the Wyrde Woods, what bliss would a whole summer bring? And how much more would I find out about my parents? I had leads to follow now. Even a place where they had been, a place that was beginning to feel like a home to me. There was also the whole motorway business. Eco-terrorists and cloak-and-dagger stuff. In short: There was an alternative life waiting for me if the Head Supervisor would just give the go-ahead. In a way, I would have escaped from Neverland.

I looked at Joy and said, "I can only hope it's true."

TO BE CONTINUED

(in *Lord of the Wyrde Woods Book Two: Dance into the Wyrd*, to be published in print in February 2015. More on Willick as a lad in Brighton in the novella: *Will's War: A Story of Wartime Brighton* to be published in print in the spring of 2015. Both stories are already available on Amazon's Kindle.)

With Help from My Friends

I have discovered that when an author starts to say 'this book couldn't have possibly been written without...' they bloody well mean that. The lonely writing process is surrounded by people who motivate, encourage, correct, inspire, proofread, criticize, suggest and fortify. I will enter into far more details at the end of Lord of the Wyrde Woods Book Two: DANCE INTO THE WYRD when the adventures of Wenn and Puck in the Wyrde Woods come to an end. The following though, were absolutely essential ingredients:

Thank you to co-author Rebel Klomp, Marijke Swank, Rob Visser, Neal Callen Clark, C.J. Stone, Marcel Vankan, Joyce Keyzer, Richard Hornsby, Nicky van Hattem, Dunia Majdub, Leon van Assem, Heather Santilli, Corin Spinks, Jacqueline Gürke, Bren Hall, Laura Kellie, Hanneke van Hattem-van Velsen, Janna Gürke, Dave England, Libby Peatman, Zoe Heukels-Morffew, Marguerita Bär, Jovannah Bär, Nicole den Heeten, Collette Hornsby, Willeke Snijder, Magén Klomp, Anneke Klomp, Frank Bruggemann, Adrie Swank, Dien van Wagtendonk, Judith Dennis, Justin Webb, Jenny du Plessis, Carlo Robbé, Geert van Roosmalen, Rudyard Kipling, William Blake and William Shakespeare as well as Wenn and Puck who have become my constant companions.

As for the setting, I owe an apology to the people of Sussex. I originally intended to use only existing locations but quickly discovered I would have to go to extraordinary lengths to explain why two penniless kids were able to afford travel from one end of Sussex to the other and back again. I was still puzzling over this during a visit to Herstmonceux in Sussex, and there, sitting on top of a field overlooking the castle, I realised the answer was right in front of me. Malheur Hall was born and then shifted to the northeast corner of a microcosm of Sussex: The Wyrde Woods.

Having released myself from the obligation to stick to actual places I was then able to transports bits and pieces of Sussex locations, legends and folktales to this microcosm. In this process I borrowed on a wider front; stealing from Cornwall the legend of the Owl Man (Mawnan) and from Ireland a suitable habitat for Ufmanna. I took the legend of the Fairy Banner from Skye in Scotland and bits and pieces of woodlands from Kent, Somerset, Devon, Dorset and the Veluwe. Regardless of this, I hope the Wyrde Woods remain a celebration of Sussex, which is a remarkable place with an incredible idiom and truly has the best mud in the country. There is none finer.

When all is said and done, the Wyrde Woods exist, they are all around you, please get off the couch and go for a walk. It's all that is needed to find them as I have.

Written at Herstmonceux in Sussex, the edge of Amsterdam in the Netherlands and, of course, in the Wyrde Woods in August and September 2014.

SONGS, POEMS & REFERENCES

Cover Photograph by Corin Spinks
Taken at the graveyard of Saint Mary The Virgin Church at Glynde, East Sussex.
www.corinography.co.uk & www.flickr.com/corinography

Cover Painting by William Blake
Entitled *Oberon, Titania and Puck with Fairies Dancing* and dated 1786. (Tate collection).

Roll Me Over
A bawdy shanty which was popular with soldiers in World War Two. The author is unknown.

La Belle Dame sans Merci
Written by English poet John Keats in 1819.

Come in the stillness
A rhyme from English folklore and said to be one of the ways of summoning the Faery folk. It has been slightly adapted.

Child of the Ocean, young Siren of the Sea
Inspired by three muses at the Dutch seaside in 2013

Song of the Woodpecker
A traditional song of which the lyrics were first written down in the 1888 book "The Stag Party." It has been slightly adapted.

My thing is my own
A song collected by Thomas D'Urfey in his 1699 *Wit and Mirth, or Pills to Purge Melancholy*

Jabberwocky
Provides some words for the skirmish by Devil's Tarn. The words were invented by Lewis Carroll for the poem *Jabberwocky* in his 1871 novel *Through the Looking-Glass, and What Alice Found There.*

Now will he sit under a medlar tree
From William Shakespeare's *The Most Excellent and Lamentable Tragedie of Romeo and Juliet* printed in 1599.

Fierce Dancing: Adventures in the Underground
Published in 1997 and written by C.J. Stone (illustrations Eldad Druks). C.J. Stone has kindly given permission for the use of his work.

Amends: A Midsummer Night's Dream
William Shakespeare provided these lines, spoken by his Puck. The names Titania and Oberon are also borrowed rather cheekily from Shakespeare's woods.

GLOSSARY

abroad - anywhere not in Sussex
abusefully - insulting
afeared - afraid
afore - before
afterdoor - back door
aftername - surname
all-along-o' - because of / on account of
alltsinit - all that is in it i.e. taking all this in consideration
alikes - like
alus - alehouse (pub)
ampery - weak / unhealthy
anigh - near by
atween - between
axe - ask
axed - asked
axing - asking

bagga - badger
bandersnatch - (LEWIS CARROLL) nonsense word from Jabberwocky
bear sic - (SLANG) really cool
beazled - exhausted
beleft - believed
bellick - to bellow
beliddling - belittling
bethanks - thank you
bettermost - superlative of better.
bi-laminate - (ARCHERY) a bow made of two layers
bio-degredibble - (OWN INVENTION) bio-degradable
bostin - (SLANG) amazing
boning - (SLANG) fornicating
brabagious - no translation, but the worst thing one Sussex woman can call another Sussex woman
brill - (SLANG) brilliant
browned off - (SLANG) to irritate/anger
buff - (SLANG) attractive
bun that - (SLANG) forget that
burbling - (LEWIS CARROLL) nonsense word from Jabberwocky
by Geemeny - the exclamation 'O Gemini!' Like: Gee, Wow, Gosh
by-the-bye - by chance

caffincher - chaffinch
callow - bald (derived from the Dutch 'kaal')
catching hot - to catch a cold
catterah - (children's counting rhyme) five

caterwise - diagonally
chance-born - born out of wedlock, or a Farisee Changeling
chank - chew
charm-stuff -'unofficial' medicine, i.e. not from modern doctor or hospital
chavee - child
chipper - nipper /child
chirpsing - (SLANG) flirting
chuckle-head - idiot/fool
clinker - (SLANG) dried feces attached to the hairs of the buttocks
cloober - (SLANG) 'clooby' derived from bloody, can be used as adj., noun, etc.
cray - (SLANG) mad/crazy
codger - a miser

da - dad
dappens - as soon as
deedy - clever or industrious
deenah - (children's counting rhyme) two
devourously - voracious
dight-up - get dressed up, make yourself presentable
dinah - (children's counting rhyme) three
dingleberry - (SLANG) dried feces attached to the hairs of the buttocks
dishabill - disheveled
dissing - (SLANG) making fun of/ making a fool of
disyer - this here
doant - don't
doe - (children's counting rhyme) four
dooby - (SLANG) very dumb
douchenoggin - (SLANG) friendly insult
douchebaggery - (SLANG) behaviour which is below any sort of par
dour - to put out a candle
dozzle - a small portion
drackly - directly
draggle-tail - a woman of dubious morals
Drefan - (ANGLO-SAXON) trouble
druv - driven. From 'Sussex won't be druv'
duguth - (ANGLO-SAXON) a band of warriors
dunnamy - don't know how many
dursn't - dare not
duzzick - a chore / a day's work

eena - (children's counting rhyme) one
e'enamost - almost
ellynge - miserable / lonely
enow - enough
et - eaten

fambly - family

Farisee - of the Faere Folk (Faerie)
fax - (SLANG) fuck
faxed - (SLANG) fucked
faxing - (SLANG) fucking
fit - (SLANG) in a good shape / sexually attractive
flabbergastation - (OWN INVENTION) own invention for 'flabbergasted'
flaffing about - (SLANG) hanging around
fluttergrub - somebody who likes to potter around in the earth
forename - first name
foredoor - front door
forever ago - (WENN) a long time ago
Forlorn Hoper - (WENN) Wenn's invention for resident of Nowhere Place
forrard - forward
fresh - tipsy
frumious - (LEWIS CARROLL) nonsense word from Jabberwocky
FUBAR - (SLANG) Fucked Up Beyond All Recognition
furriners - foreigners (anybody not from Sussex)

gaffer - grandfather
gammer - grandmother
gark - look at
garm - mud
generally-always - almost always
giggle-some - giggly
Geemeny - from the expression 'O Gemini!'
gobbet - a mouth full of something
Goody - a titular address, usually for an older woman
gormed up - all dirty on account of mud
grabby - covered in mud
graft - (SLANG) to fancy
gret - (SLANG) cigarette or hand rolled cigarette
grummut - an awkward boy
grump - someone who is grumpy
gubber - mud
gurt - great
gwoan - going

hag-ridden - having a nightmare
Heolstor - (ANGLO-SAXON) dark
Heortréow - (ANGLO-SAXON) literally Heart Tree
hickory-boo - (Archery) hickory wood, bamboo
hindesideafore - the wrong way round
hot spice - (SLANG) a sexy girl

howsumdever - however (also used as howsumever)
hugger-mugger - in disorder / without system

ike - mud
ingenurious - ingenious
innard - inward
insultive - (SLANG) insulting

jaunce - a (weary) journey
jes - just
jiggered - surprised
jubjub - (LEWIS CARROLL) nonsense word from Jabberwocky
justly - just so

ken - to know someone, from the Dutch 'kennen'.
knucker - dragon / large worm

lamentable - adjective used instead of 'very'
legend - (SLANG) something that is really cool
letbehow'twill - let it be how it will
les - let's
liddle - little
lifer - (WENN) Wenn's invention for veteran caretaker at Nowhere Place
lippy - someone quick to give commentary
loped - to run off - possible from 'eloped' or the Dutch 'loopt'
Lunnon - London
Lunnoner - Londoner

mack moment - (SLANG) the moment two people realise they are about to have sex
maene wudu - (ANGLO-SAXON) Man's Wood / Common Wood
mam - mum/mom
Master Dobbs - Sussex name for the household elf
mawkin - a scarecrow
maun - must not
mayhap - perhaps
middling - a commonly used adjective which can mean anything at all
misagift - mistaken
moil - trouble
moist - (SLANG) sad, pathetic
most-in-general - usually / generally
mucked-up - all-in confusion
Mus - master
Mus Reynard - a fox

nary - any
naun - no / not / none
negatons - (SLANG) negative vibes
none-the-better - drunk
no-ways - no way

oakum - nonsense
onnard - onward
Ole Brock - badger
OTF - (SLANG) Opportunity to Fuck
otherwhiles - at other times / otherwise
outlandish - used to describe someone not
from Sussex
outyer - out here

parring - (SLANG) showing disrespect
peert - lively, charming
peg away - to eat or drink enthousiastically
peng - (SLANG) really cool
piff - (SLANG) cool
plaguey - troublesome
poking - (SLANG) making fun of
pranging out - (SLANG) being scared
preggers - (SLANG) pregnant
prensley - presently
primed - lightly drunk
print-moonlight - clear moonlight
puck stool - toad stool / mushroom
pug - mud
purty - pretty

quiddy - What did you say? From French
Que dis tu?

ravtile - (SLANG) the worst possible insult
you can call someone
reafe up- to get really excited and
enthousiastic about something
real beast - (SLANG) really cool
recollect - remember
recollections - memories
rheummatics - rheumatism though it was
used more generically
robbut - rabbit
rolling about - fornication. Not sure if this
was Sussex but I left it like it was.

safe dreams - (OWN) My own variation of
sweet dreams
scaddle - wild / mischievous / thievish.
scamble - to create confusion
scrazed - scratched and bruised
scritch owl - barn owl
scorching - (SLANG) being disrespectful
scorse - exchange
scrowse - angry, dark, scowling

242

set - obstinate
shatter - a great number or quantity
Sheeres - the Shires. This would include
places like Surrey, but also Manchuria and
Arizona. Basically, anywhere that is not
Sussex.
Sheere-folk - people from the Shires, i.e.
not from Sussex
Sheere-man - a man from the Shires, i.e.
not from Sussex
shimper - to shine brightly
shims - an apparition, from the Dutch
'Schim'
shirty - easily offended
shruck - shrieked / yelled
sic - (SLANG) cool
sirageous - SLANG) a widely applicable
adjective expressing something is positive
skag - (SLANG) someone who eats rotten
fetuses
skreel - a scream or a shriek
slab - mud
sleech - mud
slob - mud
slubber - to slip in mud
slurry - mud
smeech - a dirty black smoke or mist
smeery - mud
smoking crow and getting blunted -
(SLANG) smoking pot and getting stoned
snooty - (WENN) Wenn's invention for
optimistic newby caretakers at Nowhere
Place
snotgoggs - yew berries
snoule - a small quantity
snuffy - angry
sodgers - soldiers
somewhen - sometimes
somewhen t'other-day - the day before
yesterday / just about any day before
yesterday
some-one-time - occasionally
soodling - a slow meandering walk
spake - (SLANG) a hefty insult, usually
used as a comeback when just insulted
yourself
sprite - (OWN INVENTION) spirit. I
wanted something that sounded a bit
differently.
squimbly - feeling unwell
streale - arrow
stodge - mud
stride - a long walk (usually any
destination outside of Sussex)
stuckish - stuck in a manner of thinking
stug - mud

suddent - suddenly

surelye - surely, often used to for emphasis, the spelling is widespread in old texts and Broad Sussex dictionaries.

swag - (SLANG) attitude, arrogance, sense of own attractiveness

swymy - giddy / faint

tarn - small lake

tater - potato

teats - breasts

teddious - tedious

telling - counting (Sussex with Dutch origin)

tessy - to be angry

timmersome - timid

thereaways - there about / that way

there is everything o' something and something o' everything - explanation for something that isn't really understood.

tiffy - touchy / irritable

tossicated - very intoxicated

trolling - (SLANG) fooling someone

tulgey - (LEWIS CARROLL) nonsense word from Jabberwocky

tmight - it might

twack - (SLANG) insult, not very nice

twere - it were

twill - it will

twould - it would

unbeknownst - unknown

Ufmanna - (ANGLO-SAXON) literally Owl Man

unnacountable - an adjective which can be used for just about anything. Used often.

vlothered - agitated/ flustered

waer-wyrd - (ANGLO-SAXON) to speak carefully, to choose one's words wisely

Waus - (HISTORICAL) from the French nickname for Willikin of the Weald.

Wazzock - (SLANG) know it all

weard - (ANGLO-SAXON) protect, defend

well stacked - (SLANG) big boobs

wheelah - (children's counting rhyme) six

whiffling - (LEWIS CARROLL) nonsense word from Jabberwocky

whiler - (children's counting rhyme) seven

widdershins - anti-clockwise

wind shaken - thin, puny, weak

Wodewose - mythical creature of the wood. Ranging from wild man to wood spirit.

wurreld - world

Wyrde - properly the 'Wyrd'

yarbs - herbs

yetner - not yet

ye can cut yern stick - do as you please

yoked - (SLANG) muscular, well built

Yuletide - Christmas

Zackly - exactly.